CONFESSING
A MURDER

Nicholas Drayson

Jonathan Cape
London

Publisher's Introduction

THE MANUSCRIPT OF THIS book has a mysterious provenance. Though written in English, it was discovered in Holland in 1988 in the attic of a large private house near Groningen. Legal proceedings are continuing over ownership of the document, but all parties agree that it was found unbound in a cardboard stationery box, together with other documents which mostly comprised household accounts of the same house, dated from July 1910 to March 1916. There is presumably a connection between these accounts and the manuscript, though the present owner of the house can shed no light on the matter. Exhaustive enquiries among the family of the previous owners have failed to produce any clues as to its provenance. An analysis of the paper and typeface of the original manuscript was commissioned from the late Dr Kenneth K. Pollward of Oakdale, Connecticut. He reported that the manuscript was typed using a Remington Elite portable typewriter (American, date of manufacture 1898–1912) on Becker paper (English, date of manufacture 1913).

When the manuscript for this book was first submitted to us for publication in 1988, we assumed that the events described were fictitious. Although many of the names can be easily identified, notably those of Charles Darwin ('Bobby'), his brother Erasmus ('Philos') and other members of the Darwin family, as well as the English naturalist Alfred Russel Wallace and several other minor characters, few of the events described are found in other contemporary accounts. Nowhere is the author of this book referred to in Darwin's own voluminous correspondence, which has long been available to scholars[1] and whose life has been meticulously researched.[2] Most of the plants and animals described by the author, plausible though they sound, do not correspond with any species previously described or presently known to science.

However, it was clear that many of the events described here are compatible with contemporary descriptions. For example, the schoolboy prank referred to of 'raising the doctor' (waking up the headmaster of Shrewsbury School, Dr Samuel Butler, by jumping around above his bedroom) is also referred to by Darwin. Darwin refers in his diary to an occasion when an innocent boy was beaten for this offence – though without naming the boy. The manuscript refers at some length to Darwin's visit to Australia on the *Beagle*. Again, this is not incompatible with Darwin's own somewhat sketchy account of that time in his 1839 book, *Journal of Researches into the Geology and Natural History of the Various Countries visited by H.M.S. Beagle*. Meticulous checking of the events described in this manuscript against several other published historical records suggested that at least parts of the story might be genuine. Although one or two inconsistencies occur in the chronology of the story – which the astute reader may spot – these are no more than can be accounted for by memory lapses of a seventy-three-year-old man. For a full and detailed account of historical concurrences, the reader is referred to the 1993 paper by Dr N.R. Drayson.[3]

The references to the English naturalist Alfred Russel Wallace are more problematical. Wallace described his travels in the East Indies in his book *The Malay Archipelago*. In this book,

---

[1] Notably the Darwin collection in Cambridge University Library. Twelve volumes of an estimated thirty volumes of Darwin's complete correspondence have now been published by Cambridge University Press.
[2] Darwin's biographies include 1887, F. Darwin; 1956, Newson; 1957, Smith and Kennedy; 1988, R.D. Keynes; 1990, J. Bowlby; 1995, J. Browne.
[3] 'New light on the Darwin-Wallace controversy', *Archives of Natural History* 20(3), pp. 13–26.

although he describes some of the incidents referred to in the present manuscript, he nowhere mentions a character who might be identified with the author. Wallace certainly spent some time with Sir James Brooke in Sarawak, and 'for three years had the services of a young Englishman, Mr Charles Allen' whom he sometimes refers to as 'Charley'. Wallace's book, published in 1869 – five years after his return from what became an eight-year trip – was dedicated to Charles Darwin. However, it is clearly stated in the present manuscript that Wallace's account of his own discovery of the idea of natural selection is false – that he was not, as he claimed, in Ternate in the Moluccas when the idea came to him, but in Sarawak, and that the idea was not his own. In this light, other parts of Wallace's account of that period of his life are open to question.

The author's detailed descriptions of plants and animals on the island are another matter. Without exception they are unknown to science. Being unqualified to pass judgment on the likelihood that they could be genuine descriptions of animals now extinct, the present publisher decided to submit them to several more qualified authorities for comments on their actual or possible existence.[4] The descriptions engendered considerable controversy. Although all the authorities consulted agreed that none of the animals described in this manuscript now exist, there was no consensus on whether they could once have. Several dismissed the accounts as amusing and imaginative confabulations. Others commented that although the descriptions were plausible, the fact that no other descriptions of the animals have ever been published made their present or past existence highly unlikely. One, an entomologist, strongly felt that at least some of them probably had existed. Noting what he called their 'overall biological harmony', he cited Charles Darwin's description of the fauna of the Galapagos Islands; if Darwin had found there that 'Most of the organic productions

---

[4] Specific comments here are anonymous, but see acknowledgments in Drayson 1993 for the names of those consulted.

are aboriginal creations, found nowhere else', why should this
not also be true of other islands? Another entomologist, though
generally sceptical of the reality of the island fauna, noted that
the area in question had long been of interest to lepidopterists.
In 1936 the German lepidopterist and coleopterist, Gustav
Erich von Hamelin, postulated the existence of just such a
vanished landmass south of Borneo in his monograph on the
larger moths of Borneo and the Celebes.[5] Hamelin noted
that large numbers of *Urania splendens* – a moth well known
for its annual mass migrations between the main islands of
Borneo, Java, Sumatra and their surrounding islands – regularly
perished in the Java Sea around the location given in the
manuscript. A similar phenomenon had been observed in the
region of Krakatau after the eruption of 1883. Von Hamelin
suggested that the moths were, in fact, trying to reach an
island that had also recently disappeared, probably in a volcanic
eruption.

Could this, then, be a genuine autobiographical account?
If so, it was of major historical importance. There remained,
however, one glaring and apparently insurmountable anomaly.
The islands so carefully described in the manuscript do not
exist. There is no land at around 115 degrees east of Greenwich
and about 6 degrees below the equator, let alone such a large
feature as the author describes. Neither are the islands shown
on nineteenth-century British Admiralty charts. If the islands
were a figment of the author's imagination, why not its flora
and fauna, as well the events and characters described in the
manuscript? The manuscript appeared to be no more than an
elaborate, though plausible, fiction. As such we decided not to
publish. In 1998, we changed our minds.

In February 1998 Dr Bors Nillsen of the Scripps Institute of
Oceanography published his analysis of bathymetric data taken

[5] 'Neue Indienische Lepidoptera der Berliner zoologische Museum', *Internationale entomoligische Zeitschrift* 1, pp. 1–166.

during the 1995 International Ocean Drilling Program on a routine charting voyage through the Indonesian archipelago.[6] The data revealed a large magnetic and geological anomaly centred at 115°16′E, 6°11′S, measuring some twenty-six kilometres (about fifteen nautical miles) across. Nillsen concluded that the most likely explanation for this feature was that it was the submarine remains of a very large extinct volcano. Could this be all that remained of the mysterious islands? But if this were so, how was it that no accounts of either the islands or their disappearance had been found during our initial research? The answer soon became clear. Krakatau.

On 27 August 1883, the Indonesian island of Krakatau, or 'Krakatoa' as it is often erroneously called,[7] was almost completely destroyed in a series of enormous volcanic eruptions. The island, in the straits between Java and Sumatra, had been rumbling and smoking for several months previously. There had been a small eruption on 20 May 1883, and further small eruptions began on 26 August. The 'big bang' occurred the following day. In a gigantic explosion which was heard as far away as central Australia, almost the whole island was destroyed. Seismic shock waves were recorded in London and Washington. The eruption generated 130-foot tidal waves along the coasts of Java and Sumatra; whole towns vanished, over 36,000 people were killed. According to the captain of a coastal steamer[8] visiting the area a few days after the event, 'This was truly a scene of the Last Judgment.'

The eruption of Krakatau was the largest in the world in living memory. European scientists rushed to investigate. In England, the Royal Society formed a Krakatoa (*sic*) Committee. The Committee, convened in 1884, examined hundreds of logs, journals, notes and memoirs. In 1888 it published its

---

[6] 'Bathymetry of the Java and Sunda Seas', *Oceanography* 34, pp. 126–67.
[7] As in the 1967 Hollywood film *Krakatoa, East of Java*. Neither the correct spelling nor the correct location appealed to the producers of this film; Krakatau is west of Java.
[8] Captain T.H. Lindeman of the *Gouvenor-Generaal Loudon*.

results.[9] It was in this document, buried within the detail of scores of eyewitness accounts, scientific analysis and theoretical interpretation, that we found clear evidence of the existence and fate of the mysterious island.

Not only was the eruption of Krakatau in 1883 preceded, like many large eruptions, by smaller seismic events (earthquakes, landslips and small tidal waves caused by submarine activity were recorded all round the Sunda Sea), it also provided the trigger for subsequent seismic activity in the area. All of this activity was noted by the Krakatoa Committee of the Royal Society, including a report by Thomas Edward MacGillivray, then master of the merchantman *The Hibernian*.[10] In August 1883 MacGillivray was on the Australian run and, having been becalmed *en route* from Macassar (now Ujung Pandang) to Batavia (now Jakarta), was drifting south of Borneo. In his log for 27 August, he recorded that he heard an explosion ('like a twelve-pounder going off on the gun-deck') at 2.47 GMT. Precisely four minutes after this, a tidal wave about two feet high approached along a broad front from the south. Twenty-two minutes later he saw a second wave coming from the west. The second wave was about the same amplitude as the first. The Krakatoa Committee tried to fit the observations from MacGillivray's log into the pattern of eruptions, waves and reflected waves from the Krakatoa eruption, which began at 2.27 GMT. Tidal waves can travel at over 400 knots (700kph) in deep water – just over half the speed of sound. They are somewhat slower in shallow water. The tidal wave from Krakatoa was estimated to have travelled at about 320 knots (about 600 kph). It could not have reached *The Hibernian*, sixteen hundred nautical miles away, four minutes after the sound of the explosion. They concluded that MacGillivray's observation, if accepted, 'suggests a contemporaneous or near-contemporaneous event

[9] G.J. Symonds (ed.), *The Report of the Krakatoa Committee of the Royal Society*.
[10] For other accounts of the eruption, see also 1902, E. Metzger, 'Krakatau' *Nature* 29: 241–4.

in the south, around latitude 115 degrees east, longitude 6 degrees south'. But MacGillivray's wave was one of several dozen 'near-contemporaneous' events noted in the report, and no further investigation was carried out.

An earlier report of a landmass in this position is found in the 1847 report of the Swiss geologist Heinrich Zollinger, who made detailed investigations of many of the volcanoes of the East Indies.[11] Bakuakau was the name given by the inhabitants of the southern Celebes (now Sulawesi) to a series of small volcanic islands about two hundred nautical miles south of the main island of Celebes. Zollinger did not visit the islands himself, but his report notes that the six (*sic*) islands appeared to comprise the remains of a large volcano, now extinct. The largest central island contained a more recent cone which was still smoking. Zollinger recorded the islands as uninhabited, noting that his informants, the Bugis,[12] occasionally visited the islands but thought them of little importance due to their remoteness from local and European sea lanes, and that they were not popular with Moluccan trepang fisherman as the strong currents in the area made landing difficult. Bakuakau was recorded (as 'Bakuoka') on one Dutch chart of the 1850s,[13] but not included in the first major British Admiralty chart of the Australia to Singapore routes (made coincidentally by Darwin's old ship, the *Beagle*)[14] of 1844, nor subsequently.

It is now clear that the tidal wave witnessed by MacGillivray coming from the south could have been caused by the sudden, catastrophic collapse of Bakuakau. One of the Royal Society Committee's most important and novel scientific conclusions about the eruption of Krakatau was that the major explosion had

---

[11] *Les volcanes des Indes orientales*. A report made for the Dutch East India Company.

[12] The Bugis are a coastal people of the southern Sulawesi, best known to nineteenth-century European sailors for their daring and blood-thirsty piracy.

[13] The 'Van den Berk map' is now in the collection of the Maritime Museum of Western Australia in Fremantle (AN234/2).

[14] HMS *Beagle* was then commanded by John Lort Stokes, who had been assistant surveyor at the time of Darwin's voyage.

been caused not by the sudden release of molten rock or volcanic gas, but by steam. During the initial activity, a hollow gas–filled chamber had formed within the island. Seawater had gushed into this chamber through large fissures, and on contact with the molten lava within had immediately vaporised. It was this explosive pressure that caused the final devastating eruption. A further conclusion was that although millions of tons of dust and rock had been blown into the atmosphere (causing spectacular sunsets around the world for years afterwards), the exterior of the island had largely remained intact, the ejected material mostly comprising gas, ash and pumice from within the volcano. The release of this material, however, left an enormous hollow chamber beneath the island. After the final eruption the island had collapsed inwards into this chamber. Krakatau was still there, but it had disappeared beneath the sea.

But not all volcanic mountains immediately collapse after a large eruption. Very occasionally the hollow chamber within the volcano remains stable for centuries, even millennia. This is the case for the famous Bornean volcano of Bukit Lembang, with its spectacular caves, and appears to have been the case for Bakuakau.[15] Volcanic material in the sediments around Bakuakau have not yet been dated isotopically, but rough estimates based on sediment accumulation suggest a date of late Pliocene/early Pleistocene for the last eruption.[16] The shell around the hollow chamber remaining from Bakuakau's last eruption thus remained intact for some 1.5–2.5 million years. The shell only became unstable following the eruption of Krakatau, presumably as a result of the enormous shock waves that it generated. The shell that was Bakuakau collapsed into the hollow chamber within. The islands which had formed the extinct volcano disappeared beneath the sea.

[15] The 'dungbat cave' referred to in the manuscript, which was explored by the author, was probably not of sufficient size to be the main chamber. This suggests that there may have been not one chamber, but many adjoining or interconnecting chambers.
[16] 1998, B. Nillsen, 'Bathymetry of the Java and Sunda Seas', *Oceanography* 34, p. 161.

The sudden disappearance of Bakuakau would have resulted in the extinction of all its life forms. But just how likely is it that such a unique and diverse flora and fauna, with its blood-sucking mistletoes and terrestrial holothurians, could ever have originally existed on so small an island? Modern evolutionary theory gives some support to the possibility. It has long been known that island faunas and floras, especially isolated ones, contain more than their fair share of endemic species. The Galapagos Islands, whose flora and fauna were investigated so thoroughly by Darwin, are a case in point. The Galapagos Islands are also volcanic and relatively young in the geological sense, having risen from the sea between 1 and 2 million years ago. Most of the animals on the islands, including the giant tortoises, marine iguanas and the famous Darwin's finches are found nowhere else; of the twenty-six land birds collected by Darwin (and later described by John Gould), no less than twenty-five are endemic. Yet, as Darwin himself postulated at the time, it is almost certain that they all derived from similar species which had floated or flown across the eight hundred kilometres of ocean from the South American mainland. It is widely accepted today that the thirteen species of finch now on the islands derive from a single species, perhaps even a single fertilised female, which was blown on to the islands from the mainland, where the species may still exist unchanged. It is clear from studies of this and other islands that this process of speciation – where one species gives rise to one or more different species – is greatly accelerated in such a situation. It would therefore be expected that an island such as Bakuakau, with its remoteness from other landmasses and its age (roughly the same as the Galapagos), would contain a large number of indigenous species.

It is now almost certain that a volcanic island existed at the same position as that referred to in the manuscript, and that it disappeared in 1883. It may well have contained plants and animals such as those described. Many descriptions of the people and events which appear in the manuscript concur with those described in other sources. There is, however, one piece missing from the puzzle. The author clearly states in his manuscript that he was going to seal it within a glass vessel, together with a specimen of the golden scarab for which he searched so long. No such insect was found in the box which contained the typed transcription in the house in Holland, nor have exhaustive searches in museums and private collections throughout Europe uncovered it. Despite this small but tantalising omission, we have decided to present this book as a true account of the natural history of a small island in the Java Sea, and the life of a remarkable man.

In his general description of the island, the author refers to a geological and topographical 'sketch'. This was not found with the manuscript, but in order to help readers understand the text more easily, the publishers have commissioned just such a sketch, based on the descriptions found in the manuscript. This forms the frontispiece of the present volume.

The identity of the author has been the subject of much research. An examination of available records – school and university attendance, ships' passenger lists, Australian medical registers, etc. – has narrowed the field to two possible names. At this time neither can be confirmed as the author, and the manuscript has been left anonymous – as, we presume, the author intended it should be. The manuscript was untitled. In a letter to his friend Joseph Hooker in 1854, Charles Darwin wrote that revealing his thoughts on the mechanism of evolution, with their denial of a literal interpretation of the biblical account of creation, felt like 'confessing a murder'. We have chosen this phrase for the title of the book.

Editor's Notes

THE TYPEWRITTEN TRANSCRIPTION ON which this edition is based is clearly legible and almost free from typographical or grammatical errors. How far it resembles the original version, which was presumably handwritten, is impossible to say. Because there are surprisingly few spelling mistakes in the typescript, I have assumed that these at least have been corrected by the transcriber; due to its polished form, it is likely that some editing has already been done.

In style, the typescript is typical of formal prose in the mid- to late nineteenth century. Paragraphs and sentences are often long (sometimes tortuously so), the sentences with many subordinate clauses; punctuation marks, especially commas, are freely used; the use of parentheses within sentences is more frequent than usual at the time (but not anachronistic). The quotations from poetry within the text are all from John Milton, and are also typical of the time. However, together with the use of verbatim conversation and the often somewhat didactic tone, they suggest that the author wrote his account with publication in mind; such inclusions are rare in letters or bona fide journals. The spelling is internally consistent, though obsolete forms are not uncommon – e.g. 'misseltow' for mistletoe, 'tripang' for trepang, 'sociable' rather than 'social' insects. The universal use of the verbal suffix -ise rather than –ize is unusual for the time but not unknown. With such a clearly comprehendible original, I have decided not to emend either the style or punctuation, other than by replacing the underlining of the typescript with italics. In this edition sentence length, structure and punctuation – though perhaps a little old-fashioned to modern readers – are as in the original transcription.

Much research has been done on the biological and historical references contained in the manuscript. Although some of this research will be of interest both to the general reader and the scholar, I have decided not to refer to it at length in this edition. Such a process would have required the use of copious footnotes, and frequent extraneous explanations would only interrupt the flow of the text. The reader will find that the author himself answers most of the questions he raises during his narrative. The few footnotes which have been inserted are intended purely to help the reader when it is not clear from the text who, what or where is being referred to.

Nicholas Drayson BSc, DJS, MSc, PhD
Caxton Underhill, England

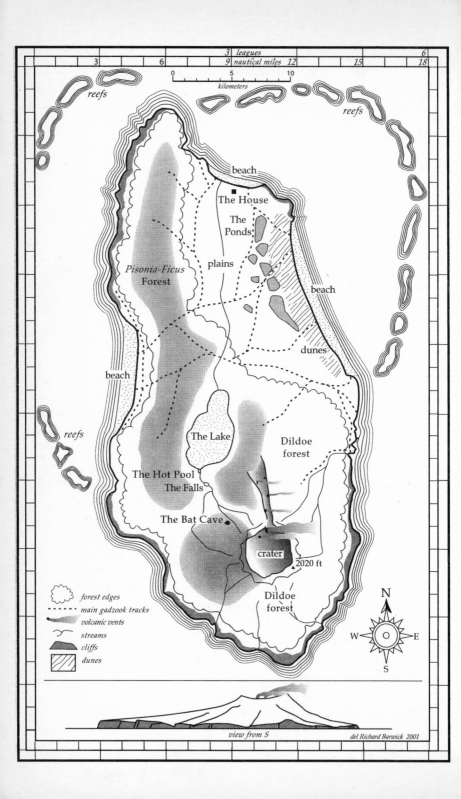

Chapter 1

TO BEGIN IN THE present. It is the year 1883; the month, so far as I can judge it, is June. I am writing these words on a small island in the Java Sea, about a hundred leagues south of the Celebes. My island is about nine leagues long by four broad, its southern end being largely mountainous, or should I say that it is largely one mountain, and that of considerable height (by rough trigonometry, I have estimated its summit at 2,060 feet). If you consult your Lyell, the mountain fits well his *Crater of Elevation*, much resembling those of St Jago and Mauritius, being conical, with an open crater at the summit, and presumably formed by similar volcanic processes. That the mountain was once a volcano can also be deduced from the gasps of sulphurous smoke and steam which still issue from the many vents of various sizes around its peak (most of these vents are no more than the size of a fist, but there is one, near the top of the mountain, into which a man might easily fall). My mountain has been most active of late. But though the mountain resembles those to be found in other parts, the plants and animals which share my island are like none I have ever seen. In 'these enchanted isles, this land of rifted rocks whose entrance leads to Hell, live dire chimeras'. Though I have discovered none of the giant tortoises nor sea-faring lizards which have made other islands famous, I have discovered wonders enough. Here live plants which suck the blood of birds, and birds which hibernate under water. Here spiders eat bats and frogs eat each other. Here live gadzocks and here, deep inside the mountain, lives the golden scarab.

*　　*　　*

It is sweet to name a thing, for is it not by naming that we gain possession? On my island I have named everything. The mountain and the forest, the gadzocks, the plants and the animals, all are mine. I named Philos, and he was mine, but who will name me? The mountain speaks to me, but it does not listen. It talks of greater things, of tides and time. I listen. I have not much time left now, but my story must be told. Schooldays in England and dear Philos, and when I first met his brother Bobby (I did not name Bobby, but it is of Bobby that I most want to tell). Then Edinburgh and Cambridge days, and the true story of Emma and how our love forced me into lonely exile in Australia. I must also tell of the Theory, how that fool Wallace got hold of it from Charley and robbed me of my dearest friend. I will tell you all about Charley Allen. There have been times when I have blamed Charley, and others when I have thanked him for the hope he gave me. But hope, though it glitter and shine, is ever a false coin. Acceptance proves a truer currency than hope, and I know now that I will never leave this island.

We saw gadzocks even before we came ashore, at first taking them for piles of sargassum weed washed up on the beach, perhaps the strange nests of the sargassum birds which we had already seen on our passage through the reef. Then Charley thought he saw one of these piles of seaweed move and lifted the glass to his eye.

'Gadzoks!' he said (or so it sounded, in his Somerset accent), 'I believe they are alive.' And thus I named them.

Gadzocks rather resemble small, shaggy goats, though completely without horns (and what need have they of horns with no-one to fight against, not even each other?). They are no doubt closely related to the anoas of the Celebes,[17] although a

---

[17] The lowland anoas, *Bubalus depressicornis*, and mountain anoas, *B. quarlesi*, are small water buffalo-like bovids now found only on the Indonesian island of Sulawesi (formerly the Celebes).

fraction of the size. The males are not larger than the females, but smaller, and there are many more bulls on the island than there are cows. The animals seldom eat grass, surviving mostly on a diet of seaweed; and the meat of the gadzock, even from a calf, is so rank as to make year-old salt pork seem an alderman's delight. But they are gentle creatures, and their lives are of some interest to the naturalist and to the philosopher.

Gadzocks feed almost exclusively on the sargassum weed that is so plentiful in the waters around the island, and is always found in quantities washed ashore on one beach or another, depending on the winds. The weed is, of course, rich in sodium chloride, at such a level as to make it inedible to most animals. Gadzocks, however, relish the stuff, and are able to circumvent the toxic effects of the salt by voiding it in their urine. The urine is indeed so saturated with salt that it precipitates to crystalline form almost immediately on excretion. Among the males this produces no unusual feature. Not so with the females. Unlike the domestic cow and other ruminants, female gadzocks do not hold their tails aloft during micturition; their tails are thus regularly soaked in this concentrated liquor, and accumulate great cakes of salt, pale yellow in colour and up to three pounds in weight, giving them a most distinctive appearance. Such a weight of salt must surely be a hindrance to so small an animal, but its effect is mitigated by the fact that the salt appears to serve as a kind of signal or advertisement. During the mating season, it is those cows with the heaviest and most visible accumulations which attract the most bulls.

I have mentioned that there are many more bull gadzocks on my island than cows, the proportion being roughly one to eight. You might assume, as I did myself at first, that this would lead to intense competition among the bulls for the cows. I soon found that the reverse appears to be the case. It is the females who compete. I have now spent three full seasons on my island and have twice witnessed the wondrous sight of the gadzocks' courtship. Early one morning on a given day in September, at the end of the little rains, the bulls gather silently on the beach on the eastern side of the island, which I can see from the hut where I am now writing these words. The females, three hundred or more, emerge from the bush and take up position on the sand-dunes above the beach. As the sun rises, they present their rumps towards the first rays of light and towards the bulls assembled on the strand below, and begin to wave their salt-encrusted tails to and fro like slow, yellow pendulums. The bulls, singly or in small groups, promenade up and down the beach, murmuring gently, as if in low conversation. Having, as it were, inspected the wares, each bull joins company with the female of his choice. Some do this within minutes, others may take several hours to decide. Each cow thus acquires a seraglio of male gadzocks, the largest number I have observed being thirteen. There is no physical coercion in this arrangement, but I have noticed a clear correlation between the size and colour of a cow's tail adornment and the number of bulls she attracts; the greater the accumulation of salt on her tail, and the brighter the colour, the larger her entourage. When towards evening the cow is satisfied that no more bulls will join her, she offers herself to each of them in turn. Each bull mounts and mates with her, and from the grunting and groaning from both partners in the procedure, I take it that the activity is not without some pleasure. The bulls themselves are peaceable animals. I have never seen the smallest sign of aggression from or between them.

This system is unusual. Not only is it the females which compete for the attention of the males, but the rivalry is totally amicable. There is no force or coercion, and all animals are able to enjoy sexual union at the completion of the ritual. All are content.

I remarked upon this fact to Charley, some few weeks after we arrived on the island in the August of 1879. We had already been witness to the gadzock's mating rituals, and when we came across a pair of the animals lying together in the shade of a fig tree, quietly ruminating, I wondered out loud whether there was any animal more content than a gadzock, more happy with its lot. Though Charley had become increasingly surly of late, with just the two of us on the island I was eager for any conversation.

'How can an animal be happy?' said Charley, his soft accent failing to mask a contemptuous tone.

'Are we, then, the only creatures to feel happiness?' I said.

'Of course,' said Charley. 'These gadzocks as you call them, why, they're not even aware that they're alive. No animal is. Besides, how can happiness be possible without its reverse? If these animals are *always* content, as you say they are, how can they be aware of it? Without night, there can be no day. Without down, where is up?'

'But surely,' I said, 'emotions are different. Love can be known where hate is unknown, happiness recognised without sadness.'

In the twenty-four years I had known Charley I had come to realise that his materialistic view of the world was not open to question, but decided to continue my argument.

'And are you also saying', said I, 'that self-awareness, that rational thought, is the sole prerogative of men?'

'Show me that it is not,' said Charley.

'There are countless examples. Do you not remember the ape which your English naturalist owned? Not content with being given the brandy that it so relished by the teaspoon, it stole the key to its master's tantalus and died from its greed. Intelligence misapplied, to be sure, but intelligence none the less. And is not love possessed by species other than man? We see love, both maternal and romantic, among many birds and beasts. If, as we both believe, a man is but the next step from an ape, which is itself but the next step from a shrew, and so on, then might not both intelligence and love be similarly graded?'

'It seems to me that anything you say *might* be the case,' said Charley. 'You have not shown me that it *is* the case.'

'You surely will not deny that animals feel pleasure? Only look at the gadzocks.'

'Pleasure is not happiness,' said Charley. 'Besides, who is to say that animals love in the way that men love?'

'We have our own observations to guide us.'

'Then all I have to say is that my observations are not your observations.'

Though I continued to argue my case, Charley would have none of it. I have sometimes thought that all the woes of mankind can be put down to this one cause; that we value ourselves too highly.

Eleven weeks after courtship, female gadzocks give birth quickly and painlessly, not to a single calf, as usually happens with our domestic beasts, but to a whole litter. Three is the usual number, though litters of both two and four are not uncommon, gadzocks, like our domestic cattle, having four teats. But unlike any ruminant that I know of, every one of these first calves is male. Just as gestation is short, so is weaning. The calves, though small at birth, are suckled for five weeks, at the end of which their mothers give each of them over to the charge of one of the adult males. The calves at this stage are hardly the size of a common terrier, but eagerly follow their guardians, who show the greatest tenderness and concern to their new charges. The pairs of young and old spend the next two years of their lives together, staying more or less separate from others of their species, it being the task of the older to care for the younger and show it where to find food and water.

The gadzocks, whether singly, in pairs, or in mating groups, appear to move around my island at random, staying in one area for a week or two, then moving elsewhere, the whole island, indeed, being criss-crossed with their paths. Though the southern and western sides of the mountain fall steeply to the sea, its northern and eastern slopes are gentler, descending gradually into more or less level country (the sketch will give you a clearer idea of the island's geology and topography).[18] The island is small enough that the gadzocks can never be far from a beach where they can find their food. They spend about six hours each day feeding, though they use not the sun for their clock but the tides. At each low tide, be it day or night, every gadzock on my island will be found on the beach, feeding on the seaweed left stranded by the retreated water. For the rest of the time they retire to the bush and the forests, where they can usually be found lying in the shade of a tree, peacefully ruminating. Another discovery I have made about gadzocks is this; among the bulls, Greek love is so common as to prove the rule. Unlike our own species, there is no inhibition, no secrecy about it. Male gadzocks nuzzle and lick, tease and tup each other as the fancy takes them. The young ones with their guardians, young with young, old with old. It is a joyous thing to see.

I have not yet mentioned the cows. As soon as the first litter of males is weaned and departed, the female mates again with the remaining members of her seraglio. Her second litter invariably comprises one or more females. The heifers are not adopted out, but stay with their mother, from whom they continue to suckle. Not until ten months have passed are they full-grown, and independent. Thus up to eight young are born each year to each female.

Whether one male fathers all the young in a litter or each has a different father, I cannot say. The females appear to mate with whichever males enter their seraglio, so perhaps each mating results in a single calf. Nor can I say how it comes about that all calves of the first litter are male, all the second female. Last year I attempted a breeding experiment, using animals which I had captured and penned, but they refused to mate

---

[18] No such sketch has been found.

(my experience in breeding pigeons and shell parrots proved little use in crossing gadzocks). I would have liked to try to determine the matter afresh, perhaps by marking the animals in some way and observing them in nature, but I fear the mountain has other plans.

One more thing I would like to determine about gadzocks is this; who really choses whom? Yankee sealers say that in southern waters bull sea-elephants own harems, into which they coerce females against their will, then fight other males for possession of yet more females. It has occurred to me recently that this may simply be a matter of viewpoint. If we look at it from the females' side, might the females not be choosing which male they wish to be attached to? The fighting among the male sea-elephants simply gives the females the opportunity to decide which is the stronger, and so the best father for their offspring, and to judge and choose their mate accordingly. And so for gadzocks. Are the females seducing the males, or are the males choosing the females? Who is to say? And who is to say whether, those years ago in Shrewsbury, did I choose Philos, or did he choose me?

By now you will be remembering your Malthus, and thinking that such a high rate of procreation of gadzocks on so small an island should soon lead to the animals exhausting the supply of food. And so it would, were it not for the fact that the males greatly outnumber the females, a circumstance which has interesting implications for population growth. Although each female produces up to eight young each year (and most of these seem to survive to breeding age), I calculate the annual increase from births at no more than one-sixth. As the mortality rate of the animals is about the same, the result is no net increase in population. I have named the species *Bovulus alleni*, and from my observations the gadzocks on the island number no more than seventeen hundred.

I only once shot a gadzock. I shot it for meat, the day after Charley and I arrived here, but such was its flavour that I declared that I would rather eat the seaweed they feed on. Had it tasted well, I still would not have had the heart to shoot another; like all the animals here, they are so tame and trusting that there is small joy in killing one. Charley killed many gadzocks. Had he not died, he may well have killed them all.

Chapter 2

KILLING HAS NEVER been my pleasure, yet I have taken many lives. Poison has been my favourite tool, and how fresh to me even now is my first experience of the art. It was the summer when the Iron Duke routed old Boney at Waterloo (I remember asking my stepfather why the church bells were ringing on a Friday). It was 1815, and I must have been six years old.

I never knew my parents, having been fostered from before memory began to an old couple (or so they seemed to me) in a remote cottage in the Shropshire hills. The cottage, with its surrounding meadows, woods and streams, was my world, and looking back at them now the guardians of my world were right enough in their way. 'Gaffer' and 'Gammer' I called them, and their other names are not important now. They fed me and watered me and clothed me, they took me to church on Sundays. The old man taught me to read from the Bible and Milton, the only two books in the house, and he beat me when I was bad. The old woman ensured that I was familiar with the use of soap, and of mop and broom. They took care of me, but they did not care for me. The old man had formerly been a gardener at some great house, and spent most of his time in his small cottage garden. He tended and planted it with great care, though never with flowers and shrubs, only with things to eat. Peas in the spring, beans and gooseberries and lettuce in the summer, apples, beets and turnips in the autumn, potatoes and cabbages in the winter, and carrots all year round. The old man was proud and jealous of his work, and waged merciless war

11

on all creatures that dared to fly or crawl over the low stone wall into his vegetable haven. Earwigs and sparrows were his special bane, and the only time I remember him smiling was when, having gathered up the earwigs each morning from the broken pipes he laid about the garden, he would tip them into the fire; or when he reached into the sparrow trap to crush each little feathered head between thumb and forefinger. The old woman had no pleasures, and hardly left the house. She baked our bread each morning, cooked our dinner each day, and sewed our clothes each evening, in summer by the window or in winter by the fire. Living thus, away from town and village, with no brothers or sisters, and no friends of my own age, I grew into a strange and solitary child. Though I enjoyed my book reading, above all I learned to read nature.

Most of my days were spent outdoors, year round. In the springtime I could tell which patch of briar the jenny wren would choose for her nest, and whether the magpie would find it and rob it. I became particularly fond of newts, and knew which rocks they would be hiding under in winter and when they would be down in the pond in spring to lay their eggs, each wrapped up inside the curled leaf of a water weed. I knew where in the woods the morels would appear in autumn, I could see at a glance whether the track through the bracken was a broad badger highway or a slim fox path, but above all I acquired a particular fondness for beetles.

Should you ask this rheumaticky old man today why he was fascinated by beetles, his reply would be, 'Have you ever tried to catch a dragonfly?' But how did it really start? Why, as a child, did I favour beetles, rather than birds, or even rocks? It is true that insects are beautiful and all children love beautiful things, but I think that what first attracted me to insects, and to beetles in particular, was their 'otherness'. As a young child, I instinctively knew what it would be like to be a fox or a pigeon, animals which have warm red blood like ours, and flesh and bones, who bark and coo as we do, who have eyes like ours which must surely see the world as we do. But who knows what a beetle sees? Just as I could not look into a beetle's eyes, I could not look out of them. Though I could *see* beetles, I could not imagine *being* one, and I am sure it was this that first attracted me to them. The world of a ladybird or a cockchafer was just as real as mine but existed in parallel with my own. Though we were each of us aware of the other's existence we shared few perceptions or experiences, and I thus made the discovery in my early childhood that there was much more to life than I could ever know (when Hamlet spoke to Horatio of the scope of his philosophy, had his eye been caught by a humble beetle?).

This early epistemological musing was not to the exclusion of more empirical pursuits. All my spare time was taken up in the acquisition and examination of every beetle I came across, in an attempt to find out about them as much as I could. I tried to keep my pursuit secret from the old woman and the old man, who would have killed them all, and having no-one to tell me the names of most of the species that I found, I invented my own. There was the big black Cherry Beetle, which oozed red liquid when I picked it up; the little red and black Smoker, which fired off a volley of tiny white clouds when disturbed; the Green Beetle (not to be confused with the Green Runner), which I found in summer only on dog roses. In the pond at the edge of the forest lived the Big Nipper, difficult to catch and even more difficult to hold, and the Stinker, the smell of whose white exudation I can still conjure up in my olfactory imagination. I had names for scores of my little friends, for so I thought of them, and never dreamed of killing them (had not naming them given me possession enough?). The man who first introduced me to killing was a man of God.

The old couple had few visitors to the cottage, for it was an isolated place and they appeared to have no relatives or friends. Our only regular guest was the local parson, a mild and distracted man, who would appear at the cottage door once a month, unprompted and unannounced, always wearing the same black habit and always giving the same greeting. It was his custom to address both men and boys as 'sir' and women and girls as 'ma'am', so after the obligatory, 'Good day to you, sir, good day ma'am, and a good day to you too, sir,' the parson would be shown to the best chair beside the fire and offered a cup of tea and some bread and butter, which he always accepted after some small protest, while I would be stood before him to hear my latest sins described in serious horror by my stepfather. During one such visit my stepfather was informing the parson how I had recently acquired the habit of secretly bringing home horrid crawling things, beetles and the like, when the parson's normally placid features acquired a shadow of animation. Interrupting my stepfather with one raised hand, he turned to me with an unexpected and incongruous smile.

'So,' he intoned, 'we have an entomologist among us. You must tell me, sir, what you have discovered.'

Hesitatingly, I began to describe my beetles and their habits to the parson, who to my great surprise became almost excited, nodding vigorously at each new piece of information.

'Yes, yes,' he would say, 'that must be the so-and-so,' using strange long words for each beetle I mentioned. The parson then declared to my astonished step-parents that, far from attempting to break me of this perversity, they should be encouraging my new hobby.

'It is by such study that we here can most easily divine the mind of our Creator,' he piously informed them, leaving them to work out whether he meant that every Christian might share this insight, or that it was limited to those of us living in his particular parish. The parson then announced that he would be pleased to supply me with the basic equipment to enable me to continue my divination. He was as good as his word, and on his next visit brought with him a wooden box, containing a paper packet of exceptionally long and thin pins, a cork board, and an empty jar. The jar looked harmless enough, of clear glass though with half an inch of some sort of paste in the bottom which smelled faintly of cherry stones.

'This', said the parson, 'is your killing jar.'

The parson told me that he had set a few crystals of poison beneath a thin layer of plaster of Paris at the bottom of the jar, and explained in words completely new to me the use of this and the other items; how a specimen should be placed into the jar and the lid closed. The specimen would be soon be killed by the cyanide, and as soon as it was dead it should be pinned through the thorax on to the setting board with its legs and antennae extended. When it had dried, the specimen could be transferred to a piece of card, preferably inside a box, and clearly labelled with species, date and location.

'And don't forget to write your name on the label, too,' he added.

I did as the parson said, and the first insect I put into my killing jar was a large male stag beetle. Such a slow and handsome creature, it took one day and one night to die, one day and one night of crawling and slipping up the sides of its invisible prison, and for that day and night I watched and wept continuously. When the beetle was dead, I took it from the jar as the parson told me, pinned it on to the cork board that the parson had given me, set its legs, and wrote out my little label.

As a child I had already begun to realise, and have often noticed since, what great divide exists between people who are aware of the natural world and those who are not. The difference strikes me most strongly when, while in conversation with someone, my eye is caught by some small movement or unusual shape. Usually a glance is enough to confirm to myself that the speck crossing the sky has the rising and falling trajectory of a sparrow rather than the arrowed flight of a starling, or that the small black spot on the ground has the solid form of a cricket rather than the misty appearance of a spider. The interruption caused to the conversation by this glance is so slight as to have no effect. If my companion is of a like mind, aware of the natural world, he will have registered my glance. Perhaps he will have followed it and confirmed for himself the object of my attention. Perhaps he will merely have noted to himself that my concentration has been momentarily diverted and, intuitively understanding that the cause is something natural but not remarkable, refrained from seeking its identity. If, on the other hand, my companion is one of those people to whom a bird in flight or a spider in a web is all but invisible unless it is pointed out to them, he will either not notice that my attention to him has lapsed, or will ask what I am looking at. Being peripheral to his interest, the creatures of the natural world are peripheral to his vision. They have a lesser existence. Those with other sensitivities, perhaps to race, or sex, or even to style of dress, may feel similarly divided from their fellows, but the gulf between those who notice the natural world and those who do not seems to me more fundamental, and has long been a source of fascination to me. We surely all of us start out with a curiosity about the natural world. In many it is later lost or subverted. Is it thus a childish trait, an anachronism in an adult? This is a point on which I am undecided.

One afternoon in the summer of 1816 I returned from an expedition to the river marsh beyond the woods, jars full and pockets bulging, to find a black horse tied up outside the gate. The parson rode a grey mare. As I approached the cottage I could hear men's voices within, but when I sought to enter the old woman stopped me at the door, telling me that we needed more firewood. I knew well that the wood box was full (had I not filled it myself that morning?), but off I went, back to the woods, and when I returned with my bundle the black horse was gone. As I stacked up my load on top of the box, the old people stood silently by the table. The old man exchanged a quick glance with the old woman.

'I have something to tell you,' he said. 'You are seven years old now, and the Trustees have decided that next year you must go to school.'

'In Shrewsbury,' said the woman, nodding her head in approval of her own words. 'Doctor Butler's.'

'The carriage is coming tomorrow,' added the old man.

That was all. For the rest of the evening, everything was as it always had been. We ate our bread and broth in silence, after supper the old man took down his Bible and began to read, and as dusk fell and the owl began its regular evening enquiry from the tall sycamore on the edge of the forest, I was sent upstairs to my cot.

Until that moment I had never heard of the 'Trustees', yet though I can remember feeling some curiosity about the word itself, I felt none about the people it represented. As children do, I simply assumed that this was the kind of thing that happened to everyone. Shrewsbury, though, was a different matter. I had never once been beyond the local village, let alone travelled as far as the town, though we could see the distant towers of St Chad's and St Alkmund's from the top of our hill. The town was both a place of mystery and attraction. I had a vague idea of what school was; I knew that it was a place for children, yet although, as I say, I had little experience of other children, the idea interested me. That night I lay awake a long time in my small room, gazing out of the window at the moonlit clouds and pondering over the changes which were about to happen. It was not until long after the old couple were themselves abed and snoring that I finally fell asleep.

I awoke the following morning to a clear sunny day. As usual, the cock was crowing in its pen, and as usual it was porrage for breakfast. As usual, the meal was eaten in complete silence. But a carriage did indeed arrive soon afterwards (I suppose I must have seen a carriage, though I am sure that I had never been inside one), and I found that the old woman had already packed up my small bundle of belongings, among which I was pleased to see was my insect box and other paraphernalia. The old man spoke a couple of words to the driver, opened the door, told me to load my bag and myself inside, then closed the door of the carriage behind me. No further words were spoken; the old man simply nodded to the driver, and off we went. The old woman did not leave the house. I left the cottage without the slightest fear or regret, and if my step-parents had any, I was unaware of them. Was that a strange way to treat a human child? Perhaps so.

My first memories of Shrewsbury were of crossing the English bridge into a sudden wave of sounds and smells. It was a market day (though I did not know it then) and the streets seemed to be full of people and animals, shouting and braying. My driver had also to shout to clear the way, but before I had time to make any sense of the hustle and bustle around me, we had driven through the double gates of the school, they had been shut behind us, and the carriage door was opened by a tall boy, clearly somewhat older than myself. He called for another boy to take my bundle, and bade me follow him. When I hesitated, he smiled.

'Don't worry, young'un,' he said. 'Doctor Butler wants to see you, and I doubt that he'll eat you this time.'

We entered a large building and walked a short way down the hall to a closed door. The tall boy knocked once, waited for a 'Come' from within, opened the door and ushered me into the room.

A man was sitting at a great desk, his head bent low. For what seemed like several minutes, he did not look up, and he said not a word. The only sound within the room was the ticking of a clock on the mantelpiece, while through the closed window came fainter sounds, of boys calling and shouting in the yard outside, and fainter still, the noises of the town. I could hear my own breathing, and with each inhalation came smells I did not recognise, of books and furniture wax and tobacco. On the desk beside the inkwell lay a brown and chipped clay pipe, from which arose a thin spiral of white smoke. The rest of the desk was covered with papers and open books, and more books lined the shelves around the room, all of different sizes and colours and, as far as I could read them, all with different titles. I could never have imagined that so many books could have been written. Then I realised that Doctor Butler was looking at me. He had not raised his head, but he had raised his eyes and was examining me intently from beneath his brows.

'Yes, there is a family resemblance,' he said. He looked at me for several seconds more. 'Yes.' Then he dropped his eyes once again towards the papers on his desk.

'Thank you, Erasmus,' he said to the tall boy, adding, as we headed towards the door, 'Give him a bath.'

I had not the slightest idea what Doctor Butler had meant. Family resemblance to the old man and the old woman, to the tall boy, to boys in general? I did not have the chance to dwell at length on this question. Within minutes I had been handed over to the school matron who took me outside to the pump, where she directed two of the servant boys to strip me and scrub me, to the great amusement of my fellow pupils. I was not in the slightest embarrassed (having not yet learned that exquisite emotion), but rather puzzled by this treatment. Was it a punishment, I wondered, and if so, for what? The doctor's enigmatic statement quite vanished from my mind, and it was not until many years later that I even recalled the words.

To such a solitary child, my new schoolmates were strange specimens indeed, and spending as we did almost all our time together, I had much opportunity to observe them. My school lessons were quite different from the clumsy methods the old man had used to teach me. They consisted of reading a variety of texts, then reciting from them, answering questions about them, and copying from them. This novelty of words I greatly enjoyed, and I became an eager student of Greek and Latin (that

I should be able to talk in tongues like the people of the Bible greatly amused me). Not only did all of us boys study together, we played together and ate together, and slept together, four to a bed, in the single attic room that formed the dormitory. This room was reached through a trapdoor in the ceiling, up a heavy ladder which was put up each night and taken down each morning by the porter. For the first few weeks at school I would hardly sleep at night, such was my excitement at these novel arrangements. After the others were asleep I would creep from my bed and, taking the candle from the small shelf by the trapdoor, would wander around the dormitory, gazing fascinated at the sleeping faces of my fellow-pupils. I remember thinking then that it is not so much death that is the leveller, but simple sleep. The rich man's son and the poor orphan, the virtuous and the wicked, the happy and the sad, are all one to blind Morpheus. But though all the boys looked alike in their sleep, they none of them looked like me. These creatures came from another world, and I could no more see into their closed eyes than I could into a beetle's. The Doctor himself was also a mystery to me. How could one man know so much, and why did everyone laugh so much when he made a joke that was not funny? Yet I enjoyed my learning, the history and geography of ancient lands, the epics of Homer, the odes of Horace. Doctor Butler himself instructed us in the classics, being particularly fond of Greek drama. He delighted to stage the tragedies of Aeschylus, Euripides and Sophocles, taking the parts of the main characters himself, with us boys as the chorus. So I became entranced by stories of the powerlessness of men against the gods, the fickleness of fate and randomness of reward. Such stories seemed to mirror my own experiences. I learned, too, the inevitability of hubris being punished by ruin, though I never thought then to apply these lessons to my own behaviour.

Philos told me that he fell in love with me the day he saw me step out of the carriage at Doctor Butler's school. It was, he said, my good looks that first attracted him, then my aloofness (who were all these people, what was I meant to say, how was I meant to play?). Five years older than I, yet still looking very much a boy, it was gentle Philos who spoke to me despite my silence, who took me into his laboratory, despite my feigned indifference, to show me his crystals and sublimates; it was Philos who walked with me in the woods, reciting to me the names of the flowers and birds, and of his friends and family. And it was Philos who looked out for me, who protected me, who cared for me, who stood up for me against the bully Corfield and interceded with the Doctor that I might sleep in his bed. Philos, gentle philosopher; thus I named him, and thus he soon became mine. But what attracted me to him? It was not love, for I had never learned to love. I remember that I felt a certain awe for this lofty being who knew everything, dealt easily with everybody. That he was handsome I had no doubt; tall for his twelve years, fine-featured, his forehead already high, his mouth resolute. Yet though clever of tongue, he had about him a gentleness that glowed like a light within, and he was loved by both masters and boys. I now wonder if I was attracted not by Philos himself, but by his very love for me. I had never been loved, and this new feeling of being adored, of being caressed and admired, felt wonderful. Who could resist? Not I. Did I ever love Philos? I do not know, but I thank him for his love then, and his steadfastness in years to come, and I thank him for introducing me to his little brother. And I thank Philos for introducing me to the love of men. It is nonsense that such love should be condemned. Among male gadzocks there is no such nicety; perhaps that is why they are such peaceable creatures.

I had been at school nearly a year when Philos arrived back from spending the weekend at home and said, 'You must come and meet the family. My brother will be coming to school soon. He must meet you.'

I had already seen his house; Philos had pointed out The Mount to me often enough on our walks together, a fine new building on the outskirts of town, not a mile from the school by road, more than two if we took the river path. I was curious to accept his invitation, yet diffident. This would be something new, something unfamiliar, and my recent experiences had given me a surfeit of the unfamiliar. But in the end I could no more resist an invitation from Philos than I could stop the beat of my heart, and with his usual effortless efficiency Philos arranged an exeat for us both on the following Sunday. On that day, as the castle clock struck nine, Philos and I did not follow the other boys to the right as we filed out of the chapel, but walked straight through the great school gates and into Castle Street, free men for a day.

Philos had already told me all about his young brother, Bobby, and his three sisters, Catherine, Elizabeth and Caroline. His mother had recently died (an event which I knew to be momentous but I confess had no more meaning to me than reading that Caesar's mother died), but his father the doctor (a *real* doctor, Philos insisted, a medical man, not like Doctor Butler) was still very much alive, and as we strolled together over the Welsh bridge on that warm summer morning, he again described the family to me, and the grand lunch we would soon enjoy. Cook prepared the same meal for every Sunday lunch; meat pie and vegetables, and baked apples to finish.

'And after lunch we'll take a walk, and you can do some of your wretched beetling,' my friend assured me.

Our appetites lending speed to our feet, we arrived at the gates of The Mount as the distant clock struck the quarter hour, but before going up to the house itself Philos insisted that we should look for his brother. Philos had already told me that his father greatly esteemed asparagus, and in early summer it was always young Bobby's task to pick some for the doctor's lunch. Bobby was almost sure to be in the asparagus patch now. We walked over the lawn past a great linden, and made towards a patch of feathery green.

'Yes, there he is,' said Philos, pointing to a dark shape among the foliage.

At first all I could see among the vegetation was a large quantity of brown hair, then there appeared beneath it a large and rounded nose. Intent as this person was on his harvesting, I had much opportunity to observe this nose as we approached, and it was only when the figure raised his head at his brother's hullo that his other features became visible and I saw they belonged to a boy of about my own age. As he recognised his brother his mouth opened in the widest grin, while his eyebrows rose to almost meet his hair. The two brothers greeted other with much affection, then Philos turned to me.

'This is Bobby,' he said and, muttering something about it being time to milk the cow, left us alone together.

What should I do, what should I say? I felt shy to the point of fear, but how quickly this young brother of Philos put me at my ease. He briefly enquired of me my name, then immediately asked if I would help him with his task of picking asparagus, showing me which shoots to pick, and how to break them off near the ground. Once thus occupied, my panic subsided and I was soon at my ease. I remember thinking what a friendly chap this Bobby was (though my eyes continued to be fixed by that nose), and thinking what a strange vegetable we were picking, so different from the turnips and cabbages I was accustomed to. The asparagus smelt so odd at first that I could not imagine eating it, but once my new friend's wide smile had persuaded me that it was safe, I took a bite from the end of one of the green shoots (it was thus that I acquired a taste for asparagus which I have never lost, and I still prefer eating my asparagus raw). As we sat together eating and counting out the spears of asparagus for the doctor's lunch (he required, I was informed, at least three dozen), I recalled Philos's words.

'Your brother didn't say you had a cow,' I said. My friend

looked puzzled, then, realising to what I was referring, burst into laughter.

'No, no, he hasn't gone to milk a real cow,' he said. 'My brother has gone to get another advance from Father, that's all. I think you'll like Father.'

While we sat thus talking away and munching on our raw asparagus, I noticed a skipjack crawling up my new friend's stocking. I reached over to pick the little beetle off, and if Bobby was surprised that I had never eaten asparagus, I was surprised that he had never seen a skipjack perform. Surely everyone knew that if you turned one of these beetles on its back, it would leap into the air with a click? Bobby was so enthralled at this small discovery, and we became so engrossed in searching under rocks and bark for more beetles, that the cook had to come out and fetch both us and the asparagus in for lunch.

Chapter 3

IF I HAD BEEN impressed with what I had so far seen of the garden and grand house, I was even more impressed with the doctor. By the time Bobby and I arrived in the dining room Philos was already at the table, as were his assorted sisters. Just as we two had squeezed into our chairs, their father appeared. He was the largest man I had ever seen. Though not as tall as Doctor Butler, his width very nearly equalled his height, and after lowering himself carefully into his chair and spreading his vast girth with an equally vast napkin, he nodded towards me, smiled warmly around the table at his children, and called out to the cook for his 'sparrow-grass'. As the steaming bowl of asparagus appeared, he looked over towards me.

'No good for children, sparrow-grass, bad for your kidneys. Good to see you, lad.'

He piled his plate high with the bright green vegetable and, after carefully spooning out the last drops of melted butter, he spoke again.

'Makes your piss stink.'

I assumed that the great doctor was saying this for my benefit, though what he was talking about I had no idea. But it was of little matter; I was already busy trying to follow the excited chatter around the table, the teasing and bantering, in which the doctor himself soon joined with much enthusiasm. Things were different here, I realised. Here was not the silence of the cottage, nor the uneasy politeness of school. I looked over towards Philos. His eyes were shining as he recounted to two

25

of his sisters the latest story from school, to which his younger brother listened eagerly. It was clear that Philos loved each of his sisters, yet this love did not stop him loving Bobby. All loved him. Their father, beaming as he wiped the butter from his mouth, loved them all, and though he commanded their respect, it was clearly a respect freely given, born of love rather than fear. The whole household seemed to run on love, and it was again brought home to me that love is not something innate, it is something which is learned. I could see all this at a glance, but it was like looking through a window-pane. Though I could see, I could not touch. Nor, on my side of the glass, could I be touched.

Yet though I could not touch I could feel, and the feeling I recall from that first meeting with Philos's family was the most strong and burning jealousy. It was as if Philos's love for his own and only brother, and his brother's for him, was a calculated blow to my own happiness. I, who had never known love before, now wanted all of Philos's love for myself. As I listened to the happy conversation of my hosts I seethed and boiled within, yet I am sure that my jealousy passed unnoticed by the family. After the doctor had finished his asparagus, the cook removed the empty plate from in front of the doctor and replaced it with a large covered dish.

'Ah, good,' said the doctor, winking at me as the cook removed the lid. 'Rat pie!'

It was indeed a handsome pie, though I had never before heard of people eating rats. Elizabeth, the eldest sister, explained to me that the rats were from Uncle Jos's cat farm. Uncle Jos was immensely rich, she said, and had made all his money from this wonderful farm.

'Cat fur,' she said simply.

'Ah yes, cat fur, that's the thing,' said Philos, as his father sliced open the pie. 'Lovely stuff, comes in all colours and patterns, all lengths. Sells for a fortune. Not hard to breed are cats, and no trouble with food. Why, once you set up a cat farm, it runs itself. Isn't that right, Father?'

'Indeed so,' the doctor gravely replied, leaning forward as much as his great girth would allow to inhale the fragrant steam.

'You see,' Philos continued, again turning to me and passing me a plate, 'cats eat rats. And rats, they'll eat anything.'

'They'll eat anything, will rats,' confirmed his father. 'Like pigs. Pigs'll eat anything – corn, kale, meat. You remember them pigs of old Bradge, Lizzy?'

'Finest pork in the county, Father,' said Elizabeth.

'Aye. You can't beat a knacker when it comes to good pork.'

There was a brief silence as the doctor continued serving out the pie. I watched, mesmerised, as each plate was passed down the table. No-one had yet been given a piece with a thin tail sticking out.

'Uncle Jos's idea was this, see,' said Philos, gesturing at me to begin. 'You haven't heard about it?'

I shook my head, but left the pie untouched before me.

'Well,' said Philos, 'it's simple. You buy a few kittens' ('Always find kittens,' said the doctor through a mouthful of pie) 'and you buy a few rats. How much will a few rats cost, a few pennies from the ratcatcher? You feed up the rats' ('They'll eat anything, will rats,' interjected the doctor) 'and they'll begin to breed. When the young rats are good and fat you feed 'em to the kittens. In no time the kittens are cats, and they're having kittens, more kittens than you know what to do with. That's when you start making your money. You kill the cats and skin 'em. Sells for a fortune, cat fur.'

Though the pie indeed smelled delicious, still I had not picked up my knife and fork. Philos picked up his own knife and waved it in my direction.

'Now here comes the clever bit; what are you to do with the

27

cat carcasses, eh?' he said. 'Not much use for cat meat, not round these parts.'

Bobby interrupted. 'I'm sure I remember reading that the Tartars are fond of cat,' he said. 'Perhaps you could sell the dead cats to them. Or was it the Mongols? You should know, Catty.'

His younger sister ignored the remark.

'No need, Bobby dear, no need,' said Philos. 'Remember, rats'll eat anything, will rats. You feed 'em to the rats, see?'

The doctor smiled and nodded.

'The rats eat the cats, the cats eat the rats,' continued Philos. 'Once you set up a cat fur farm, why, it's like coining money.'

'But,' said Philos to me, the corners of his mouth turned sadly down, 'as I'm sure I don't have to tell you, rats breed faster than cats. Poor Uncle Jos has more rats than he knows what to do with.'

At this, the doctor picked up a large piece of pie on his own fork and looked at it with solemn admiration.

'It's the least we can do,' he said. I watched fascinated as he put the piece of pie into his mouth, chewed it slowly, swallowed, and gave a deeply satisfied sigh. 'The least we can do.'

'But surely,' I began, and it was only then that I noticed Philos staring at me with an expression which I could not decipher. I looked around the table at the rest of the family. All were completely silent, all were looking at me. Then from Bobby came a small repressed squeak, and that was enough. The whole family burst into laughter loud enough to set the glasses rattling on the sideboard. Oh, I had been well quizzed.

Just as Philos had promised, after our baked apples and cream we three boys set out for a walk along the river and up behind the town. In my memory it was a perfect English summer afternoon, the rooks and jackdaws cawing in the fields, the stock doves warbling from the trees, a yellowhammer calling from every hedgerow. Bumblebees droned among the dead-nettles, and beetles were about in great number. Orange and black soldier beetles patrolled the cow parsley, tiger beetles (my Green Runners) scuttled across the path before us, there was even a large green and purple longhorn displaying itself, as if already killed and pinned, on the leaf of a bramble where we crossed a stile. Though I had not forgotten the incident of the rat pie, I was not sure whether to be amused or angry at the trick that had been played on me. Then, in the meadow below the wood (where Philos and I had often gone alone), I spotted a small animal lying in the grass just off the path. I hushed my friends and crept towards it. The leveret could have been no more than a week old, yet it looked perfect, its bright eye shining, its ears flat along its back, its fur the colour of the warm grass in which it lay. It was completely sure of its own invisibility, as though wishing were enough. I was within a spit of the little thing, yet it stayed so still that I could even see the beat of its heart. Never had I seen anything so alive, so beautiful. Sounds I had been so aware of before, the jackdaws and rooks in the churchyard, the chaffinch singing in the ash, faded away. The only two things in the world were me and the little leveret, and all life was in its eye. And then it was dead. As I had slipped away into my own world of silent admiration, Bobby had quietly pulled a marble from his pocket. Hooking his forefinger around the small stone globe, he had raised it above his head and shied it at the target. It was a perfect shot, striking the leveret right below the ear.

'Well done, young'un,' said Philos, laughing, as he picked up the small, dead form.

I said nothing, I could not. With life had disappeared beauty. I took the little leveret from Philos's hand. It was limp and warm. I could smell the blood that trickled down past its now-closed eye, and my own eyes were prickling strangely. But Bobby, his eyes were shining, and in his bloody victory he looked to me then even more beautiful than the hare. Are we not strange animals?

*   *   *

There are no hares on my island. The only mammals which I have discovered, other than the gadzocks and the several kinds of bat, are two species of mice, one of which is unusual for its voice, the other for its aquatic habit. This latter, though no larger than a house mouse, is an excellent swimmer, living and feeding mainly on the reeds and rushes which grow around the freshwater lake and ponds. The reed mice construct small nests of the leaves of a species of aquatic sedge, much as the English harvest mouse does among grass stems, and I have spent much time in investigating their economy. It was while I was observing one of these mice, which I have named *Mus aquaticus*, in the construction of its nest, that I discovered the mudswallows.

The long rains here are from the end of November to the beginning of February. During this season the skies are often overcast for days or weeks at a time, and rain is of more or less daily occurrence. If the island can be said to have a winter season, it is this, marked as it is by a decrease in temperature of four or five degrees (though still warmer than most Englishmen are used to in summer), and a distinct lull in the activity of the animal life of the island. This being the period that precedes that when birds begin nesting, and during which many of them choose to moult, the avian life of my island is more subdued than at other times. Few birds are visible, either on the wing or in the bush, and during my first such season here I noticed on my walks to the lake that, although flies were still about in considerable numbers, the swallows, which had been constantly present up to then, were no more to be seen hawking over the lake.

To a bird as swift and aerial as a swallow, it is presumably of little consequence or difficulty, during bad weather, to fly away to where conditions are more favourable, even if the journey involves crossing a hundred leagues of ocean. The Reverend White of Selbourne made frequent observations of swallows flying before a summer storm, and sailors out at sea have made similar observations. Though I had not seen any swallows leaving my island, I had noticed them, young and old, massing in the reedbeds around the lake for some weeks previously, much as you might see the swallows and martins of England doing in September, prior to their autumn departure. I therefore assumed that the swallows' absence in November was due to them having left the island, and that when the rains stopped, they would return.

One February dawn, 'under the opening eyelids of the morn', as I was watching a reed mouse weaving a new nest (I had discovered that the female constructs a separate nest for each offspring in her litter, though to what purpose I know not), my eye was distracted by a movement in the water among the reeds. My first thought was that it had been made by a swimming reed mouse, or by a fish, but I soon saw that whatever had made the movement was now about to emerge from the water and climb one of the reed-stems. The creature was neither mouse nor fish. It was brown and rather slimy, being still covered in mud from the bed of the lake. As I watched this strange creature ascend the reed, I could see that it was doing so by means of two clawed feet, which it placed one over the other on the stem, so slowly pulling itself clear of the water. When it had reached a point a yard or so above the water, where the sun was already warming the tops of the reeds, the creature rested for a few moments in the sunlight, before spreading out two long, narrow wings. As the sunlight slowly dried the mud, I recognised the strange creature as a swallow. I looked around, and more muddy swallows were emerging from the water, or were already perched on other reeds, wings outstretched, warming themselves, and shaking out and preening their feathers in the morning sunlight. The swallows had not migrated during the island winter, they had hibernated.

I have named the mudswallow *Hirundo gilbertii*. By dissection, I have discovered that the birds' crops are full of fine gravel when they emerge from the water. Presumably this is swallowed before, rather than during, immersion to act as a counterweight to their natural buoyancy, but how a creature of so active a constitution can remain alive under water for many weeks, is one puzzle which, I fear, neither I, nor the Theory, can answer. I intend to make further observations on the subject.

On our return to The Mount after our walk, I ran up to Bobby's father to tell him that his son had just killed a hare. His reaction was immediate. What, his son, the son of a gentleman, poaching on private land like a common criminal? Bobby did not deny his crime, nor indeed could he have, the leveret's blood being still fresh on his fingers. Red-handed the doctor caught Bobby, and red-arsed he beat him. Innocent though my betrayal may have appeared, I well knew what the doctor's reaction would be, and I well remember that Bobby's punishment felt like my revenge, but my revenge for what? For being teased by him and Philos about the rat pie; for killing my hare; for being loved and admired by Philos, who loved me; for having a family, where I had none? And was my retaliation against Bobby, or was it against Philos? I do not know why we betray the things we love.

A few weeks later, Bobby himself started school. I must have been sleeping better by then, for I was awoken in the middle of the night by all the boys yelling and stamping around on the dormitory floor. When someone shouted '*Cave!*', I was still only half-awake, so that when Doctor Butler, woken by the ruckus, stormed upstairs and climbed the ladder, he found me apparently the only one awake, still sitting up in bed trying to make sense of it all. It was me he pulled out of bed by my ear, me he ordered downstairs, and me he flogged. Did Bobby plan it? Was this his own revenge?

I have often observed that the morality of children is not so much based on what is right and wrong, but on what is and is not fair. As a child myself, I had no thoughts one way or the other as to whether flogging in general was a good thing; it had always been just part of life. But that I should be flogged for the actions of others, this I knew to be unfair. Despite what the stories of Sophocles and Euripides might say, it made nonsense of the relationship between the cause and the effect on which, children or adults, our modern world rests. And a thought has just occurred to me, that Bobby knew this too. It has just occurred to me that perhaps that is why thereafter he became even more friendly. He was trying to set things to right again, to restore to his own world the balance which this small piece of randomness had threatened. Thus began the friendship which was to shape my life.

Chapter 4

WHAT IS THE DIFFERENCE between a lake and a pond? Just another small riddle that enters my mind uninvited and refuses to leave until I provide an explanation. The question, though small, is insistent. It will be not be satisfied that it is simply to do with size. 'What size?' it demands. 'At exactly what point does a large pond become a small lake?' While my mind ponders the riddle anew, I drop my guard and in slips another: 'If you cannot say, can any man?' Then I begin to wonder whether, if no man can answer a question, is it a question at all? So small questions lead to larger ones, until they exceed the compass of our thought and vanish away.

Was it really Charley who caused so much that I have regretted? It was he who betrayed the Theory, it was he who brought me here. But was it not I who told him the Theory, and I who eagerly agreed to come on the search for the golden scarab? The closer I look for causes, the less I see. Yet I am curiously content, and if there is anyone to thank for my present state of contentment, perhaps it is Charley. Without him, I would never have come to know the natural history of this island.

Despite my occasional epistemological confusion, I have no difficulty distinguishing the lake on my island from the ponds. The lake is near the centre of the island, near the foot of the mountain and some four leagues from my house. It is approximately circular and about half a league across, and as well as supporting several species of aquatic plants, it is home to a large number of birds, including one spoonbill, two ibises, and three or four species of heron (it is probable that both the white and the grey short-necked herons here belong to the same species, but I have not yet confirmed this by dissection). The ponds are quite distinct from the lake, and are fed not by streams but by groundwater, which, welling up from its subterranean source, is trapped by a layer of clay which extends over much of the low-lying eastern half of the island, the product, I suspect, of the weathering of an ancient sheet of basalt which poured down from the volcano at some time in the distant past. The ponds rise and fall but little, regardless of season, and are home to a most interesting frog.

All of yesterday the mountain was hidden in cloud, and this morning I awoke to rain, the first for more than a month, and unusual for this time of year. Though the mountain has been speaking to me much of late (make haste, make haste), this morning it was silent, and the only sounds I could hear were the dripping of the raindrops on my roof and the calling of the yellow frogs.

I often hear the frogs from my house, though it is a mile to the ponds from here. I first heard them a few weeks after our arrival, a procession of single sharp taps, between a drum-beat and a smack, which I did not recognise as frog noises, and wondered what could be their origin. That the sounds must be coming from animals of some sort I had no doubt, and so loud were they that I at first thought that the animals must be of considerable size. When I approached the shore of one of the ponds the noises suddenly stopped, and it was then that it occurred to me that, although the call was like none I had ever heard, the callers could only be frogs, for you will have yourself observed how calling frogs all stop together, and then all start together (such unconfident beasts, to so much rely on the audible support of their fellows). When, after much careful stalking among the tall *Typhus* which lined the pond, I eventually found one of the animals, I discovered that although my initial assumption about its dimensions had been an overestimate, the animal was indeed of considerable size, easily covering the palm of my hand. It was a handsome beast, bright yellow with a single green stripe on each flank, and was further remarkable from its mouth having the appearance of an enormous smile, stretching right across its face from one eye to the other, and giving the frog a most amused and amusing expression.

Since that first discovery I have devoted much time to studying these amphibians. My immediate assumption had been that, as in others of their ilk, the calling frogs were all male, yet search though I might I could find no member of the opposite sex. After several more searches over the next few months, I had almost given up on this puzzle when, strolling by the pond one evening to take my pipe, I chanced to see a V-shaped ripple on the water. The sight took me right back to Shrewsbury days, to strolling by the river with Bobby on a winter afternoon and seeing a water vole swimming in the Severn, and I watched eagerly to see if the creature which was creating the disturbance would swim ashore.

It was clearly in no hurry to do so. For several minutes it coursed up and down the pond, about two yards from the edge, invisible but for its ripple. As it did so, I noticed that the frogs, which had become silent on my arrival at the pond, began to call with renewed vigour. I also noticed for the first time that these calls produced their own distinctive ripples on the surface of the pond, now easily visible in the evening light. The ripples were semicircular in shape, radiating from the point at which the frogs called. After ten or so minutes of swimming back and forth, the creature in the pond turned towards one of the calling frogs on the shore. I moved slowly towards a spot on the bank a little away from the frog, yet close enough to maintain a clear view. I could just make out the frog on the shoreline, see its semicircular ripple fanning out with each sound, and see the creature moving towards it. As it reached shallow water, the mysterious creature at last revealed itself to be another frog, though not one-tenth the size of the large one. The large frog stopped calling, slowly raised itself up on its forelegs, and opened its enormous, smiling mouth to reveal a large red tongue surrounded by a startling white mucosa. The small frog crawled purposefully through the shallows to within a few inches of the edge of the pond. It paused briefly, then with a single spring disappeared into the gaping white maw of its larger relative, which immediately snapped shut.

I was at a loss to explain this action. It was clear that the larger frog had just eaten the smaller, yet it also seemed clear that the smaller had leaped to its fate of its own accord. I immediately thought of angler fishes, which lure smaller fish close to them with a wiggling 'bait' on their forward-pointing fin-spine, then gobble them up. Did this frog use a similar technique? Was its large red tongue somehow so attractive to the smaller frog that the hapless animal actually jumped down the throat of its predator? More observation was necessary. I began to spend what became many hours of watching the smiling frogs; what I discovered, I will now describe.

My first discovery was that the small swimming frog almost always swam towards the frog on the bank which had the loudest call, and I was able to demonstrate that it was not the sound itself which was the attraction, but the size of the ripple. I managed to create ripples myself, striking the water with a small wooden paddle, which I fashioned for the purpose. After some experiment I managed to create a regularly shaped ripple, and found that the harder I struck the water, and the larger the wave I made, the more likely I was to attract a swimming frog (though the sound made by my paddle was a simple splash, quite dissimilar to the sharp tap of the calling frogs). Having thus attracted a swimming frog, I had no difficulty in catching it by hand and dispatching it by pithing (for this technique of introducing a sailmaker's needle into the cranium of a frog through the occipital aperture, I have to thank Professor Grant in Edinburgh).

I had assumed that the swimming frogs were females, for it is well known that, almost universally among the Salientia, it is the males which call and the females which are attracted to the call. Dissection revealed that the small frog was a male, its abdomen containing two large testes. These organs were indeed so large that they occupied most of the abdominal cavity, the alimentary system having degenerated to such a size as to preclude effective digestion. The male frog was also remarkable for the size and shape of its nuptial pads. Unlike most of its order, these were not simple rough callosities on the wrist, which function to facilitate holding the female during sexual conjunction, but large and soft. To use a human analogy, they resembled a soft wart rather than a hard corn.

I also caught and dissected several of the large calling frogs, which I found to be exclusively female. The reproductive tract, consisting mainly of a dark mass of half developed ova, occupied almost the entire abdomen, again at the expense of the alimentary tract (these frogs, unlike the smaller ones, were well supplied with masses of yellow fat, both within the abdominal cavity and subcutaneously). I noted in particular that the stomachs of the females were shrunken to such a size that would hardly admit a No.4 shot. It seemed impossible that a stomach of such size could contain one of the male frogs that I had witnessed several of them swallowing.

It was becoming clear that the swimming frogs and calling frogs were no more than the male and female of the same species. But if this were so, how could I explain the apparent cannibalism of the males by the females? By continuing my observations of the frogs at the pond, I was able to at last catch a female seconds after she had eaten a male. I immediately dispatched her and returned proudly to my house, frog in pocket. Once home, I carefully pinned my specimen out on a board and prepared my instruments. Lifting the skin of the abdomen with the forceps in my left hand and inserting my scalpel into the vent, I cut up towards the thorax, opening the abdomen while taking great care not to damage the internal organs. On reaching the ribs, I made incisions first to the left and then to the right, pinning back the two flaps thus formed to fully expose the contents of the abdomen. There was the heart, there were the large egg masses. I lifted the eggs aside to expose the alimentary canal. The stomach was empty. The small swimming frog, which I had seen with my own eyes being swallowed by the larger animal not half an hour before, was nowhere to be seen.

I cut through the corner of the mouth to the throat and across to the ribs, laying bare the pharynx, yet still the male frog was nowhere to be seen. The large red tongue lay there, bulbous and contracted on its bed of white mucosa, but no male frog. It could not have been digested in so short a time, of that I was sure. It must have fallen or crawled out of the female's mouth during the trip from pond to home in my pocket. I felt in my pocket, but found nothing. Cursing myself for my carelessness, I was about to throw out the specimen when I noticed a slight movement of the tongue. My first thought was that the movement was an involuntary spasm, a not-uncommon phenomenon in fresh muscle tissue, yet when I observed it for the second time it seemed slow for such a reaction, a rolling rather than a twitching. Probing carefully with my needle, I discovered, at the base of the tongue, an opening in the floor of the mouth. It was inside this opening that I at last found the male frog.

The male had not been swallowed at all, but had crawled, or been directed, into this oral diverticulum, the female's sublingual pouch. The male frog was still alive and quite active, though when I tried to remove it I found that it was firmly attached to the female by its nuptial pads, which it had inserted into two smaller diverticula on the dorsal surface of the pouch. They had become so swollen as to prevent easy withdrawal.

What was the point of this strange behaviour? More observation, and several more dissections, revealed the answer. The two frogs are indeed of the same species. The males are attracted to the females by means of the ripples they make on the ponds. The females, on seeing a male approach, open their brightly coloured mouths, providing a clear target for the males to jump towards. On entering the female's mouth, the male enters the sublingual pouch and immediately attaches itself by inserting its highly vascularised nuptial pads into two corresponding pits on the upper surface of the chamber, which are similarly vascularised. It seems probable that this system acts as a kind of placenta, through which nourishment is exchanged between host and guest, as the male frog remains inside the female for some weeks, during which time neither eats, both being solely nourished by the fat stores within the female. It is during this period that the female lays her eggs. These are not, however, fertilised externally, as is the rule among amphibians. The male, still within the female's sublingual pouch, rather excretes his sperm into the female's pharynx, from where it passes unchanged down the atrophied alimentary tract, eventually fertilising the eggs internally within the female's cloaca. The fertilised eggs are then expelled in the normal way and whipped up by the female's back legs into foamy masses, as is the general rule with other ranids. At the end of the breeding season (which seems variable, simply depending on sufficient rain to fill the ponds and swamps), the female's reproductive tract is empty of eggs and her alimentary system begins to regenerate. The male's does not. His job is now over, and further dissections of females at the end of spawning have revealed that the first meal most females take after their long fast comprises a male frog. I have named the frogs *Rana grantii*. Unusually, they call only during daylight.

The ability to pith frogs was only one of the skills I acquired through the teaching of Professor Robert Grant, late of Edinburgh University. He was also of great help in enabling me to hone my agapitic abilities. Just as there are musicians who are technically brilliant but cannot express the intention of a piece of music, or painters who amaze with their virtuosity of the brush and palette but cannot capture the soul of their subject, so there are those who are skilled at the arts of love while having no concept of the meaning. Though insensitive to the essence of love, I had become expert at creating its form. At school I had already begun to explore this art on other boys than Philos, and masters too. While my days were filled with classics and mathematics, my nights were spent in other studies. Lessons in how to read the hearts of men; experiments in how to attract, how to fan that attraction with indifference, how to fuel it with jealousy; the sport of flattery and control, the use of silence to punish and intrigue. When, in 1822, Philos left Shrewsbury for Edinburgh to study medicine like his father and grandfather before him, I had no intention of releasing him from my well-honed hook. As a desert yearns for rain, so I yearned for his love, and so began a weekly correspondence filled with declarations of affection and oaths of constancy.

Philos's letters to me were no less affectionate, but also brought news of his life in Scotland, and it was thus that I first heard about Grant. Grant was one of Philos's teachers, and for the past year it seemed that all I read was 'Grant said this' and 'Grant did that'. When, in the middle of 1826, Bobby also left for the Northern capital, the Trustees agreed that I could accompany him. It soon became clear to me that Philos and Grant were more than good friends. I had never stopped wanting Philos's total affection. Just as I had been jealous of Bobby, I was jealous of Grant, and I lost little time in planning my campaign.

Chapter 5

FOR THE FIRST TIME in my life, my plans went awry. I had felt confident of arranging matters so that Philos would be forced to chose between me and his new suitor. My years of practice had not been in vain: a judicious prescription of ardour and petulance, kindness and cruelty, left poor Philos so confused that after a few weeks he could take no more. But instead of simply leaving Grant, Philos decided to leave Edinburgh and move down to London to continue his medical studies there. This was not exactly the result I had counted upon, neither was I pleased to find that as the dust from this battle settled, a new threat loomed. Grant began to turn his attentions to Bobby.

I had been delighted to be moving from the confines of a boarding school to become my own man, and doubly delighted that the Trustees had agreed for me to not only accompany my friend Bobby to Edinburgh, but to undertake medical training there. Bobby had been a more reluctant recruit to the family business. Though at school he had been developing an increasing interest in natural history and in the more scientific study of the natural world, he had misgivings about whether the practice of medicine would suit him. Even though he would be joining his beloved brother, he none the less felt sure that he would miss his home and family in Shrewsbury. When Philos left for London so soon after he arrived, he felt lost, and welcomed Grant's overtures with more than his usual innocent enthusiasm. To him, Grant was no more than his brother's friend, a knowledgeable companion to replace the absent Philos on rambles around the countryside. When Grant invited Bobby to his rooms to show him his latest dissection, or let him peer through the microscope at the beauty and complexity of sponge spiculae or pollen grains, I am sure that it seemed to Bobby no more than an informal extension of lectures. But I knew well that Grant had other motives in mind. Though he professed to be interested in Bobby's mind, I knew that Grant was after his heart. And I knew just how to stop him. All it took was a little encouragement.

I had myself arranged to take private anatomy lessons with Grant, suspecting that his interest in my own anatomy might extend beyond the theoretical. Grant soon knew that I was friends with Bobby and Philos, and during our nights together would often ask casually about Philos's 'little brother'. I, pretending that I could not see behind this apparently innocent interest, answered his questions blithely. Yes, Bobby was indeed interested in natural history. Yes, he had told me that he greatly admired Grant, and that he enjoyed Grant's company. I began to embellish my replies. Bobby had mentioned to me that he looked forward all week to his Saturday excursions with Grant; he became distraught when a meeting was cancelled. In short, I soon made Grant believe that Bobby felt as strongly about him as Grant did about Bobby, but that my friend was too shy to make any overt response to Grant's subtle overtures. Indeed, I suggested, perhaps the overtures were a little too subtle, and the message was not getting across clearly. Grant asked me if perhaps I thought a more open approach was called for. Perhaps it was, I replied, and perhaps the walk over to Musselburgh that the two had planned for the following Sunday might be just the time for Grant to try it. I did not need to hear from Bobby on Monday morning what his reaction had been; Grant's black eye told it all, and his dissembling explanation to our class for his injury gave me much amusement.

But despite my jealous games, I myself admired Grant

greatly. It was Grant who first induced me to think clearly about the apparent design of nature, and the possibility of transmutation.

As old Erasmus Darwin had put it:

> First, forms minute, unseen by spheric glass
> Move on the mud, or pierce the watery mass.
> These, as successive generations bloom,
> New powers acquire and larger limbs assume.[19]

Grant was not only well versed in English theorists, he introduced me to Buffon and Lamarck. My own observations had already left me in little doubt that transmutation was a fact, that life must have evolved from simple beginnings. But how? It was surely not by Lamarck's mechanism, by some unconscious will, or exterior guidance, and it was nonsense to assert that changes acquired in life were inherited when every observation told against it. The Lamarck to whom Grant had introduced me was more philosopher than naturalist, basing his ideas of evolution more on reason than observation; as a keen student of natural philosophy in all its forms, I needed more earthy material for my theorising. Experimental evidence was needed, and it was then that I began my breeding experiments with pigeons, which I kept in a loft at my lodgings at Mount Street, and which first caused me to observe the parallels between artificial and natural selection.

I first began to keep pigeons as much for amusement as instruction. It happened that a pair of wild birds were already nesting on the sill outside my lodging when I moved there. The landlady, on first showing me the room, assured me that she would have the birds removed that very day, but she failing to keep to her pledge, I was woken each morning by their soft

---

[19] Lines from the poem 'Zoonomia' by Erasmus Darwin.

coos. I took to feeding the birds, which soon became so tame as to almost ignore my presence, and I became so familiar with them that whereas they had first seemed identical, I could soon distinguish one from another at a glance. When their squabs hatched, I became equally familiar with them. It then occurred to me that there is always *some* variation between individuals. We take this as a matter of course where our own species is concerned, but when we become familiar enough with other creatures we soon notice an equal individuality. This is, of course, the very skill which animal breeders use to identify, and then select, those individuals which they wish to use to improve the strain, and can be applied as well to pigeons as to poultry or pigs. I gained much practical experience of selection and breeding from my loft of pigeons, though rather than using my friends the wild birds, I purchased more special varieties.

Grant was amused by my 'lofty experiments' as he delighted in describing them, but being a true empiricist was always keen to discuss my results during our weekly meeting at his chambers.

'And what new chimaera have you produced this week?' he said one autumn evening, as he welcomed me at his door. I had interrupted him in some anatomical investigation. On his table by the window was a foot, clearly human, fastened to the deal in a somewhat clumsy manner with several bent nails (skilled anatomist though he was, Grant was no carpenter).

My reply was short. For many months I had been trying to produce a bird with both small beak and normal-sized feet, and my lack of success had both puzzled and vexed me.

'Come, then, and see what I have found,' he said, leading me towards the table. The upper surface of the human foot had been neatly flayed, exposing the white tendons. Taking some stout forceps, Grant pulled on one of the severed tendons above the ankle, causing the big toe to lift. As he repeated the process with four other tendons, each of the four other toes duly lifted in response.

'What do you notice?' he asked me.

I was not sure how to reply.

'The only thing I notice is how peculiar it looks to see one toe lift at a time. It looks unnatural.'

Grant slapped me heartily on the back.

'Exactly!' he said. 'We are so used to seeing all our toes curl up together, as if they are all somehow worked by the same mechanism. But you see, they are not. Each toe is perfectly capable of independent movement, do you see?' He demonstrated once more by pulling each tendon in turn. 'So why is it that they act together?'

No answer came to me. I shook my head.

'I suspect that the answer lies not here,' he poked the foot with the forceps, 'but here,' with which words he tapped his head. 'What do you think, eh?'

My response to this question was interrupted by a soft knock at the door. Bidding me be silent, Grant crossed the floor to let in a thin man of suspicious appearance.

'You have it?' said Grant, his recent passion now replaced by enthusiasm of a different kind.

The man nodded, and signalled down the steps to where a stouter man stood waiting, a heavy sack over his shoulder. As soon as he was through the door Grant closed it behind him and hurried over to the table by the window, wrenching off the dissected foot and sweeping away his instruments.

'Hold this,' he said, handing me the foot. 'Now, on to here with it.'

With much grunting and groaning the man heaved his load on to the table and lifted away the sack. Out tumbled the filthy but naked body of a girl, no more than a child, and, from the bloody dent clearly visible beneath her matted hair, clearly dead. Grant inspected the body carefully and rummaged in his desk drawer for a purse.

'Yes, this is fine,' he said.

Taking whatever coins Grant pressed into his palm, the thin man glided towards the door.

'Always a pleasure doing business with you, Professor,' he said, and the two men slipped back out on to the street. Grant came over to stand with me before the table, and put a hand on the chest of the specimen before him.

'Mr Burke really should be more careful,' he said. 'I do believe she's still warm. But I must get to work. Same time tomorrow?'

I left the room.

Why is it that we can accept the death of a beetle in the name of science, but not a human? I knew well that the infamous resurrection men, of whom every medical student of that time was either consciously aware or equally consciously unaware, thought no more of digging up a corpse from a graveyard than we would of picking up an insect from a meadow. If a corpse was not available, or the grave too well guarded, we also knew that such men were not averse to plucking from the streets some beggar or prostitute whom nobody would miss, or, if they did so, would not complain about. Medical teachers and students needed cadavers for dissection, and legitimate sources could not supply the demand. If a doctor could refine his skills on a dead body before essaying them on a patient, was this not to the benefit of the living? And removing dead bodies from graveyards, or hopeless and useless paupers from the gutters, was this such a terrible loss? If I could drop a stag beetle into my killing jar with scarcely a thought, why should not Burke use his blackjack to collect larger specimens? These were some of the thoughts which came to me as I looked down on the dead girl on Grant's dissecting table, but even as I turned them over in my mind one by one, I knew that they were wrong. Though I had no God, no scripture or commandment to decide the question for me, there was within me the undeniable conviction that any murder, however it is described or justified, cannot be condoned nor forgiven. And if I knew it well then, I know it better now.

Chapter 6

APART FROM THE MOUNTAIN'S mighty voice, my island is a quiet place. Like most tropical places, it is not subject to the same winds which are so much a feature of higher latitudes. The heat of a typical afternoon may be moderated by a slight sea breeze, a rainstorm may be accompanied by stronger squalls, but most days, and especially mornings, are usually so still that the large fronds of the cocoa-nut trees hang motionless on the trees, while the reeds and rushes which fringe the lake are silent, and not a ripple disturbs its surface.

The lake on my island is not only fringed with water plants of the usual sort, *Typha, Juncio*, etc., but is also home to a species of *Nymphaea* or water-lily. With its white, yellow-centred flowers and circular floating leaves, the plant resembles others of its tribe, and I had taken no great notice of it until, some months ago, I chanced to find one washed up on the shore of the lake. This was in itself remarkable. My previous observations had suggested to me that the lilies preferred to grow in deeper water, being seen in small groups always some yards from the edge of the lake. On retrieving the plant from the water, I was able to see that, though superficially resembling the common water-lily, it differed in several respects.

From my experience in both the northern and southern hemispheres, a typical *Nymphaea* consists of a tough and fibrous rhizome growing in mud, from which are produced the leaves and flowers, which themselves grow upwards on long stalks until they break the surface of the water, when

51

they open out to fulfil their usual functions. The species that I now had before me had a short, swollen rhizome to be sure, though it was curiously shaped and producing only a single leaf on a short stalk. The rhizome itself was distinctly bifurcate, its two equal branches resembling the condition sometimes seen in the common carrot and parsnip. On its underside I could see several of what I took to be brown roots, though they were unbranched and each contracted into a coil or helix, similar in appearance to the curious flower stalks of the ribbon weed or *Vallisneria*, which uncoil to allow the submerged female flower to reach the surface of the water. When I extended one of these roots, I found it to be nearly three yards in length. The root was elastic, and when released it sprang back to its original position. The tip alone was stiff. I immediately found myself speculating on the function of these appendages, and it occurred to me that they might serve as tendrils, like those of the *Convolvulus* or bindweed, to hold the plant to others of its kind.

On turning my attention to the plant's single leaf, I found nothing unusual apart from its singularity. Thin and leathery, though slightly spongy to the touch, the leaf was typical of any other water-lily. When I held it to the light I could see the single layer of enlarged cells that formed its surface, somewhat larger towards the edge. The underside of the leaf was sparsely covered with soft hairs or spiculae. The plant which I had found had no flower, and when I returned it to the water it floated comfortably, the leaf on the surface, the rhizome suspended a few inches below. It seemed probable to me that this water-lily did not root itself in the mud like other water-lilies, but spent all its life afloat, like a giant duck-weed. It was not until some time later that I discovered that this is only part of the story of what is a most remarkable plant.

When I returned to the lake the following day I found that the plant I had left floating near the bank was now further offshore; the following day it was further still. There it remained for a couple of days, but then continued on its passage and after about a week it had disappeared into the crowd of its fellow water-lilies floating in a small clump some hundred yards from shore. Vaguely assuming that the plant had drifted on some slow current or been blown by the wind, I dismissed the matter from my mind. It was not until some weeks later that it suddenly struck me that this could not be the case.

My insight was occasioned when, during a walk along the beach, I observed along the strand line an unusually large accumulation of by-the-wind sailors, or *Velella*. This little blue floating jellyfish has the surprising ability to tack across the surface of the sea. Though its body lies flat on the water, the little ridge on its upper surface catches the wind just so, that the animal travels at an angle to the wind. Intriguing though this ability is, the present sight of the many thousand washed up on the beach suggested that their sailing ability was somewhat limited. But the stranded *Velella* brought back to my mind the floating water-lilies, and I realised that my previous explanations for their movement and distribution must be mistaken. If the single floating specimen I had returned to the lake was blown towards its fellows by a wind, why were they not blown along too? If current had carried one, why not them all?

Perhaps this problem, and its probable solution, has already occurred to you. The simplest answer is surely that the group of water-lilies which the single one eventually joined with were not at the mercy of wind or current, but were somehow anchored. And surely the anchors must be those coiled roots, which I had initially assumed might be used to hold the floating plants one to another. I examined this explanation thoroughly and found it perfectly satisfactory, but now another question began nagging at my mind. Was it not remarkable that the single lily had been carried by current or wind straight towards its fellows? Why had it not been carried back to the shore, or away in another direction?

I am not, and never have been, a swimmer. The experience

on my first day at school of being scrubbed down beside the pump had instilled in me a lifelong dislike of cold water. I was never one to join the other boys who would risk a thrashing to slip school on a summer afternoon to go jumping and splashing about in the river. Sea-bathing has always been an anathema; the very idea of immersing myself in a liquid which stings the eyes, assaults the skin and revolts the tongue is folly almost beyond imagination. A warm bath, even on a hot day, is far more refreshing than a cold one. Yet the problem of the water-lily so needled away at my brain that a few days later you might have seen me standing naked beside the lake, dipping an unwilling toe into its unwelcoming waters.

I had hoped simply to wait until the opportunity for examining a lily was again presented by finding one washed ashore, but after combing the margins of the lake almost every day for a fortnight, I realised that I might be in for a long wait; had I not remarked to myself that the first water-lily I had found was a rare event? My curiosity daily became stronger, my patience weaker. The idea of constructing some raft or other vessel occurred to me, but the effort of such an undertaking was too daunting. Eventually my infuriating curiosity overcame even my dislike of cold-water immersion. I had no idea how deep the lake was, but I determined to brave the water and to wade out as far as I could in the hope of reaching some of the intriguing water-lilies.

The experience was as unpleasant as I had imagined it to be. The feeling of the water gradually rising up my body, from ankle to calf, from calf to knee, from knee to thigh, as I waded ever deeper into the lake was horrible. Being still some yards from my goal, I then had to endure the exquisite torture from thigh to waist, which was not something I wish ever to repeat. If the coldness of the water were not enough, to add to my discomfort was the fact that it was of such muddy opacity that after only a few paces from the shore I could not see the bottom and had to feel my way with my feet. But, with the water lapping my breast, I at last achieved my goal. I was now able to inspect these curious plants at close quarters.

My assumption about the function of the tendrils has been correct in both respects. I could feel with my feet that the plants were indeed anchored to the bottom, and see that they were also linked loosely together with more of the same structures. Each plant was similar to the one I had seen previously, consisting of a submerged rhizome from which grew a single leaf on a short stalk. I counted fifty-three leaves in this particular group. Though the tendrils appeared to link them loosely, I discovered when I tried to separate one from the raft that its attachment was in fact tenacious. The tendrils stretched when pulled, but they would not be parted other than by each being individually untangled from its fellows. Even so, I managed to separate a dozen individual plants from their brethren before the unpleasantness of my situation forced me to make for the shore, towing my botanical booty behind me. Never was shipwrecked mariner more relieved than I to leave the water's cold embrace.

I had already devised in my mind an experiment to learn more about the movement of the water-lilies. To each plant I attached a long length of twine, tied at the other end to a peg. I then returned each plant separately to the lake, at intervals of about ten yards, the pegs being firmly driven into the bank. I would now be able to observe the free movements of the plants, yet be able to retrieve them without subjecting myself to the brutal discomfort of entering the lake. Over the next days I visited the plants daily, making careful notes of not only their movements, but also of the direction of the wind and of any apparent currents in the lake. What I discovered only served to puzzle me still further. I discovered that, regardless of the strength and direction of the wind, every one of the floating plants had each morning moved further from the shore, and each one was on a direct bearing for the raft of plants from which it had been recently removed. It was as though the plants knew where they were going.

The faculty of voluntary motion is more common within the vegetable kingdom than is often thought. Who is not aware of the daily rhythm of the opening and closing of the poppy, or of how the girasol tracks the sun across the sky? The slow, inexorable bending of the sundew around its prey, or the snap of the Venus flytrap, is also known to botanist and layman alike. Yet common though motion may be, locomotion is, as far as I am aware, unknown. How was I to account for what I had now witnessed? My first inclination was to try to explain it a priori. Let us assume that the common direction taken by the plants was governed by the same stimulus; for instance, an inclination to move to deeper water. Would they not then all follow the same contour from shallow to deep, and so give the impression of purposeful navigation? As for their means of locomotion, perhaps they remained anchored to the bottom with their tendrils when the wind blew onshore, but released their hold when the wind blew offshore. This ratchet-like effect would result in movement in one direction only. Satisfying though these explanations were to my intellect, they did not satisfy my curiosity. It was only by experiment that I would discover the truth, and I resolved to begin a series of trials and explorations.

Intellect was not entirely superfluous to this procedure. It was clear that my method must involve not only confirmation, but confutation. By taking the water-lilies from the lake to the pond, where I was more easily able to control the conditions under which I observed them, I was able to show, early on, that direction was not governed by depth, but that the plants actually appeared to have some awareness of the position of their conspecifics. One plant would always move towards two or more, never the reverse, and regardless of whether it was moving from shallow to deep water or vice versa. I will not now relate the many experiments that I devised to discover how the plants detect each other at a distance, whether by light, sound, or smell, but having eliminated the former I concluded that the plants have the ability to detect some chemical exudation from their conspecifics; if they were animals, we would say that they can smell each other. The small hairs or spiculae on the underside of the leaf of each plant, not unlike those on the leaves of a nettle but with no irritant properties, are the organs which I now believe detect the presence of other plants; when I removed the spiculae from one of my experimental subjects, it moved around in a random pattern. I suspect that the hairs enable the plant to follow a gradient, not of depth, but of chemical concentration, which would naturally tend to increase as the distance from its source decreased.

I was also able to show that, though the plants do indeed anchor themselves against contrary winds, they have the capacity to move independent of wind or current; the way that they do so is no less remarkable than their sensory ability. Though possessed of neither sail nor boiler and engine, my island water-lily possesses a means of propulsion hardly less sophisticated. It is a means of locomotion so far unknown in the plant kingdom, based on the frequent and controlled expulsion of water. The finer details, both chemical and mechanical, I have yet to establish, but the basic principle is this. The tapered ends of the bifurcated rhizome each contain a hollow tube, about the thickness of an ordinary wheat straw. The tubes are lined with large vesicles, and it is these vesicles which provide the force. You may be familiar with the humble bladderwort, a plant apparently innocuous, yet whose roots contain small hollow capsules which prove anything but harmless to any small animalcule which brushes past one. On contact, a trapdoor on the capsule springs open, and with a rush of water the prey is sucked into the trap, where it dies and is digested. A similar principle is involved in the action of the vesicles lining the water-lily's rhizomic tubes, except, as it were, in reverse. The effect of the bladderwort's trap is produced by the walls of the capsules absorbing water from the interior, thus creating a negative pressure within, which, when the door is opened, results in a quick influx of water. The water within the vesicles in my water-lily, each of which is also furnished with a door, or valve, opening into the tube, is under positive pressure. At a certain signal or pressure (I know not which) the valve opens. The result is a rapid expulsion of water into the tube. Although the vesicles are each no larger than a grain of rice, thousands of them line each tube, constantly absorbing water from the surrounding tissue and expelling it under pressure into the tube. The water can only exit by one route, the opening at the back of the rhizome. The two small but steady jets of water being directed backwards from the submerged rhizome naturally result in a forward motion to the plant in general, and it is thus that the water-lily is propelled across the lake.

It has so far been beyond my ability to elucidate the exact mechanism of the valves, nor how their opening is triggered. The plant clearly has some overall control over the timing or amount of water released by each vesicle, as it is able to adjust the relative flow of water from the two tubes and so direct movement; more flow from the right-hand tube results in a turn to the left, and vice versa. Nor have I been able to prove to my satisfaction how the ability of the plant to detect its fellows is linked to its ability to move and steer towards them. I have found no area of apparent histological specialisation which might correspond to a brain, and suspect that the process is controlled by chemical infusion within the plant.

The role of the tendrilous roots in the process of motion is also of interest, as they too are capable of motion. When wind or current is sufficient to overcome the relatively weak propulsive force of the rhizome, the plant simply 'drops anchor'. The tendrils extend downwards, their hook-like tips grip the bottom of the lake and hold the plant in place until conditions improve and it is once again able to make its way towards its desired destination. I have named the plant *Nymphaea peregrina*. A more ingenious system is difficult to imagine.

There were water-lilies at Holyrood House before they filled in the old pond in the west garden. In Edinburgh, the garden had become a favourite hunting ground of mine; as soon as spring arrived I would often spend an afternoon searching the pond for water insects, or examining the rocks of the old abbey for early beetles. It was here that, one May afternoon in 1827, Bobby first told me that he had become disenchanted with his life in Scotland. It was partly the unpleasantness with Grant, he explained, and partly his general distaste of the whole business of doctoring. He would never get used to the sight of blood, nor the necessity to cause pain in order to cure. He had decided to give up his medical studies and move down to Cambridge, where he planned to begin studying for holy orders. I was not surprised that Bobby wished to give up medicine, but the idea that my friend should take to the Church was both shocking and disturbing to me. I was young enough to try to change his mind.

'Can you not see that your heart is not in it?' I asked him. 'Even your Church would think it sacrilege to enter orders guided by your head and not your heart.'

'On the contrary, dear friend,' replied Bobby with depressing good humour. 'It is the head which must rule. Perhaps if you read what Pearson has to say on the Creed, as I have been doing, all will become clear. I think it would surprise you to know just how much logic there is in the Anglican doctrine, if you only look with a careful and unprejudiced eye.'

'I'm not talking about doctrine or dogma, Bobby, I'm talking about belief. You are a man of medicine, a man of science; can you honestly say that you believe every word of the Bible?'

My friend looked at me with genuine surprise.

'Why, yes,' he said, and I realised with some surprise that as far as Bobby was concerned that was the end of our conversation on the matter. It was as if the competing theories of science and religion occupied separated parts of Bobby's brain, comfortably separated by an ill-defined but impenetrable wall of complacency and tradition.

Bobby still had to persuade his father to the move. The doctor had set his heart on at least one of his sons following the path taken by him and his father before him into medical practice, and though Philos was still enrolled at Cambridge and taking lessons at medical school in London, he had revealed in a letter to me that he only did so to keep the old man happy, and that he had no intention of ever taking up a practice, and I suspected that his father knew as much. At first, the doctor would have nothing to do with Bobby's move. He had no intention of seeing his younger son become an idle, sporting man, as he assumed would be Bobby's probable fate should he move to the softer South. But Bobby was ever a charmer, and his father could no more resist him than could I. In the summer of 1827, Bobby received a letter from the doctor agreeing to his move to Cambridge.

Chapter 7

IN EDINBURGH I WAS myself becoming restless. The enjoyment I took in playing and landing Grant had already palled, and I was having some difficulties with money. My tuition and board were paid for, as had been my school fees, by the Trustees, those shadowy figures who had appeared in my life when I first went to school, and who had provided for me ever since, though I knew no more about them then than I had when I first heard the word. They seemed to have always been part of my life. The Trustees had paid for my schooling, and when the time came, the Trustees agreed to pay for my university education. Since arriving in Edinburgh I had been provided with a small monthly sum for personal expenses, while my bills for tuition and boarding were sent to a firm of Shrewsbury solicitors and I heard no more about them. But while at first my allowance had been quite adequate for the usual disbursements, I had now outgrown my old style of life. Where I once drank ale, I now drank claret; where I once wore linen, I now wore silk. Philos had been generous up to a point (as was Grant), but the local tradesmen were becoming impatient with my debts. I had taken no examinations, but I had picked up enough of the rudiments of medicine to impress my teachers, and had also increased my knowledge and love of natural history, not only from lectures and field excursions with Grant and Jameson, but from less formal tutors like John Edmonton and Ian M'Arthur.[20] The more I knew, the more I wanted to know, and Cambridge seemed the place to increase my knowledge. With some trepidation, I wrote to the Trustees asking to continue my medical studies in Cambridge. They agreed to my move without demur.

How I loved those days at Cambridge; new hearts to conquer, new fields to explore, new beetles to collect, and Bobby. I arrived from Edinburgh the term after Bobby and had been delighted to find that he was about to move into a room at Christ's. I was thus able to take over his lodgings above the tobacconist's shop in Sydney Street, just over the road from the college. Despite his early fascination with my skipjack in the asparagus patch, Bobby had since shown no great enthusiasm for beetles; at school he had preferred chemical experiments, in Edinburgh it was plants, birds and hunting. I was pleased to find that in Cambridge my enthusiasm for insects at last began to rub off on him; when he first gave up a day's beagling for a day's beetling, my heart fairly soared. The memories of those days are fresh with me still. Punting on the Cam, Bobby draped over the bow, net in hand, ready to scoop up each unwary *Gyrinus* or *Dytiscus*. Chasing a rare *Panagaeus crux* over the fens, our hearts full of laughter, our boots full of water, then gathering glowing *Lampyris* from the hedgerows on our walk home. That famous time on our excursion to Gaminlay Heath with Henslow, when my friend was so eager to capture another *Melasis flabeillicornis* that he put a *Brachinus* in his mouth to give him a free hand and it fired off its little cannon in his mouth, so that he not only spat it out but dropped the others (have you forgiven me yet, Bobby, for laughing at you then?). Beetles and friendship, what more could there be to life? But I was by no means Bobby's only friend. One day a microscope

[20] John Edmonstone (sic) was a freed American slave brought from the West Indies to England in the early 1820s by the eccentric naturalist Charles Waterton, who instructed him in taxidermy. Edmonstone later taught his art in Edinburgh. Ian M'Arthur has not been identified.

arrived at his rooms, an anonymous gift from someone 'who has long doubted whether Mr Darwin's talents or his sincerity be the more worthy of admiration'? How that gift delighted and puzzled him, until he finally decided that it must have come from his friend Herbert, though Herbert continued to deny it. I was so jealous I could have strangled the little cripple. I knew who had really sent it, though I could not say. But what I remember most is summer days chasing beetles through the countryside, and winter nights in Bobby's rooms at Christ's, preparing slides of dragonfly wings and beetle genitalia, or just talking and smoking. If ever I was truly happy, it was then.

I have my own instrument with me here on my island (an old Coddington,[21] Bobby, just like yours), and still take much pleasure in the microscopic world. Though I have long considered a microscope to be an indispensable tool for scientific investigations, I more and more value it as an aid to aesthetic appreciation. The sculpture that is a pollen grain, the matchless mosaic of a butterfly's wing, the world inside a drop of ditchwater, all these exist without a microscope, but they are hidden. But 'beauty is Nature's coin, must not be hoarded'; while the microscope does not create beauty, it *reveals* it. Beauty revealed is more sublime than beauty created, and what is more beautiful than life? A stone is a stone is a stone. Though it may possess beauty, of form or colour, it is a dead beauty, static, unchanging. But a feather, a bird, a flock, in these are found not only the beauty of being, but the beauty of becoming. You may argue that all things are becoming. The mountains rise up and are worn away, the land becomes sea and the sea becomes land. But these are apparent to us only in thought, not in observation. Our time is in minutes and days, not aeons. Life alone is on our scale of things. Feathers fanned in flight, a blackbird hopping quick-eyed across the lawn, a

[21] An English manufacturer of microscopes, 1806–1861.

skein of geese arrowing purposefully towards the horizon; I marvel not only at their form, but at their motion. I, too, am in motion; I, too, am becoming. I long sought to find from where comes this appreciation, this apprehension, of beauty. I now know that this was a foolish quest. Beauty is.

Those Cambridge days were surely when Bobby and I were at our most eager for new aesthetic experience. I can remember today the rapturous look on Bobby's face when he took me to the Fitz to show me his favourite painting, of Venus I think.[22] I, in turn, could not wait to show him my own favourite object. On a previous visit to the museum I had found myself, more or less by accident, in the antiquities gallery. Among a jumble of Ancient British coins, Roman pottery and Egyptian funerary paraphernalia I noticed what I at first thought to be a small gold brooch. Closer inspection revealed it to be the most exquisite representation of a sacred scarab, apparently cast in solid gold.[23] A coin of slightly baser metal slipped into the curator's hand enabled me to hold the wondrous thing in my own. The scarab was indeed of solid gold; though no more than an inch and a half in length, it was surprisingly heavy for something so small. I took from my pocket the lens which was always about my person and took the beetle over to the window to better examine it. The detail was superb, even down to the individual segments and claws on each leg, which were tucked in close to the body, greatly resembling the natural posture of a dead beetle. I could only surmise that whoever made it had used a real insect to make the mould in which it had been cast. This treasure had once belonged, the curator assured me with all the certainty of complete ignorance, to 'Tommily the First'. I was delighted to find on my second visit that Bobby was as entranced by the miniature golden statue as I was. A coin again liberated

---

[22] Presumably Titian's *Venus*, still in the Fitzwilliam museum in Cambridge.
[23] This piece is no longer in the museum and its identity is unknown.

the specimen from its case, and Bobby was able, as I had, to examine it finely.

'What say you to your painting now?' I asked him.

'I say I would rather this in my cabinet than all the paintings in England on my wall,' said Bobby. 'It is the most exquisite thing I have ever seen.'

I handed him my lens for him to examine it more closely.

'What would you say – a *Copris*?' said Bobby.

'Undoubtedly,' I said.

Bobby handed the golden beetle back to its obliging guardian.

'So tell me, my friend, why, when we have seen this Egyptian marvel, we have not seen the English *Copris*?' and with that he declared that he would not rest until we had found the golden scarab's English cousin.

How many Cambridgeshire cowpats did we turn in search of the elusive *Copris lunaris*? We never did find one, but found some consolation with a rare *Typhaeus*, and I think I was as proud as my friend was to see his name in Stephens[24] with a new record for the county.

I have so far counted 1,763 species of beetle on my island, chief among which are the Rhynchophora (one of which, a weevil similar to the *Apion pisi* of England, though considerably smaller, is become quite a pest on my pea plants), the Clavicornia (including many Tenebrionids, though curiously, not a single Carabid), and the Phytophaga. A score of other families are present in smaller numbers. The three largest families presumably represent the earliest arrivals on the island, which have since speciated to take over the positions occupied in other places by a more diverse coleopteran fauna. Among the Phytophaga, for instance, one species of *Chrysomelus* feeds on aphids, another on dung, which food is more usually associated

[24] *Illustrations of British Insects* was published in serial form by James Stephens from 1826 to 1848.

respectively with the Coccinellidae and the Lammellicornia. The dung eater is of particular interest.

There is a beetle in Australia, *Macropocopris symbioticus*, which lives in the anus of wallabies, eating its dung *in situ* (though Australia has several species of dung beetle, none seem inclined to eat the dung of our introduced domestic animals, as the result of which I fear that not many years hence, Australians will find themselves completely buried in the excrement of their own livestock). But most dung beetles fly to dung after it has been deposited, from which they fashion a ball and roll it away to bury it and lay their single egg within. Since, as a child, I first saw a little *Aphodius* perform this Sisyphean task, it has been a procedure which has fascinated me (you have yourself written at some length, Bobby, on the utility of the humble earthworm in turning over the soil, but what untold good these little beetles do, cleaning up the fields of ordure, returning the plant matter to the soil from which it derived). The Chrysomelid beetle on my island uses a different method to ensure its young are fed. The habit of most of the Chrysomelidae I have come across is to lay their eggs on the food plants which their larvae eat, the eggs being generally laid in batches, either as a rosette around a stem, or as a flat sheet on a leaf. My island Chrysomelid lays its eggs singly, and it lays them not on dung, the food on which they exclusively subsist, but on seaweed.

This beetle, which I have named *Cassida rhynophilus*, was the first insect I came across on the island. On first seeing the gadzocks, Charley and I were curious to observe that every one of them appeared to be suffering from a pair of brown callosities on their noses. Closer inspection revealed these were not in fact part of the animal, but large domed beetles, of which there always appear to be two, clinging, limpet-like, to the bare skin of the animal's nose, their legs invisible under their carapaces. The strength with which the beetles clung to their hosts was most remarkable, it being quite impossible to pull them off with the fingers, yet it was clear that the beetles were able to leave their station whenever they wished. While watching gadzocks grazing on the beach, I would see a beetle detach itself from a nose every now and then, to fly down on to the sargassum weed on which the gadzock was feeding. At first, I assumed that the beetles must themselves be eating the seaweed, but by close observation I discovered that they were not feeding, but laying eggs. Each beetle would crawl briskly about the pile of sargassum, depositing an egg here, an egg there, before returning to its post on the gadzock's nose. The eggs were always laid on the pile of sargassum on which the gadzock was feeding at the time, never any other, so it was clear that they must almost always be consumed by the gadzock, along with the weed. What could be the usefulness of such a habit? The only way I could think to discover the answer was to use the method by which Bobby and I tried so hard to discover our Cambridgeshire *Copris*; by thoroughly investigating large quantities of dung.

My research, though somewhat distasteful, was successful. The beetles' eggs are indeed eaten by the gadzocks, but, having an exceedingly tough shell, they pass undigested through the animal. They are thus eventually deposited whole within the fresh dung. After they leave the animal the grubs hatch from the egg (by what stimulus I have been unable to discover), and immediately begin to feed. Gadzocks are considerably smaller than domestic cattle, and their pats are correspondingly small. It is probable that each contains sufficient nourishment for the complete development of only one beetle. This supposition is supported by the fact that although I have found up to half a dozen eggs or newly hatched grubs in a single pat, I have never found more than a single fully grown grub or pupa. Presumably the survivor has killed, and probably eaten, its siblings (what unseen battles are fought in every cowpat, what unknown competition exists for every natural production).

*　　*　　*

67

I have also discovered much about the adult beetles. They are almost always found in pairs on the nose of a gadzock, each pair consisting of one male and one female. The male beetle remains on the gadzock's nose at all times, but while the female is laying her eggs, he is not idle, it being his task to defend the nose. During the female's absence, the male is kept constantly busy fighting off other beetles which try to land on the vacant territory. This fighting consists of each beetle trying to insert his (or her) head underneath the carapace of its rival, then pushing and lifting, so trying to break the grip of the other. These battles often last for several minutes, which has given me the opportunity to test the outcome of these battles with some accuracy. By marking the combatants with coloured gum, I have discovered that the resident beetle is victorious seventy-nine times out of eighty. These odds are still not enough to discourage potential rivals, of which there are always a few, both males and females, always to be found buzzing around the gadzocks, on the lookout for an unoccupied nose, and this despite many beetles, both adults and grubs, falling prey to birds (a species of heron, I think identical to the Reef heron of other tropical parts, is often seen on the beaches, probing the gadzock dung with its long bill). The adult beetles appear to subsist entirely on the gadzocks' nasal mucus. The gadzocks seem little inconvenienced by their passengers; fond though I am of beetles, I think that even I would prefer one living on my nose to up my arse.

I suppose it was not all beetles in Cambridge. Though my studies in medicine and natural philosophy took up most days, few hours were spent in sleep (when you are young, 'what hath night to do with sleep?'). Most nights were given to pleasure, when with Bobby and with other friends I enjoyed great Bucklandian dinners of hawk and hernshaw, and learned to smoke and drink and gamble, and took more lascivious lessons at Mrs Duke's establishment. But it is the beetles that I remember best, and the day that Bobby took me to Maer Hall and introduced me to his cousin Emma.

Chapter 8

'WHAT ARE YOU DOING this vacation?' Bobby asked me one early summer morning in the year of 1831, as we breakfasted together in my rooms in Sydney Street.

I said that I had no plans.

'I am going to Maer Hall, you must come too. You must come and meet my Uncle Jos and Aunt Bess, and my cousins. Say you will.'

I had known of Bobby's Uncle Jos ever since that first visit to his home in Shrewsbury, and Bobby had often spoken to me of Maer Hall, which I think he preferred even over The Mount. To him, it was 'Bliss Castle', a second home, where he was loved and fêted and, above all, accepted. Knowing this, I said I would be delighted to come. I was considerably less delighted when I found that Bobby planned to ride on ahead, and I was expected to share a coach with his cousin Fox and Sappho, his disgusting hound.

If ever there was a puppy which should have been drowned at birth, it was Sappho; if ever a child, Fox. Bobby had introduced me to both only days after I arrived in Cambridge. Fox had nearly completed his own studies for holy orders and, my oath, he was a bore. In so many ways still a child, yet trudging happily towards old age, his inevitable country vicarage seemed already complete with inevitable wife, half a dozen inevitable children and an equal number of dogs, among whom would no doubt be the stinking, drooling apple of his eye, Sappho. He would be a conscientious parson, and probably develop a special interest in the Orchidaceae of southern Britain. I pitied his poor parishioners. The Bible was ever his final authority, God was in every sentence he uttered, and if I rather despaired of Bobby then, I believe that his cousin Fox was largely to blame.

I cannot remember ever having a God. Though, as a child, I went to church every Sunday since I could remember, first with my foster-parents and later at school, the God who to everyone else seemed so familiar, to whom we all prayed, whose thoughts and deeds and judgments were apparently of the gravest importance to everyone, was nothing to me. The very word God seemed to have no meaning, while the stories from the Bible, of Abraham, Moses, David, even Jesus, though interesting, were of no more relevance than those I heard at school about the long-dead kings of history. I felt no distress at this vacancy. Despite the enthusiasm with which others, including Bobby, embraced their religion, it never occurred to me that I was missing anything, that everyone else knew something I did not, or had something I had not. I was quite sure that there was no God, and I was quite sure that I was right. When, at school, we had learned simple theology, with its putative arguments for the existence of God from first cause, from design, or whatever, I found them simply ridiculous, not even worth the trouble of countering. As for William Paley, he was a fool, his God a cul-de-sac to reason. He diverted men from the path to truth and beauty, he barred the way of the real explanations for the way things are, especially the question which especially intrigued me, of the relationships between living things. This question, to which I gave so much thought at school, was not then of the slightest interest to Bobby. Even later, when we were medical students in Edinburgh, though Bobby had seemed as intrigued as Philos and I to hear Grant's daring talk of transmutation and Lamarck, as soon as he went to Cambridge to study holy orders, he slipped back into the arms of God, the great designer. Paley was his Bible, each flower and animal another 'watch on the heath'. In all this he was constantly encouraged by his cousin Fox. But much as I despised Fox, it was him I have to thank for helping me to first distil in my own mind what had previously been no more than a series of disconnected hypotheses. It was during my conversation with Fox that I came to know the Theory.

On the morning of our departure for Maer Hall, I arrived at the King's Arms in good time to secure a seat on the Nottingham coach.[25] The coachman assured me that there was still plenty of room inside, so while an ostler heaved my bag on to the roof, I climbed aboard. There was only one other person in the coach. Fox had arrived before me, and was sprawled over one seat; Sappho was on the other, shedding hair and saliva in equal abundance. The low growl with which she greeted my entry to the coach showed me that she had no intention of moving from the seat. Though he had not yet taken orders, Fox was already in the habit of wearing the dark garb of a parson. He had acquired a broad-brimmed hat from some relative's visit to Rome, which he insisted on wearing as his normal headgear, and which was now held carefully in his lap. I suppose that Fox was about as pleased to see me as I was to see him, but he greeted me with an almost professional cordiality.

'Delighted you could come,' he assured me. 'Aren't we, Sapphy?'

The hound looked up at me with only the smallest pretence of enthusiasm. I squeezed in beside Fox, and no sooner had I done so than the horn was sounded and we were off. The journey looked like being a long one.

Our conversation started, I remember, with you, Bobby. Fox was immensely proud of his family connections (why one should be either proud, or ashamed, of one's relations I have never been able to fathom; one does not choose them). Did I know that you and he were cousins? I had surely heard of your

[25] Though Maer Hall is in Shropshire, it was presumably necessary to change coaches at Nottingham.

maternal grandfather, he was one of the leading manufacturers in the country, but did I know that your paternal grandfather, Fox's great-uncle, had been asked by the king himself to be his personal physician, and had refused? How was that for importance? Did I also know that this same grandfather was a poet of great repute? Of course, I knew all this and more besides. Philos had told me things about the family that even Fox was not aware of, such as what had really happened to your grandfather's first wife, and about his 'Mrs Parker' and the bastards he had by her, and about his two lawful sons who had died by their own hands. I had also read your grandfather's poetry, greatly enjoying the speculations on transmutation which it contained, and the subtle atheism that it espoused (I suspected that Fox had not read a poem since school).

'Yes, your great-uncle,' I said, giving what I hoped was a beatific smile, 'a fine poet indeed. And in these days of so much humbug and cant, it is so reassuring to find a man who actually lived by the credo he avowed.'

'Why, yes,' agreed Fox, with some enthusiasm. 'You are referring to his "Botanic Garden", I suppose.' (Perhaps he had read one poem, after all.)

'A wonderful work indeed, but it is his "Temple of Nature" which I particularly admire. For it is true, is it not, that the purest love we can aspire to is sexual love?'

Fox gave me a look that was half-shocked, half-quizzical.

'Surely you remember those immortal lines,' I continued. '"Hail the Deities of Sexual Love, and sex to sex the willing world unite!"'

I was delighted to see from Fox's immediate blush that I had scored.

'I also admire, as I'm sure you do, your great-uncle's "Zoonomia". Never mind God; transmutation, that's the thing.'

So pale did Fox's face become that I thought that this second barb might have finished him, but he rallied. Giving me a look of infinite pity and scorn, a look straight from the pulpit, he said softly, 'I am sure, sir, that my uncle meant no such thing. I am quite sure that my uncle would countenance no theory that goes against what the Bible teaches us, and I am equally sure that neither would I.'

'You mean, sir,' I replied, 'that it goes against what William Paley teaches us.'

'The Reverend Paley is right,' said Fox. 'Transmutation is wrong. How can we look at the miracle that is a flower, and not see evidence of design? How can we look at the form and actions of the bee which pollinates that flower, without being sure that it, too, was intended thus by an all-wise creator? Paley must be right. Just as the intricate mechanism of a watch points surely to man's creation, so the whole of nature points just as surely to God's creation.'

'But what if I told you how such things might come about *without* God?'

'Without God? Without God! Very well, my atheistic naturalist,' said Fox smugly, 'pray tell me.'

Pious bore though he was, I assumed that Fox was not without a brain. We had a long journey ahead of us. Pray tell him, I would.

'Let us return', I said, 'to your great-uncle. Perhaps you remember his clever phrase to describe how the two sexes choose a mate. He called it the "Law of Battle".'

Fox thought for a second. 'Yes, yes, I remember. Fighting stags, that sort of thing?'

'I think we can assume that is what he meant,' I said. 'It is a common enough thing in this world to see males of the species fighting each other for females, is it not?'

Fox nodded and, looking across at Sappho, said, 'Just like those naughty dogs, eh, Sapphy? But your master soon got rid of them for you.'

From the way Sappho looked at her master, she was clearly in some doubt whether or not she agreed with the treatment that had been meted out to her suitors. Life with Fox could not be easy, even for a dog. Her head flopped back on the seat, and she began drooling with more than usual abandon.

'But your uncle got only half way,' I continued, 'for the law of battle, as we shall see, is not just between males for mates. Now, have you read Malthus?'

'Who?'

'The great political economist, Thomas Robert Malthus. You must have read his *Essay on the Principle of Population*?'

Fox replied that he most probably had read it, but could not recall.

'Well, perhaps if I may summarise what he said, you will remember.'

Fox tilted his head and turned down his mouth in grudging agreement.

'Firstly, Malthus points out that as we humans breed, our populations tend to grow. The human population of England is growing, the population of France is growing, the population of the whole world is growing, is it not?'

'Yes, I can see that,' said Fox; continuing with a smile, 'But it is surely no more than what God has ordained for man.'

'Just for the moment, let us look at this growth mathematically rather than theologically. Now, can you tell me how this growth comes about?'

'Why, it is surely quite simple,' said Fox, after a moment's thought. 'If each couple has more than two children, and if they survive and themselves have more than two children, then such growth is inevitable.'

'My dear Fox, your mathematics are faultless,' I said. 'But what about your geometry? You will have no doubt noted that this growth is geometrical. The more the population grows, the more there is to grow, and the more it then grows.'

'This is no more than the theory of compound interest, my friend. But what is the point you are trying to make?'

'I shall be coming to it soon. You may remember that Malthus also noted that the amount of food that a country produces can also increase. In England, each year, we drain more land, we use improved methods and varieties, and so our harvest, on average, also grows.'

'As I was telling my dear Uncle Robert only last month, sometimes there seems no limit to the Lord's beneficence.'

'Let us keep to the mathematics just a little longer, my dear Fox,' said I, pausing only to swallow the gorge that rose in my throat at this pompous platitude. Sappho yawned widely. 'Able calculator that you clearly are, you will appreciate that this increase in food is *not* geometrical. We might be able to add a bit here, by clearing some woodland or draining another swamp, and add a bit there, by using a new strain of wheat or cattle, but the overall increase in production is just that – additional rather than geometrical.'

'Yes, I can see that.'

'So what is the inevitable result?'

I looked at Fox expectantly. He seemed to be having some difficulty in finding an answer to my question, so after several silent seconds I answered it myself.

'It is surely that the increase in population will eventually exceed the growth in the supply of food.'

From the way Fox furrowed his eyebrows and pursed his mouth in concentration, I feared that I had lost him. Eventually, however, he admitted that this was indeed so.

'And then what must happen?'

Fox thought for a while longer, before giving his triumphant conclusion.

'Why, we will simply buy food from abroad.'

'Excellent,' I said, forcing a smile (I may have been correct in my assumption that Fox had a brain, but it was clearly not a large one). I was determined to go on with my argument.

'Now let us look at our globe as a whole. The number of people, we have agreed, is growing geometrically, the amount of food is growing arithmetically. What then will happen?'

'Well, eventually there won't be enough food.'

'You are absolutely right, Fox,' I said, 'we cannot import food from the moon and there will not be enough food for everybody, even to buy from abroad. So some people will start going hungry. There will be famine. And then what will happen? What happens when there is famine?'

'People die,' said Fox, and gave a sad sigh. 'But it is God's way. Surely it is not for us here on earth to question God's way?'

'As I said at the beginning, my dear Fox, let us try to leave God aside for the time being. But as you say, when there is famine, people die. And they die not only from hunger, but from the war and plague which accompany the famine.'

'This is unfortunately so. But not all die.'

'Exactly so,' I said, pleased that Fox appeared to be at last grasping the argument. 'This is my point. Not all will die, but who will be the survivors?'

'We will, I suppose,' said Fox.

'Who do you mean by "we"?'

'Us, here in England.'

'Yes,' I said, 'we probably will. But why us? Why will we English survive famine and disease and war?'

'Because we're better.'

'You are right, my dear Fox, you have hit the nail on the head,' I said. 'We are better. We are stronger, and healthier. We are richer, and our army and navy are better equipped.'

The frown lifted from Fox's forehead, and he gave a small smile. He liked being told he was right.

'Now look around you,' I said, motioning outside. 'What do you see?'

Fox looked out through the coach window at the muddy verge and the hedges and fields beyond.

'It is not just humans that are breeding and increasing, is it, Fox? Look there. Every dandelion along this road has a hundred seeds; every butterfly lays a hundred eggs. There is not room on this earth for every dandelion, there is not food enough for every caterpillar. What happens to them all?'

'I suppose a lot of them die.'

'Yes, a lot of them die. In fact, most of them die. But which ones die?'

'What do you mean?'

'Which ones die, and which ones live? If there is only room in a field for one more dandelion, which is the seed that fills that vacancy? If there is only food for one more caterpillar, which caterpillar gets that food?'

'I don't know,' said Fox, 'it could be any of them.'

'Yes, yes, a certain amount of luck is involved. One dandelion seed might get caught in a spider's web, another might be blown out to sea. But among those that land on the earth, which one survives? Among all the caterpillars which hatch on a nettle, which one grows up to be a butterfly?'

'I'm not sure what you want me to say.'

'Look at the nations on earth,' I said, 'are they all the same? Are people the same, are all the apples on a tree alike, are all the puppies in a litter identical?'

'No, there is much variation among them all.'

'Yes, there is much variation. As with nations, so some individuals are healthier, or stronger, or better armed than others. Now, you remember your great-uncle's "Law of Battle". In nature, is not every individual constantly at war, attacking its prey, defending itself against its predators, in never-ending competition with members of its own species and others for the limited supplies of food, and shelter, and mates? So just as we can say which nation will survive famines and wars, which seed or caterpillar will survive the war that is constantly being fought in nature?'

'Clearly it will be the one which is stronger, or healthier, or better defended.'

'Exactly so. It is the strongest which survive.'

To me this seemed as clear as day. Only the strongest survived. I survived.

'And now you can see', I continued, 'that God has had no place in this argument.'

Fox looked at me. He had again turned quite pale.

'I see it,' he said at length, 'but I don't like it.'

'Why not?' I said.

'That God has no place in your argument is tantamount to saying that He has no place in the world. This is surely blasphemy.'

'Then call me blasphemer,' I said with a smile. 'But I am right, am I not?'

Fox was silent.

Satisfied though I was with my little victory, until that moment I had not realised how deeply my argument might affect Fox. I had no belief in his God. Where was the benevolent father in my life, where the loving saviour? It was nothing to me to leave God out of nature completely. But to Fox, and I suspect also to you, my dear Bobby, God was the foundation on which rested his whole philosophy. Paley's divine watchmaker was not just necessary to account for the beauty of the natural world, he was necessary to justify Fox's place in that world. Place and purpose. Without God to design his world, to assure him of the rightness of his existence, nothing remained but an awful void. All this I saw as that small flash of doubt and terror passed over Fox's face.

But within a minute, Fox's silence was broken by a strange rumbling noise. It took me only a second to realise that it was coming from Sappho, who had been drooling copiously for some time. As she pushed herself up on to her front legs I only just had time to grab the nearest thing within my reach and hold it in front of me before her great maw opened. Fox almost leaped from his seat as the stinking stream shot towards us, but I at least was safe. Held before me, shielding me from the stinking tide, was Fox's hat.

For the rest of our journey to Shrewsbury we conversed no more, Fox frantically consulting his dog-eared Bible while at the same time trying to hold his hat out of the window, I deep in my own thoughts. Was this what would become of you, Bobby? Was your intellect already being stifled by certainty, your enthusiasm buried by dogma? Would you emerge from Cambridge with a vision fit only for unlit parish churches, your ardour slowly cooling in some underheated vicarage? Flitting sparrow or soaring swift, which would you be?

Chapter 9

OF THE THIRTY-THREE SPECIES of birds I have now identified which live here all year round, five are seabirds, many of which nest in the *Pisonia* forest on the north of my island. Among them are large numbers of noddy terns, which build their crude nests among the branches of the *Pisonia* trees, despite the fact that they are much inconvenienced by the seeds of the tree sticking to their feathers (I have found *Pisonia* trees on almost every small island I have visited in the East Indies, and suspect that the terns and other seabirds are the main means of their dispersal). But there is another plant on my island which makes use of the birds: it is a misseltow.

Though my interest in natural history has always been more zoological than botanical, I have long been fascinated by misseltows. First the English species, which roots itself in the bark of an oak or an apple, drawing its nourishment from the very sap of its unwitting host, and whose white berries are so attractive to thrushes, which, wiping their beaks free of the sticky seeds, spread them to other trees, where they germinate and grow. Then the dozens of species of misseltow in Australia, which have an even more intimate arrangement between plant and bird. For wherever there is misseltow you will find a small red bird, which feeds almost exclusively on the berries, often building its pendant nest on the plant itself. Like the thrush, this bird is also the agent of the seeds' dispersal, but rather than wiping the seeds from its beak on to the branch of a tree, this bird swallows the berries whole, then defecates the seeds on to a tree. Uniquely among any birds I have seen, this bird squats not across the branch when defecating, but along it, thus being sure to deposit its dung on to the branch rather than letting it fall to the ground. This bird seems the main, if not sole, agent of seed dispersal for all the Australian species of misseltow, and is called the 'misseltow-bird' by the settlers. Here on the island there exists a misseltow which has developed yet another arrangement.

I soon noted in Australia how often the foliage of a misseltow resembles that of the tree on which it grows; the species which grow on wattles have broad leaves of a bright green, those which inhabit gum trees often have leaves of a dusky hue, while one growing on a she-oak has long slender leaves like pine needles, almost exactly mimicking those of its host. Why this is so I have never been able to explain (when I asked young Hooker[26] to answer this question, neither he, nor his father, could give a satisfactory explanation). When I came to this island I found a similar situation existing; the leaves of the misseltow here resemble those of its host, the *Pisonia*, so exactly that it was some time before I noticed the plant at all. That I eventually did so was due more to culinary than botanical investigation.

My diet here is reasonably varied; fish and cocoa-nuts are plentiful (though more difficult to gather now that Charley is no longer here to climb the trees); there is a spinach growing along the shore to furnish salad for my table, and I grow peas and Indian corn from seeds which I carried with me in my stores; several trees provide fruit almost all year round, many of which can be dried and kept. I have also discovered that the eggs of the noddies eat well. Though hardly bigger than acorns, noddy eggs are always plentiful. It is no great feat to gather them by the score, as the birds nest low in the trees, and are so tame that I can take an egg from beneath a bird on the nest without suffering so much as a pecked finger. Because the birds nest

[26] This reference suggests that the author had met the English botanist Joseph Dalton Hooker on his visit to Australia in 1840 as surgeon and botanist on HMS *Erabus*.

year round, there are at all times not only eggs but nestlings, which grow as fat as squabs on their rich diet of fish. Having eaten and enjoyed in Australia the squabs of the 'mutton bird' (a species of puffin), I thought to try some of these fat young noddies as food, anticipating no difficulty in procuring my meat, for the nestlings are as docile as their parents. But when I first tried to remove a squab from its nest, I discovered that it was tethered by what appeared to be a short piece of cord attached to one of its legs. The cord was smooth, somewhat resembling the root of an onion, slightly pink in colour, and though it was flexible it was extremely strong. Only by cutting it with a knife could I remove the young bird from the nest, when I saw that the cord was not tied to the bird's leg, as I had initially supposed, but appeared to be growing from it. On its cut end was what looked like a drop of blood. I was much puzzled by this. Could it be some device of the parent to prevent the chick falling from the nest? This seemed unlikely; the answer would only be found by dissection. Taking the young bird with me, I returned to my hut, where my scalpel and forceps soon revealed the truth.

The cord was attached to the bird just under the thigh, but it was not tied on. It rather appeared to be growing from the skin. By cutting open the leg, I could clearly trace its path, at first subcutaneous, then intramuscular, along the thigh, past the sacrum and into the abdomen. Here it ramified into dozens of fine threads extending throughout the abdominal cavity. My immediate thought was that this was some parasitic worm, although when I had cut it, and afterwards, it had given not the slightest sign of movement. Microscopic examination showed its internal structure to be almost completely undifferentiated, comprising no more than a hollow tube (my examination also confirmed that the red liquid was indeed blood). Yet it must surely be animal. Perhaps the rest of the creature, the part that I had left in the nest, would provide more information.

The following day I returned to the *Pisonia* forest, where I soon found another nestling similarly attached to its nest by a pink tube emerging from beneath its thigh. This time, however, I did not cut the tube, but carefully traced its course. It extended for about eight inches into and through the structure of the nest, but its other end was not free. The tube ended in the living tree, merging with the bark as if growing from it. Near the point where it merged, I saw the unmistakable long red flowers, not of a *Pisonia*, but of a *Loranthus*. It was not a worm feeding on the blood of the young noddy, it was a misseltow.

I have now investigated the matter thoroughly. There is not the slightest doubt that the misseltow is indeed a vampire, sucking the blood of noddy chicks as they lie in the nest. The mechanism by which this vampirism occurs is this. The adult noddies seem oblivious to the threat posed by the plant, appearing to nest on it as readily as on the *Pisonia* itself (I suspect that this may be largely due to, and may explain, the great resemblance between the foliage of the two plants). Furthermore, the numbers of birds in the *Pisonia* forest are so large that every misseltow is assured of a nest on it or near it. I have discovered that the plants do not grow the parasitic roots at all times. The roots are produced only in response to guano, though not that which the adult birds use to cement together their nests, but only that which the voracious young birds produce, which they do in considerable quantities, ejecting it in a fluid stream from the side of the nest after every meal. I was able to test this response of the plant by collecting some nestling guano and placing a small amount on to a branch of a misseltow on which there was a nesting bird, still with eggs; within twelve hours of this treatment the plant had produced a single hair-like root some three inches long, growing from the place where I had put the guano. The tiny root extends through the nest and, on reaching the interior, develops on its tip a small swelling, resembling the root on the end of a plucked hair. Though small, this swelling is extremely sticky, fixing firmly to anything that touches it. Once stuck to a nestling, the root quickly penetrates the skin (though without causing the bird any apparent distress), and continues to grow within the body, lengthening and swelling to the thickness of the cord I had first observed. The noddy nestlings appear oblivious to their strange tethers. They stay on the nest for about ten weeks before fledging, during which time they are constantly fed by both parents, and remain active. The parasite, which I have named *Loranthus sterniphagus*, does not remain attached to its host for long. After eight weeks the root begins to wither, eventually dropping away to leave the newly fledged noddy free to leave the nest.

Not all the nestlings were parasitised by the misseltow, yet I was surprised to find no apparent difference in size and health of those chicks which were parasitised and those which were not. The parasitised chicks seemed to grow no less fast than the others, and showed all normal stages of development. Again, it was my culinary investigation which provided the answer to this conundrum. As I had suspected, the noddy squabs did indeed provide good eating, being fat and tender, though with rather more of the kipper than the capon. But in preparing them for the table I found that some of them contained, within their muscular tissue, many hundreds of small cysts, which dissection revealed to be the cysticerci of a tapeworm. Though I was sure that thorough cooking would render these parasites harmless, I preferred to avoid them, and sought a way to recognise which squabs would contain these cysts and which would not. I discovered after some time that if a squab had been parasitised by the vampire plant, it would have no cysts, whereas one which had not been so parasitised was sure to contain them. It therefore appears that the misseltow, in return for its meal, renders the birds a service by somehow inoculating them against the worm. If one did not have the Theory, one might almost believe that God had designed it so.

By the time we arrived in Shrewsbury, Fox had regained his usual smug composure. I realised that my words had been as water off the back of a duck; religion had triumphed over logic, faith conquered reason. It was growing dusk, but a carriage was waiting for us at the inn, its lanterns all alight, and after a short drive out of town we turned off the road at a pretty little white gatehouse to enter a long avenue flanked by fences.

The picture of my first view of Maer Hall is still in my mind; the house, the trees with the hills behind, and Bobby on the front steps, for had not Sappho set the other dogs barking to announce our arrival? As I alighted to my friend's embrace, another man appeared at the door.

'May I introduce you to my Uncle Jos.'

The man who stepped forward to shake my hand was both shorter and rounder than Bobby, but from his broad forehead and prominent nose, there could be no doubt that the two were from the same stock.

'Welcome,' he said with a wide smile, 'I can't tell you how pleased I am to meet you at last.'

That is all he said, but from his simple words and the way he said them, I had the immediate and somewhat strange feeling that it was true, that this man really had been looking forward to meeting me for a long time. Before I had time to analyse this feeling, a smaller figure stepped out from behind him.

'Ah, there you are, my dear,' said Jos, with the fondest smile, and turned to me again. 'The rest of the family are in town, I fear, but may I introduce you to my youngest daughter, Emma.'

A young woman stepped forward. Simply dressed in a white dress gathered at the narrow waist by a green silk sash, she put out her hand.

'Any friend of cousin Bobby's is a friend to us all,' said Emma, and as I took her hand in mine I felt as if I had at last come home.

Chapter 10

I SETTLED IN QUICKLY to Maer Hall, despite frequent encoun-
ters with Fox, who would waylay me at every opportunity to
force on me some or other fatuous rebuttal to our conversation
in the coach. On the third day of my stay Fox, Bobby and their
Uncle Jos decided over breakfast on some rough shooting over
the estate; though the morning was fine and sunny, I declined
an offer to join them, having neither desire nor aptitude for
such sport. Instead I asked to examine Jos's collection of books,
which I had briefly seen on first coming to the house and which
I now saw an opportunity to examine more fully. Bobby's uncle
had no objection to my request, and as soon as the three men
had left the house with their guns, dogs and beaters, I took
my coffee into the library. It was not a large room, but it was
light and airy, and lined with books from floor to ceiling. A
small table had been set up near the window. Here I placed
my cup, and began my inspection. I found the collection to be
well stocked with all the usual classical histories and religious
tracts; here was Herodotus, here Juvenal, here Cowper. A whole
shelf was occupied by my old friends Sophocles and Euripides.
The library also contained a large and carefully chosen selection
of works on natural history. Two shelves were filled by the
complete set of Buffon, that poor vain man who seriously
imagined he had described every animal that exists. Next
to him were the beautifully illustrated works of Lewin the
elder, several editions of White, and a well-thumbed Kirby
and Spence. I took down a slim folio that I had not before

come across, John Lewin's *Natural History of Lepidopterous Insects of New South Wales*, and immediately found myself transported to that strange new land. Here were wonders indeed, magnificent insects whose features were so minutely produced in the illustrations that they appeared as real. I was so absorbed by my find that it was only when I heard a small sound and looked up from the book that I noticed that Emma had entered the room.

Women had always been peripheral to my life. I had never known a real mother or sister, never had a female friend; the closest I had come to any members of the opposite sex was to Bobby's sisters, whom I regarded as I would have some pretty, but rather strange, butterflies. With Bobby's other female cousins at Maer, and with his Aunt Bess in particular, I had developed during my stay so far no more than a cold cordiality. With Emma, it was different. Though I felt no physical attraction towards her, there was something about her reserved self-confidence, so 'sober, steadfast and demure', and about her very femaleness, that fascinated me. Since our first introduction when I arrived I had hardly spoken two words to her, yet I had often noticed her sitting by the window in the drawing room, or in the garden under the chestnut tree, always with a book in her hands. Emma was carrying a book now, and came over to where I sat.

'Ah, I see that you have found one of my favourites,' she said.

She was again wearing a long white dress, her bonnet pushed back on to her shoulders where it hung by a green ribbon around her neck. The spray of wistaria which she had tucked into the ribbon told me that she had just come in from the garden. I arose from my chair and turned the volume towards her.

'And what is it that you like about this particular book?' I asked.

'Oh, the beauty, simply the beauty,' said Emma. She gazed down at the plate at which the book lay open on the desk, a coloured etching of a fine sphynx moth, with its impressive caterpillar.

'You find all insects beautiful, Miss Emma?'

Emma appeared to take this question with great seriousness, for she gave it some thought before replying.

'All God's creations have their own beauty, though it is often hidden from our eyes. Do you not agree?'

I took her question equally seriously.

'About the ubiquity of beauty in nature, I do; about the relationship of all creatures to God, I am not so sure.'

A small frown gathered on Emma's brow, and I saw that she was about to make a comment on my statement when I noticed something on her shoulder. A bee must have settled on her dress when she was in the garden. It was about to crawl on to her bare neck. As I opened my mouth to warn her of the danger, Emma, seeing that my gaze had been diverted, herself looked down. In doing so she turned her head and her chin touched her shoulder, so pressing down on the bee. She gave an immediate sharp cry of pain as she felt the sting, her hand flying up to her neck.

'No, don't touch it,' I cried, my sudden command having the effect of making her drop her arm and stand quite still.

'Yes, that's it, stay like that. Now just give me a moment.'

I reached quickly into my pocket and took out a small bundle of cloth. I had long made a habit of carrying on my person, wrapped up in a piece of linen, a pair of entomological forceps. Taking Emma's chin with one hand, I turned her head towards the window and moved my own head close to hers, the better to see the small black sting that the bee had left in Emma's neck, its poison sac still pumping. Gripping the sting with the forceps as close to the tip as I could, I pulled it out with a small jerk. It was at this moment that Emma's mother, attracted by her shout, entered the room.

Though I did not at the time understand the look on Bess's face as she stood at the library door to see my hand still cupping

Emma's chin, my face still close to hers, I shall never forget it. Emma immediately flew to her mother and clung to her neck, at last allowing herself to express her natural reaction to the pain and surprise of the bee sting. Bess said not a word, but as she stroked Emma's head and dried her tears with a handkerchief, her eyes continued to stare at me, her face such a perfect beacon of contempt and loathing that I could myself find no words. It was Emma who spoke first.

'It was a bee, Mother, a bee,' she said, and showed her mother the place, already reddening, from which I had extracted the sting. Making the small sounds of a mother hen, Bess shepherded her daughter out of the room, yet her eyes never left mine until she was out of sight, and all the while they continued to burn with the same cold fury.

When Emma's father returned with Fox and Bobby from their sport, the first thing he heard about was the story of the bee. Emma told him how my prompt action had saved her from much worse pain and suffering, to which my friend Bobby eagerly assented.

'It is most important in these cases, Uncle, that the sting is removed as soon as possible. As long as it remains in the wound, it continues to inject its poison. People have died from the effects of a single sting.'

Jos was visibly impressed with these words.

'Why then, sir,' he said, taking his wife's and daughter's hands. 'We have to thank you for saving our daughter's life.'

I smiled in slight embarrassment; I had done but a small service, and no more than any other man would have done.

'It always pays to have a medical man in the house,' said Bobby, putting his hand on my shoulder, 'but it pays even more to have an entomologist. Why, how many people besides my friend here do you know who would carry a pair of forceps with them?'

Jos laughed, Emma smiled, and the matter was over. But

Emma's mother did not smile, and on her face were clear echoes of the look she had given me when she had been summoned to the library by Emma's cry, and had found us head to head by the window.

I have been stung several times by bees over my many years, the effects of a sting seeming to increase each time I am stung, and I am now wary of any insect 'with honied thigh that at her flowery work doth sing'. I was therefore in no rush to investigate the habits of the large black bee, about the size of a bumblebee but with a faster and more purposeful flight, which is one of the most prominent among the insect fauna of my island, and which I had first noticed during my investigation of the land cucumber,[27] this bee being the main pollination agent of the dildo plants, which flower in profusion on the mountain in February. I had noticed during my investigation of the carnivorous misseltow that many of the smaller branches of the *Pisonia* contained neatly made holes, the size of my little finger, which I assumed to be made by the larva of some cossid moth or longicorn beetle. They are, in fact, made by the bee.

The insect which makes the hole is a species of *Xylocopa* or carpenter bee, which, like its smaller English (and Australian) cousins, nests within the stem of a plant. I have frequently noted the Australian species nesting in the soft-wooded stalks of black boy flowers; my island bee nests in the soft-wooded *Pisonia*. Choosing a vertical twig, of a diameter slightly larger than the span of her legs, the bee takes a firm grip and begins to chew at the outside of the twig, the scraping of her large jaws being clearly audible, the fine shower of *frass* (as our German friends so eloquently describe it) which falls from her drilling clearly visible. She continues to chew without rest, working her body around in a circle, until she has made a neat hole of sufficient size just to admit her body. It takes the bee only

---

[27] Fully described in Chapter 14.

a few minutes to penetrate the outer woody layer into the soft pith within, and within a few more minutes she has chewed her way out of sight. Over the next half hour, her head occasionally emerges with some pith in her jaws, until she has excavated to a sufficient depth within the twig to make her nest.

Like others of her ilk, the material which she uses to construct her brood chambers is not wax, like the honey bee, but propolis, gathered from the nearest convenient source. For this giant *Xylocopa* that source could not be much closer, for the seeds of the misseltow, which grows on the very *Pisonia* tree where the bee is nesting, are not enclosed in gelatinous berry, as are those of most other misseltows, but with a sticky resin. Just as the noddies nest all year round on my island, the misseltow is always in flower and its fruits, too, can be found at any month. The bee gathers the misseltow seeds, one by one, in her jaws and carries them into the nest chamber. Here she removes the resinous coating and uses it to construct her cells. The cells, of which there are invariably six, are arranged one on top of the other within the hollow stem. Each is well stocked with a paste of pollen and honey, on to which is laid a single egg. It is a remarkable fact that, although the bottommost egg must necessarily be laid first, it is always the topmost egg which hatches first, the others hatching in strict descending order. This ensures that each young bee develops, matures and leaves the nest before the ones beneath it, and there is no congestion in the gangway. How this order is ensured, I do not know.

The bee has no further use for the seeds after she has scraped off the propolis, and removes them from the nest. They are still so sticky from the little resin remaining that she finds it impossible simply to drop them outside the nest, and is forced to wipe them from her jaws. The nearest thing to her nest is invariably the branch of a *Pisonia*. Here the misseltow seeds stay affixed until their germination is triggered by the next rain. A more useful arrangement for both plant and insect is hard to imagine.

* * *

The beauty in natural relationships is similar to that which, I imagine, mathematicians find in numerical ones, and I am often tempted to theorise on exactly how such relationships have developed. In this case, I suppose that at one time there was no connection between bees and misseltow; the bees on this island gathered their propolis from other plants to make their nests (much as English bees use the resin from poplar buds), and the misseltow's seeds were spread by another agent, presumably a bird. Then grew one misseltow which had rather more resinous berries. This the bees discovered, and used for their purposes. The seeds of this different misseltow were spread so efficiently by the bees that it increased and, breeding true, became a new species. This new species was now in competition for space with the ancestral species, a competition in which it succeeded, eventually becoming the dominant type. By this time there were not enough of the fleshy-berried species to maintain the population of seed-dispersing birds, who themselves gradually died out. With their demise, the final demise of the original misseltow swiftly followed. The only species of misseltow that remained on the island was the new one; a natural selection, indeed.

And what of the misseltow's carnivory? What is the 'missing link' between the English misseltow, sucking the sap from an apple tree, and my misseltow sucking blood from a bird? Let us suppose, again, that the remote ancestor of the vampire plant was an ordinary misseltow, which just happened to live on the same tree as the one the noddies choose for nesting. I have observed that among the thousands of noddies which hatch here each year, many hundreds die in the nest, from one cause or another, whether it be sunstroke from being too exposed, or starvation if some misfortune befalls their parents. If the nest containing the dead chick is in a misseltow plant, could it not be that the plant's roots, which are naturally adventitious, might grow into the corpse, thus gaining accidental access to a rich source of nourishment? Those plants whose roots were more adventitious would be more likely to find this source of nourishment, and would be favoured, gradually usurping the places of the less-favoured plants. From this it is but a short step to evolving the ability to take advantage not only of the occasional dead nestling, but the much more numerous living birds.

Despite Fox's imperviousness to logical argument, back in Cambridge I would sometimes half-heartedly bring up the subject of evolution with Bobby. I was restrained from a full debate because I was myself aware of many difficulties with the Theory. How was it that similar species, which must have shared ancestry in the relatively recent past, were sometimes found not as neighbours, but existing on different continents? How could there have been time enough for the gradual accumulation of differences which distinguish present species, it being clear from present experience that nature does not make great leaps. How could I explain the presence in some species of organs which appeared to serve no function? What happened to the intermediate forms between evolving species, which are not present now nor apparent in the fossil record? These problems caused me such uncertainty that for some time I gave up on my attempts to sow in my Bobby the seeds of religious doubt, and to nurture them within him. I became resigned to the knowledge that his simple soul was being drawn to a life in the Church; the only doubts he faced were whether to aspire for a country curacy, like the one his cousin Fox had already obtained, or to try for a teaching billet at Cambridge. I myself still had two years at Cambridge, and either a tutorship or a curacy would at least give Bobby time to come beetling with me. Though we had almost given up on finding our elusive English scarab, we had not lost our keenness for the hunt. When Bobby passed his examinations (to my great surprise, as it seemed to me that my friend had been spending more time at his beetles than his books), and while he was making up his mind what to do next, there was time aplenty for more beetling.

But the seeds I had planted had not failed, had they, Bobby? Like the seeds of the misseltow, they had merely been lying dormant on the branch, and the drops which watered those seeds were the words of Herr Alexander von Humboldt. If I had not given you that book of Humboldt's travels and adventures to taste, would you have acquired so strong a thirst for travels of your own, Bobby? Would you have been ready for Henslow's suggestion, in that hot summer of 1831, that you leave England, your friends and your family to go on a five-year voyage round the world on a flat-bottomed bathtub of a boat, with a man who, you told me with some amusement, had serious misgivings about the shape of your nose? I was sad to see you go, but I could at least give myself the satisfaction that I had saved you from following Fox into religious obscurity. Yet still you might be lost. How was I to ensure your lasting safety? I think that it was at this time I first realised that perhaps you might be saved by the Theory.

But that gift was yet to come. When I came down to Plymouth dockside to see the *Beagle* off, the only gift I brought with me was a small cardboard box, of exactly the type we had used so many times to pin out our beetles. And when you opened it, and saw inside the *Copris lunaris*, the beetle for which we had spent so many Cambridge days searching in vain, seeing the smile that spread across your face was like feeling the sun on a winter's morning. And as the tears appeared in your eyes and you embraced me with such warmth and affection, I found my own cheeks were wet. But the tears that ran down my face to mingle with the salty Solent did not mean that I was sorry that you were going, Bobby. I was pleased that you had escaped the destiny I feared. Here at last was the great adventure, perhaps a chance to make a name for yourself with new discoveries in new worlds.

As we finally parted at the Plymouth docks, I suspect that

theories of evolution were probably the last thing on your mind. And perhaps the last person on your mind was Emma. What was Emma to you but a comfortable cousin, a substitute sister in your second home, and had not Fanny Owen also come to see you off? But Emma had been on my mind ever since we first met at Maer Hall. Long after I left Maer, it was her memory which stayed with me. When, after you had finally left on your voyage,[28] Philos again invited me to Maer to spend Christmas with 'the family', a large part of the reason I accepted was that I knew I would again see Emma.

[28] After being forced three times by bad weather to postpone departure, the *Beagle* finally sailed from Plymouth on 27 December 1831.

Chapter 11

IT WAS LATE ON Christmas Eve in 1831 that I arrived for my second visit to Maer Hall. I had left Cambridge early that morning and, after a long, cold coach journey (I would have welcomed even Sappho to keep my feet warm that day), I arrived at the Hall long after dark. I had already seen the lights of the house from the gatehouse at the bottom of the drive, and as the carriage neared the front door I could hear music and laughter. Someone must have been watching from the window, for as we pulled up outside Jos himself opened the door and hurried me inside. The party was in its full swing. In the drawing room sat Bess, with their children Frank and Fanny, and I think Elizabeth and Charlotte and Harry were also there. Several neighbours had been invited with their children, most of whom seemed to be piling their plates high with as much ham and chicken as they would hold, and Philos had already come up from town and was standing at the piano singing a melancholy song with the most enormous smile on his face. At the piano, playing the accompaniment, was Emma.

Almost as soon as I had been fed and watered, Emma asked me to sing. I could not refuse, but despite Emma's best endeavours to ameliorate the sound of my voice with liberal use of the forte pedal, it was generally decided that the party had had enough of music and that it was time for some games. I immediately found myself the object of one such game, which was being arranged with equal amounts of serious discussion and helpless giggling by the children. Each man of us was to be taken into the hall, stood under the misseltow, and blindfolded, whereupon we would be kissed by all the ladies in turn, our task being to guess which kiss came from whom. Jos went first, and much sport he made of it, pushing out his lips, and grasping the kisser for another if he felt he had been given short measure. When it was Philos's turn he showed such remarkable accuracy in his guessing that foul play was suggested, upon which he was forced to admit that he had been looking down through the bottom of his blindfold, and recognising each kisser by her shoes. Then came my turn.

The first kiss was easy, a loud smack a few inches from my cheek from someone smelling of rosewater; who else but Aunt Bess? Then came a child's kiss, a small kiss from small lips, which I had to reach down so far to receive that I knew it could only have come from young Louisa Jane. Then came another kiss. To anyone watching, I doubt whether the third kiss would have seemed remarkable. A small, affectionate contact between friends, perhaps between brother and sister. Lips to lips, the smallest exhalation of breath; it lasted no more than a second. And perhaps if it had lasted half a second, or even four-fifths, it would have meant nothing. If the lips had been held just a little tighter, or the breath withheld, it would have passed by unnoticed. But that extra fifth part of a second, the lightest sensation of warm breath on my face, those soft, soft lips. It was a kiss such as I had never felt before. You can sometimes catch the merest glimpse of a bird on the wing, or a beetle as it disappears under the bark of a tree, yet be completely certain which bird or which beetle you have seen. If someone were to ask you how you know, what you saw, you would not be able to answer them, but you are certain all the same. It was so with that kiss. It was Emma.

That first Christmas after Bobby went away I stayed long at his uncle's house. Though Emma gave me no further sign, I had no doubt at all of her meaning. For reasons which puzzle me still, Emma had become enamoured of me. And though I was careful to give no sign that I had noticed, I was also in no doubt that she knew I had. Here was a new experience for me. Women had hardly entered into my life, let alone my heart. Despite my experiences in Cambridge, I had realised long ago that women were not to my taste, and Emma was unlikely to be the one to change my opinion. It is a nice distinction, but all I can say is that although I found her fascinating, I did not find her attractive. She was pretty enough, and charming enough in her quiet way, but I had little in common with her. Her simple-minded religiosity, the Bible-reading and visiting the poor, the Sunday school that she and her sister Fanny inflicted on the neighbourhood children, were positively anathematic to me. But yet, I could not deny that there was something about Emma, which I can only describe as a strong mental or spiritual attraction. I have also to admit that another thought occurred to me. I would soon be finishing my medical studies and, though I would then be equipped with a profession, I had been made to understand that my allowances would cease. I had no capital, and no immediate prospects. Emma was the daughter of a wealthy family. On financial grounds, a match with Emma was well worth contemplating.

There is something about the act of writing which facilitates thought. As I write these words (the tail feather of a sargassum bird makes an admirable pen), it occurs to me that my intentions for Emma may not seem like those of an honourable man, which is a thought that has never before entered my head. It is, of course, quite true. I have never been an honourable man (is it more honourable to acknowledge such a claim, or to deny it?). All my actions, even those which may appear altruistic, or at least neutral, are, and always have been, purely selfish. This is not to say that I am a cruel man. Though I suppose I am at heart a hedonist, my pleasure has never centred on hurting others, and I certainly had no plans to hurt Emma. In exchange for her money, I would have been happy to give her a peaceful life, with home and children if that was what she wanted.

Bobby, you are shocked. How could I be so heartless, so calculating. But when you yourself were contemplating marriage, you made up two lists, did you not? Oh yes, I remember your letter. On the positive side, children, a housekeeper, companionship ('better than a dog', was it not?); on the negative side, freedom for work and society, and fewer expenses ('more money for books', was it not?). Where was your heart then, Bobby? Yes, I was calculating, but perhaps no more so than many others.

A liaison between Emma and myself was unlikely to meet with the immediate approval of her father. I well knew that although Jos loved and indulged his children, none more so Fanny and Emma, the two youngest, his idea of family unions was that they should be directed more from the head than the heart. I had myself heard him speak of how he liked to 'keep things in the family', and he had made no secret of his satisfaction at the prospect of having Bobby's sister Caroline marry his son Josiah. Jos was unlikely to view a penniless student as an ideal son-in-law, nor could I see Emma being able to change his mind, dote on her as he might. The matter would not be easy. I decided that, for the while at least, I should do nothing.

We humans make so much of such affairs; should he or shouldn't he, will she or won't she? Things are surely simpler among other animals. Does a hen choose a mate for her chicks, or a bull disapprove the choice of his offspring? Yet mating, whether between humans or other animals, is seldom a completely haphazard affair, and competition for mates is among the most potent forces in the process of evolution. This can be nowhere more clearly seen than among birds.

I have already mentioned that Charley and I saw the nests of sargassum birds before we had even set foot on this island. The birds are about the size of a dunghill cock, but with longer legs, and with toes of enormous length, not unlike those of the jacana of other tropical regions. They are immaculate white below, and uniform yellowish-brown above (and so almost invisible when crouching against the plant on which they live). As far I can judge, the two sexes are outwardly identical. Sargassum birds somewhat resemble the scrub-fowl of northern Australia, and are no doubt closely related, as they incubate their eggs not by corporal heat, but by the heat engendered by the very nest they make (though you did not see the scrub-fowl in your travels, Bobby, you will surely have heard of it, or of its fellow Megapodidae in Australia, from friend Gould).[29] For their nests are no more than enormous hot-beds, raked together by the birds' large and powerful feet, inside which the hen birds lay their eggs, then abandon them to the tender warmth of the rotting vegetation. But whereas the antipodean megapodes are terrestrial, using leaves and bark for their nests, sargassum birds make their nests from the sargassum weed on which they live.

The island on which I now find myself is surrounded by four smaller islands. Together with the reefs which are common in these parts, this arrangement leads to a most intricate pattern of circular currents and whirlpools in the waters around the main island, so that the sargassum weed which abounds here, as in most tropical seas, does not form the enormous floating islands familiar to sailors in open water, such as the vast 'Sargasso Sea' of the Atlantic Ocean, but is concentrated by the currents into smaller clumps, seldom more than an acre in extent, which are given additional buoyancy by the natural inclusion of large amounts of pumice, of which rock great quantities abound in the area. The currents being strong and more or less regular, the clumps often remain in position for several months between one monsoon season and the next. This is the time that the sargassum birds choose for nesting.

[29] John Gould and his wife Elizabeth described and illustrated the birds which Darwin collected on the *Beagle* voyage, and later visited Australia to collect material for Gould's own books on Australian birds and mammals.

Sargassum birds nest and work in pairs. They use not their feet for gathering the weed, but their beaks, which are thick and strong, not unlike those of a gallinule. When I still had the use of my canoe, I would often paddle to within a few feet of them, and spent much time in observing their behaviour. To begin a nest, both birds make a large pile of pumice stones, extracting the pieces of rock from the entangling weed and carrying them one by one to the centre of the floating island, until the pile is a yard high and about three yards across. There is usually enough pumice on their own island, but I have sometimes seen the birds fly to other islands to gather the stones, which they bring back to the nest in their beaks. When the foundations are complete, the main nest construction begins. One bird grasps a strand of weed from the outer edge of its floating island, heaving with all its might until it has pulled as much as it can from the water. Its partner, who is standing ready, snips through the entangled ends of the weed, thus freeing the strand from the mass. The first bird then drags the weed to the centre of the island, while the second begins to tug at another strand (should any small fish or shrimp be lifted with the weed, it is immediately pecked up; the floating weed appears to attract enough small fry to provide the birds with all the food they need, though what they drink, I know not). Over several days, a large mound is thus built up. You will appreciate that as seaweed is piled up at the centre, so its weight causes the mound to sink; the pumice, however, gives the whole nest sufficient buoyancy that the weed rests at all times above the water. The completed mounds being a yard in height, with a circumference of ten yards, I have calculated the amount of weed moved by a single pair of birds at near twelve tons. By the time the construction is complete, the weed, now out of its natural medium, has already begun to die, and to rot; the nest is ready to receive its eggs.

The female lays her eggs not on, but in, the mound. After a brief copulation, the hen bird burrows with beak and feet into the side of the mound until she completely disappears from view, re-emerging after several minutes having laid her egg or eggs inside. The eggs are kept warm by the process of decay within the mound until they hatch, although during the period of incubation I have observed the birds removing vegetation, apparently to prevent the eggs from overheating. On hatching, the young chicks are immediately able to walk and to feed themselves. I have never observed an adult feed or in any way look after one of its progeny. The chicks are difficult to see, both from resembling in colour the weed on which they live, and from having the habit of crouching completely still at the first sign of danger. Nevertheless, they are frequently taken by frigate birds, which take a high toll on chicks at this time.

Why do birds copulate so quickly? Pigeons, shell parrots or sargassum birds, it is all the same; a flap of the wing, a twist of the tail, and it is all over. Many mammals, and even insects, may take hours over the process. An acquaintance in Sydney once told me of the pair of marsupial mice he kept at the museum, which he swore remained *in copulo* for the best part of twenty-four hours (he also delighted in relating that the male died soon after the performance, though, he took care to assure me, the animal expired with a satisfied smile on its face). Can birds enjoy so brief an encounter? I have no answer to this conundrum, and yet I have myself usually found that anticipation is more often the finer dish than consummation; it is not the carnal act itself which provides the greatest pleasure, but the courtship. If this is so, then birds, with their plumage and posturing, are hedonists indeed, and perhaps none more so than sargassum birds. For, outside the nesting season, sargassum birds court for almost every minute of every day of the year.

Although sargassum birds build their nests as pairs, they spend the greater part of the year alone, each on its own floating island of weed, and most of this time is spent in song. 'Such sweet compulsion doth in music lie', and there is no song more compelling than the song of the sargassum bird. The soft, sad contralto of the English blackbird, the nightingale's 'liquid notes that close the eye of day', the merry warble of the singing crow-shrike[30] of Australia, all are as penny-whistles to the clear silver flute of the sargassum bird. But sargassum birds are not only peerless soloists, they are orchestral players of consummate achievement.

Each day on my island, the faintest light swelling up from the eastern horizon is the cue for the first bird to begin the performance. From low out on the water comes a single, pure note. It is never the same. It may be a long note, a serious note, a note that tells of all the suffering of the world, yet all its beauty. It may be a bright note, reaching deep into the heart to confirm that all is well with the world, for how could it be otherwise? Or it may be a note of such exquisite brilliance that it must outshine the very sun, and the dawn itself will surely be an anticlimax. From out of the darkness a second singer joins the first, picking up the mood and tempo of the introduction. Another bird picks up the rhythm, keeping up a steady, repetitive undertone. Near the first singer, a neighbour joins in close harmony, while from far over the water, so faint that you can scarcely hear it, a slow soaring descant covers all with a delicate lace of sound. The concert has begun. Like true musicians, each bird responds to every other bird. From left and right, from far and near, more voices join in. Then more, and more, until from miles around a thousand voices are united. It is nearly dawn. In the east, the sky glows pink, then red, then fiery yellow. The first sunlight shoots over the rim of the ocean to reveal the singers, each facing the sun, legs straight, head up, hurling its song to the sky with open beak. Though each bird is alone on its island, all are united in music. All morning the song continues, each day a different song.

And what has this to do with courtship? Why, everything,

---

[30] Now usually known as the Australian magpie.

for the song is the courtship. For ten months of the year the birds sing to each other every morning, new tunes, old tunes, always together, always sublime, until one morning in June, just as the first ray of sunlight shoots over the horizon, there is none. Instead of the expected crescendo comes silence. Then slowly, across the water, comes a sound like the distant flutter of leaves in the wind. The birds, each of which has remained alone on its sargassum island for almost a year, are taking to the air. Each bird opens its wings, and with powerful flaps flies upwards, circling round and round, ever higher into the sky. The sound of wings grows distant as the birds rise up and up, then, when they are almost lost from sight, a different sound is heard. The birds are singing again, but they are singing a different tune. Instead of singing together, each bird now sings its own song, loud and bright. Instead of co-operation, there is competition. A thousand songs come floating down from on high, growing louder as the birds descend. A note here, a phrase there, is all that can be distinguished in that distant cacophony, yet I believe that, just as we can distinguish individual voices in a room full of people, every bird can clearly distinguish every other bird. For as the birds descend and once more become visible to the eye, you see that they are no longer flying alone. Over the months before, each has been listening to each, and from the songs they have heard has picked a mate. Recognising each other by voice alone, they find each other in the wheeling throng and, in pairs united, descend to earth.

Was this to be my destiny with Emma? Had I at last found my own mate? When I returned to Cambridge from Christmas at Maer Hall, and throughout the winter of 1832, these questions were much on my mind. I did not need to receive that first letter from her to be sure that I had indeed won her heart, nor the subsequent letters, sometimes two or three a day, which began streaming into my lodgings. There could be no doubt that Emma was enamoured of me, though why, I could not understand. I had not sought out Emma's love, I had used none of the tricks in my established repertoire of seduction. My only interest in her was one which I was sure that I had kept private, that strange fascination that I had felt. Could it be that Emma had divined these secret thoughts, or could her behaviour simply be explained as a girlish infatuation with the remover of her bee sting; did she perhaps believe Bobby's exaggerated and half-facetious claim that I had saved her life? Perhaps my bookishness appealed to the schoolma'am in Emma, perhaps she saw in my rejection of her own orthodoxy some challenge, which I have often observed is so important to a woman. Whatever the reason, I was both surprised and intrigued by the sentiments which Emma expressed so frankly in her letters, and they did nothing to dampen my own speculations about the possibilities and advantages of a union.

When each sargassum bird has united with its chosen mate and returned to earth, the pairs begin the task of selecting one of the floating islands for their nest. It is now that the previously harmonious relationship between all the individuals in the species is abandoned. Musical competition is now abandoned for physical combat, with each pair doing its utmost to claim by occupation the largest island it can. This period of competition continues until each pair has found an island of its own, and it is then that the business of nest-building and laying, which I have already described, begins. A few of these floating islands are invariably washed ashore by changing currents or in a storm, and I have been able to examine them. The greatest number of eggs I have found in one of the nests is nineteen, the usual number being about a dozen, each laid separately rather than next to its neighbours. It is no pleasant task pulling apart twelve tons of rotting weed to come by this knowledge, but I am now used to necessary tasks, however unpleasant. I have named the bird *Megapodus eumeles*. The colonists of southern Australia call the megapode of those parts the turkey or lowan, a lazy bird, for not making a proper nest and not sitting on its eggs. If they could see the amount of labour that each pair of these and their cousins must expend in creating and maintaining their incubators, they would rather think the busy sparrow a slug-a-bed. The eggs eat well.

I was myself abed in my Cambridge rooms early one winter morning when I was awoken by a messenger. He brought a note from Philos in London, telling me that Emma's sister Fanny was seriously ill and that he was leaving immediately for Shropshire. I ran to the staging inn and secured a place on the coach. I arrived at Maer Hall that very night, to find that Philos and his father had arrived the previous evening. But the great doctor had been too late, the cholera had already done its work. Emma's mother was distraught, and had taken to her room. Her father had sunk into a deep depression, hardly able to think, let alone act, and was being waited on by Philos. Though Emma had not heard that I was coming and was surprised to see me at Maer, she was clearly pleased, and eagerly accepted my offer of help. The rest of the family had little stomach for the details of death, and it had fallen to Emma to make the arrangements for Fanny's funeral and interment. Together, we visited the rector and wrote to the relations (I remember addressing a letter to you, Bobby, at Rio). Together we rode into town to discuss matters with the undertaker. Emma's mother and father seemed to accept that I had come as a concerned friend, and it felt quite natural that over those sad days I should be treated as one of the family, joining them for quiet evenings in the drawing room, Bess and Jos snoring a duet from their armchairs, Elizabeth and Charlotte gravely sewing, Emma bent over her Bible by the fireside, its dancing flames reflected in the spectacles on her nose as she searched the pages for an assurance that one day she would be reunited with her darling Fanny.

The day of the funeral dawned grey and wet. But by the time the parson had finished his oration and the sexton had begun his work, the rain had eased and Emma asked me if I would walk home with her from the church, to which I readily agreed. While the others returned to Maer Hall in carriages, Emma and I walked alone, and our conversation soon turned to the afterlife. This was a subject on which we had often conversed over the last few days, probably, I think, because Emma knew that I had no belief, while her certainty was the perfect armour against my weak Pyrrhonism. But the funeral service, despite all its talk of the inevitability of a life hereafter, had upset Emma. Death had brought doubt, and, as we walked back to the house, she began to cry. This was the first tear that I had seen fall from Emma's eyes since her sister's death, and by the time we arrived back at the house she was weeping most piteously. Though she tried hard to control herself, it soon became clear that there was no question of Emma receiving the mourners, as she had expected to do, and at my suggestion her father allowed me to take her to her room, promising I would bring her down as soon as she had composed herself.

Did I take advantage of her then? As I consoled her for her loss, carefully drying her tears with small kisses and consolations, should I have stopped her responding as she did? What would you have done, Bobby? Emma was a passionate woman, and she was not in control of herself. She did not 'yield with coy submission, modest pride, and sweet reluctant, amorous delay'; she responded to my caresses with fire. By the time Emma returned downstairs to greet her guests, we were betrothed in deed if not in name. It seemed that my future was assured.

I had reckoned without Emma's mother. Distraught though she was from Fanny's death and funeral, Bess had immediately guessed (as women will) what had happened between me and Emma; as soon as the mourners were out of the house, she hurried Emma upstairs and called for Jos. Within minutes he came down and closeted himself in the library with Bobby's father, who had returned to Maer for the funeral. I knew that it was my fate they were discussing, but I was ready to argue my case. An orphan, with neither name nor fortune, might not seem the best choice as a husband to even the youngest daughter of that great family, but I had nearly finished my medical studies. If Bobby's father and his father before him had gained wealth and position from their doctoring, could not I do the same? Besides, I had a trump card. Emma and I were now as good as wed, a fact that in a few weeks might well become apparent to all. I did not expect Emma's family to be overjoyed at our union, but would they not be forced to accept it as a *fait accompli*?

When I was myself eventually summoned to the library, I found both Jos and the doctor seated at the table. Though I saw anger on the doctor's face, Jos's expression was more difficult to read. As the footman left the room, closing the big doors behind him, the doctor looked up at me coolly, as though he was about to perform a dangerous but necessary operation. I remained standing and turned to Jos.

'You have learned what has happened, sir?'

He nodded his assent.

'Then I would like permission to marry your daughter.'

Jos gave a long sigh.

'It can't be done, lad,' he said. 'I'm sorry, it can't be done.'

'Please hear me out, sir,' I said.

The doctor raised his great bulk from the table and held up a hand.

'No,' he said, turning to Jos and getting a nod of assent. 'This business, very difficult.'

'Nothing against you, lad,' said Jos.

'But no. You can't marry her. That's that. You won't allow it, will you, Jos?'

'Indeed, I cannot,' said Jos.

At first, the doctor tried to reason with me, explaining the unsuitability of the match. Even the idea of the daughter of such a wealthy family marrying a penniless orphan was unthinkable, surely I must see that? I responded that if the doctor's own

111

father could rise from country doctor to court physician, so could I, with Emma by my side.

'It might not be quite that easy,' said the doctor, again looking to Jos for affirmation. 'There could be no question of support from the family.'

Jos looked down at the table. 'None,' he said.

But think of poor Emma; why, it would mean social ruin. I replied that neither Emma nor I cared what the world might think, that the only good opinion I valued was that of Emma herself, and that this would conquer all difficulties. The doctor then tried a different tack.

'On the other hand,' he said slowly, as if the thought had just come to him, 'perhaps it *is* a question of money.' I saw him glance again towards his brother-in-law, but Jos was only staring at his hands, which rose and fell together in quick rhythm on the table before him. 'Let us suppose you were to give up this foolish idea,' said the doctor, 'perhaps we might . . .'

'That'd be different, would that, completely different,' interrupted Jos eagerly. 'Why then, we'd be pleased to help you.' He was positively smiling. 'Very pleased.'

By now I was well immersed in the part of wronged suitor. With considerable heat I replied, 'I do not want your gold.'

My words made their mark. The doctor went quite red in the face, and Jos immediately rose to his feet to speak. But before Jos could say a word the doctor said softly, 'You've been happy enough to take it these twenty years.'

It took me some moments to understand the content of these words. Could it be so? Could it be that my friend's father and uncle were really the mysterious Trustees? It was Jos who spoke next.

'I wasn't going to tell you. No need, really. But now . . . When you were orphaned, just a little baby, well, call it charity if you like. It was my decision. I decided to give you the best I could, and I did so with glad heart. You've done well by me, I've no complaints. But I, we, cannot allow you to marry my daughter.'

'Besides,' said the doctor, as if as an aside, 'Emma is already spoken for.'

It was then that the truth struck me; they were keeping Emma for you, Bobby. Your two great families, who were already united through your father and mother, who, with your sister Caroline and cousin Josiah clearly set for a match, were destined to be even more closely bound, wanted yet firmer ties. Jos's gentle daughter and Robert's simple son were to be the ropes that would bind the families and their fortunes stronger still. Neither Emma nor I nor you had any say. Despite what had happened, the plans would go ahead, plans which I could no more change than change autumn into spring.

But 'what though the field be lost?', the game was not yet over, and this poor little orphan boy still had a trick or two up his sleeve. What if I were to tell the world what had happened? I still had Emma's letters. What if I threatened to show them to you, Bobby? Though it was looking increasingly as if I might not win Emma, surely if I played my cards wisely I need not walk away from the game empty-handed. I might not make my fortune by marrying Emma, but I might still make one by not marrying her. I was careful to let my face show none of the thoughts that whirled behind it. I said nothing, letting the silence drag on until it was Jos who finally spoke.

'Let me tell you what we had in mind,' he said. 'Nothing much needs to change. There's no reason why you shouldn't finish your studies or anything like that. I'll make sure that the money comes in just the same. I'll even add a bit. All you have to do is give us your word not to see or communicate with Emma.'

'Or my son,' added the doctor.

'You are saying, then,' I said, 'that if I agree to your conditions, you will pay me. And if I do not agree to this, this blackmail, then all my allowances will cease.'

'Your education has clearly not been in vain,' said the doctor, leaning towards me, his huge hands resting on the table. 'And by the way, don't forget. Emma can't support you. She has no income, nor would she get any from her family.'

He turned towards Jos for agreement to this statement. Jos reluctantly nodded his head.

'Not a penny,' he said.

'But what about Emma, what if . . . ?'

Jos looked up at the doctor, who again spoke.

'I'll see to that,' he said.

It was these cold words above all which made it clear to me that a union with Emma was now out of the question, but I had at least learned that the two men were willing to pay for my compliance. I now needed to find out how much. I continued to refuse their money outright. Though they kept raising their offer, at the same time bringing in the threat of yet further unnamed calumny should I refuse (threats which I knew enough to take seriously, for they were powerful men), I stuck firmly to my declaration that I loved Emma, she loved me, and married we would be. It was only when I judged that I had convinced the two men that they could not buy me, and were on the point of carrying out their threats, that I declared my hand. It had happened that, during our negotiations in the library, my eye had strayed to the bookshelves. I noticed again the book on the butterflies of New South Wales that I had been reading when Emma had come into the library those few months ago. I had thought then that, if these were the butterflies which might be found in the antipodes, what might the beetles be like? Here, perhaps, was a chance to find out. Bobby had already sailed away on his own voyage of adventure and discovery; could this be my chance to do the same? To their great surprise, I told Jos and the doctor that I would accept their final bid, but also pointed out to them that it might be worth their while to ensure against my reneging on it by a small additional expenditure. If they were to pay me the agreed sum of £1,000, and also pay my passage to New South Wales (first class), where they would arrange for a regular and substantial annuity to be paid into a bank there, they would have their guarantee that I would stay away from Emma.

The two men were so surprised by my offer they were almost grateful. A bargain was immediately struck, and that is how in June of 1832 I found myself on Bristol dock, about to board the *Sarah Rose* for Australia. Jos came to see me off from the dock. As agreed, he handed me £1,000 and an order to draw £400 on the Bank of New South Wales in Sydney on the first day of January each year.

'I am sorry it has come to this,' he said, 'but I fear there was no other way. Good luck, my boy.'

I saw that there were tears in his eyes as he spoke these words, but then he took a document from another pocket.

'My brother-in-law thought it best to take out an insurance policy on your behalf,' he said, handing me the envelope with some show of reluctance. I thanked him, and unfolded the paper. It was a statute of civil outlawry issued against me, with a warrant for my arrest should I ever set foot in England again.

That Emma was heartbroken at my departure I had no doubt. Before leaving I had received from her a last letter delivered to my Cambridge lodgings by her maid (are not maids always the most reliable of couriers?). Despair and anguish flowed from every word. Dear Emma, so quiet in company, so passionate when we were alone. I had never seen so clearly into a human heart as I did when Emma gave me of herself, but it was her words, most of all, which gave me this insight. Emma was no poet, but the artless passion of her declarations made lyrical her simple prose. Her love was as new and fresh as the first snowdrop in spring, and she opened to me as the blossom does to the light. But what of my own heart; was it, too, broken by my impending separation and exile? Was I angry or sad, or did I treat the whole event as an exciting adventure? I cannot now be sure, it is too long ago, but I suspect that my vanity sustained more damage than my heart. If I loved Emma, it was not a great love. Why did Emma love me so? Even now I sometimes lie awake at night on my island pondering on this question, and answer comes there never.

Here on my island, the night belongs to the bats. From dusk till dawn the night sky is full of their aerial acrobatics. Do you remember Grant's cat, Grendel? It would often bring him bats, as well as the more usual rats and mice and shrew-mice, but bats, as a rule, have few enemies. In Australia there is a goat bat,[31] which I think eats other bats, and I suppose some owls and hawks take a toll, but it is normally the bats themselves which prove the enemy to other creatures. Here though, the bats have a foe of an unusual kind, and one which has been of great assistance to my taxidermic endeavours.

The bats of my island are all nocturnal, emerging to 'execute their airy purposes' only when the sun has sunk well below the horizon. Each night I see them, swirling and swooping as they hunt after moths and other night-flying creatures, and it is in a clearing in the forest that each night their enemy lies in wait for them. Imagine a pair of thin horizontal lines stretched out between two trees, with a series of fine golden threads suspended vertically between them, arranged like a large gridiron some six feet square but with each of its bars no more than an inch apart. The threads are smooth and slippery, and slightly elastic. Any flying thing which hits this gossamer grid will be gently but firmly arrested, and, its momentum checked, will slide down the threads towards the ground. Now imagine that at the base of this gridiron, about two feet from the ground, is a horizontal sheet. Anything sliding down the bars of the gridiron will land on this sheet, which is so soft and elastic that trying to walk on it is like trying to walk on molasses; as one foot is raised, the other sinks, making progress impossible. The maker of this trap is not visible at first. It is hidden beneath the sheet, waiting. As a bat hits the gridiron and slides down

[31] The author is presumably referring to the ghost bat, *Macroderma gigas*, of northern Australia, which is known to prey on other bats.

on to the sheet, the creature races upside-down towards it and thrusts its poisoned fangs through the fabric of the sheet, deep into the flesh of the bat. The bat flutters a moment, then is still. The grendel has caught its dinner.

It is more after Beowulf's gruesome foe than Grant's cat that I call this giant spider the grendel. It is similar in appearance to the enormous *Epeira* spiders of other tropical parts, though perhaps even larger, and like them its silk is of a shiny yellow or golden colour. The structure of its web, however, is unlike that of the *Epeira*, nor does this spider stay in its web day after day, but, like the common *Arenea*, lies flat against the bark of a tree, where its colouring makes it almost impossible to see. As with most other spiders, it is the female which spins the web. The male of the species resembles the males of other *Epeira*, being but a tenth the size of the female, though of similar form, and being always found somewhere around the edge of the female's web (I have long suspected that the spider which you described as parasitic on your Brazilian *Epeira*, Bobby, was, in fact, the male of that species).

It occurred to me that I might make use of the grendel's trap for my own purposes. Since arriving on my island I have been attempting not only to thoroughly investigate and document its natural history, but to build up a collection of its fauna, and having one day come across a recently dead bat in a grendel's web, I had taken it home with the intention of skinning it and dissecting it. Soon after my return, however, I was afflicted with one of my headaches (a cursed infirmity to which I have long been prone), which forced me to lie abed for all that day, and the next. Flesh rots quickly in the tropics, so you may imagine my surprise, when I was able to get back to my taxidermy some two days later, at finding that after all this time the bat was in as good a condition as when I first plucked it from the grendel's web. The body showed no sign of putrefaction, the animal's flesh felt firm yet supple to the touch, and the blowflies and other insects which, even on my island, seek out corpses before they are yet cool, were nowhere to be seen. When I began my dissection I found that, though the skin itself had turned almost white and the muscles and most of the viscera were now slightly translucent, the flesh was undecayed, and contained not a drop of blood.

This change was clearly due to the spider. It must have sucked out the blood of the bat, while the poison which it used to kill its prey must be acting as some kind of systemic preservative. The next morning I collected another bat from beneath the grendel's web. After keeping it for four days, it still showed no signs of spoiling, though it had become set in rigor mortis. Over the next few weeks I collected more bats from the webs, and I found that by arranging them in whatever position I desired before this rigor took effect, I could obtain the most lifelike preserved specimens. None of the specimens showed the slightest odour, or other sign of decay.

I was eager to see if this method would work with other animals, and was delighted to find that it did so. By tossing a newly dead specimen of bird or beast into a grendel's web in the evening, by morning I had a preserved specimen (this worked for quite large animals, up to the size of a sargassum bird, though the spider would feed on an animal of that size for several days before discarding it). I now have nearly a hundred mounted specimens of various species, although best represented are the bats, of which there are three species on the island, all of the flittermouse type (apart from the dungbat, which I will later describe). No more careful cutting and cleaning skins, no more dabbing away with tow and turpentine, no more wires and wadding, no more Gardner's preservative. Here was taxidermy for dunces, indeed.

Do you also remember John Edmonton, Bobby, whose rough black hands could set a feather on a hummingbird's throat, or straighten the antenna of a gnat? I remember him well, and the receipt for Gardner's preservative that he taught us. 6 oz arsenic, 3 oz corrosive sublimate,[32] 2 oz yellow soap, 1 oz

---

[32] I.e. mercuric chloride, $HgCl_2$

camphor, thoroughly dissolved in half a pint of spirits of wine; wonderful stuff for preserving dead skins, though I suspect that it is not so good for preserving live ones. When first I learned of your illness, I wondered if this was what had caused it. A small dose of arsenic or mercury never did anyone any harm, but what with all the specimens that you must have prepared while you were on the *Beagle*, you would have had more than a small dose of both. I have named the spider *Epeira edmontonii*.

As the *Sarah Rose* sailed away from England, my feelings were mixed. I had to admit that the warrant, bought as it had clearly been with all the money and influence that those two men of property and propriety could muster, was a masterstroke. It would ensure my exile for at least enough time for Emma to recover from her own heartbreak, perhaps even until Bobby could return and himself claim her for his bride. On my first days aboard ship I was both seasick and homesick, but soon became used to my new situation. Within a few months I was able to tell myself that there were only two things that I missed about England, and I miss them still. I would pay any price on a warm day for a pint of cool English cider, and I would give any money to gently turn over a lily pad in a pond and find beneath it, hanging motionless in the water, beautiful, simple and small, a newt. To me there is something essentially English about these harmless little water-lizards, and the memory of finding a newt in a pond is the memory of all the happiness of my childhood, and the memory of all of England.

Chapter 12

No NEWTS HIDE BENEATH the lily pads in the lake on my island, though it is home to considerable numbers of small fish; on some mornings and evenings its surface seems alive with their rising and splashing as they chase after the gnats and midges which drift like mist over the water. The fish are of the Galaxiid variety, small, elongate and without scales, resembling the minnows of Australia, whose fry are taken in great quantities as whitebait when they make their annual migration up the estuaries, much as elvers are taken in England. I have only lately discovered that the island fish, too, migrate, though the circumstances of their journey are very different.

The lake is a peaceful place. Swallows skim its surface, warblers call from the reed-beds, solitary herons patrol its margins for frogs and fish. It has no exit, but is fed by a small stream which, rising on the mountain, enters the lake at the northern end. The source of the stream is a hot spring (one of several I have discovered on the mountain), and though by the time the water reaches the lake it has already lost much of its heat, it is still uncomfortable to touch. The bed of the stream is completely covered with a species of alga, resembling nothing so much as bright green hair, becoming more dense the nearer it is to the source. It is indeed so bright that the course of the stream can be traced from some distance away as a green thread winding up the mountain. How any plant can survive in water so hot, I know not. It is hot enough to set an egg.

*　　*　　*

Of all the benefits which civilisation has conferred on mankind, to my mind two stand out. One is tobacco, the other is a hot bath. I started smoking in Cambridge. For many years I had avoided the stuff, though through lack neither of opportunity nor example. Doctor Butler smoked, and it seemed to me that all the boys at school smoked, yet as a child and later as a youth, I found it strange that anyone should willingly engage in an activity that appeared to make him sick. In Edinburgh, most of my student colleagues were smokers, but there too I found their ostentatious pipework somewhat pretentious, and had no mind to enter their brotherhood. It was the simple delight of getting the stuff delivered up to my room from the shop downstairs at my lodgings in Sydney Street that first got me to try the stuff at Cambridge (three knocks on the floor for snuff, four for turkey), but since I first became enamoured of Dame Nicotiana, I have never been without her. It was Captain Forsyth of the *Sarah Rose* who told about the desirability of always carrying with me some tobacco seeds.

On leaving Bristol, our first port of call was Madeira. Captain Forsyth, a small and dapper man, was a far cry from the traditional image of the old sea salt in everything but his hands, which were as powerful and weatherbeaten as any that ever held the wheel of a ship. He had invited me to join him in a tavern that he knew of (you may remember the dockside at Funchal from your own visit, Bobby, and perhaps spent an hour or two in the same tavern),[33] and while drinking some surprisingly good wine, the captain offered me a pipe of his twist. As I was filling my pipe, I noticed within his tobacco pouch a second, smaller pouch.

'What have we here?' I asked.

'Why,' he said, taking the pouch from me, 'that's my sailor's seeds.'

[33] The author is here mistaken, as the *Beagle* did not in fact visit Madeira.

I had never heard of sailor's seeds.

'Oh, most sailors carry a few tobacco seeds with them,' said Captain Forsyth, and opened the pouch to show me the dust-like seeds within. 'Have you not heard the tale?'

I said that I had not, and as he filled his own pipe he told me the story of the sailor's seeds. I tell it to you as he told it to me.

'Many years ago,' said the captain, 'it was just after we had driven the Frenchies from the Main for the last time, as I remember, and the fleet was heading back to Portsmouth, just as we were off the Azores, a terrible storm came up, a right blow she was, and one of our frigates, lagging behind the rest of the ships, was driven on to the rocks. It was the *Lady Chatham*, under Captain Thursoe. Within minutes the old ship was breaking up, and all hands were forced to take to the boats, of which there were only two. They got the boats free of the ship all right, but were blown away heggerty-peggerty by the storm, and became separated from each other. Somehow both boats survived, and a couple of days later, when the wind was blown out, both boats were able to make landfall, each on a different island a few miles apart. The seas were still pretty rough, though, and the boats were smashed in the landing. When the wreckage of the *Lady Chatham*, and a few bodies besides, began to wash up on Fayal, it was assumed that all hands had been lost. No attempt was made to find the survivors.'

The captain paused from his narrative to carefully light his pipe, giving the task, in the manner of the best storytellers, his full attention. Satisfied with his performance, he puffed a couple of clouds of tobacco smoke into the air and continued.

'Well, nearly two years went by. Then a British man-o'-war, sailing well to the south of the Azores, saw smoke coming from a small island. The captain sent over a landing party, and discovered some of the crew of the *Lady Chatham* alive and well. They told their saviours that the other boat had landed on an island a few miles away, although they had seen no signals for several months. A landing party was dispatched to the second island. They found the crew there, right enough, but not a man of them alive. But not only were they all dead, all of them bore clear signs of having died by violence, either by pistol, or musket, or cutlass or dagger. Now why should this be so? Why had one crew survived, and the other all died so horribly?'

Captain Forsyth tamped down his tobacco with a thick-skinned thumb, applied another taper to the pipe, and took a few more meditative puffs before continuing with the story.

'Well, the answer soon became clear. The *Lady Chatham*, like most of the fleet I suppose, had picked up a little bit of booty from her recent engagement, and among this were several bales of tobacco. When orders came to abandon ship, both crews had the foresight to take a bale or two of this tobacco with them, for no-one knows more than a sailor the value of a pipe. Food he can do without for days, weeks even, but not his pipe of tobacco. When those poor men eventually made land, it was the tobacco more than anything that kept up their spirits, and helped them bear their hardships.

But after a few months, the tobacco which the men had brought with them began to run out. On both islands the men managed to catch plenty of fish, and there were cocoa-nuts, I suppose. They had food enough, but without a plentiful supply of tobacco, tempers began to shorten. Some men had been hoarding their tobacco, or believed that others had more than their fair share. Jealousy, fear and hate began to rear their heads. Men began to steal, men began to cheat, and soon men began to fight, all for a pipe of tobacco.'

The captain inspected his own pipe closely and looked up at me.

'Yes, the corpses on that island told the whole sad story. Each and every man had been killed for want of a bit of tobacco. Only one corpse was unwounded, and he had clearly been the last to die. Clutched in his hand was a smoked-out pipe, and lying by his side was an empty tobacco pouch. Though he had not been murdered, without his tobacco, he had simply lost the will to live.'

'But what of the other crew?' I said.

'Ah, well,' said the captain, 'that's the point of the story. One of the sailors in the first boat, a wise and thoughtful man, had taken with him a pinch of tobacco seeds, wrapped carefully in an oilskin pouch. The very day after his boat made land, the wise sailor planted his seeds in a secret place, and over the following weeks he tended his plants. By the time the tobacco which the sailors had brought with them was running out, and their tempers with it, the tobacco plants had grown up and were ready for harvest. And so on the first island, with tobacco aplenty, the crew continued to live in peace and harmony until they were rescued.'

The captain took another small pouch from his pocket, and passed it across to me.

'Here, take this. Fill it with tobacco seeds,' he said, indicating a small bowl on the tavern bar, 'and refill it whenever you get a chance. Carry it with you always. If it don't bring you life, it will bring you luck.'

Since then, like many a sailor still, I have always carried a small pouch of tobacco seeds about my person, and have religiously replenished it whenever I had the chance from the small bowl of tobacco seeds you will find in any tavern or chandler's shop, in any port where British sailors go. And I have had my share of luck over the last fifty years, though I never thought I would need to use the seeds. But now it is my luck to have a fine crop of tobacco on the island, and a morning pipe and an evening pipe to soothe my heart and soothe my soul, and for them I thank my own wise sailor, Captain Forsyth of the *Sarah Rose*.

I can think of no-one in particular to thank for introducing me to the hot bath, but it was the cause of considerable and frequent regret to me for my first two years on this island that

I had no way of indulging this pleasure. Even had I been able to find a pool or rocky hollow of the right size, I knew that the labour of filling it with hot water would have outweighed the pleasure of the bath, and though I had been aware of the hot streams on the mountain from early on, they were much too hot for bathing in (Charley and I would sometimes amuse ourselves by taking a sargassum bird egg or a fish wrapped in leaves to poach in the hot water for our lunch). Why it took me so long to reason that the hot water of the stream and the cold water of the lake might provide the answer to my missing indulgence, I cannot tell, though I have kicked myself for it many times since. A few months ago, the thought struck me out of the blue that the hot water and cold water must mix of themselves at some point. Though I had never properly investigated the actual place where the stream joins the lake, surrounded as it is by dense vegetation, I immediately determined to do so. In the event, it took me only an hour or so to hack my way through the bush to the point where the waters meet. The ground was steep and rocky, and the stream ended in a series of small waterfalls, at the base of which was a deep pool. When I put my hand into it, I was delighted to find that the water was the perfect temperature for a bath.

The path to the pool is now well-worn, and bathing has become part of my routine. There can be few combinations more relaxing than smoking a pipe of tobacco while sitting in a warm bath, and I often spend an hour at my twin indulgences. It was lying thus one evening last September, stretched out in the water, pipe in hand, that I first became aware of the migration of the minnows.

Since I first discovered the pool, I have been taking careful notes of its natural history. Its inhabitants comprise a single, though abundant, species of snail, a quantity of aquatic insects, notably the larvae of what appear to be four or five species of chironomids, several caddis flies and mayflies, and a large

126

predacious Mecopteran. There are also adults and larvae of two aquatic beetles, one a *Gyrinus*, or perhaps large *Orectochilus*, similar to the whirligig of English streams, the other belonging to the Hydrophilidae, probably to a new genus, whose larvae eat the water-snails. The adult beetles appear to feed mainly on the bright green alga from the hot stream, small clumps of which are continually being washed down over the waterfall. This particular day, on coming down to my evening bath, I was surprised to see, swimming in the warm water of the pool, several small fish, about the size and form of the minnows in the lake. But they were not the pale brown colour of the lake fish, they were bright red.

The next day when I returned to the pool, I found more of the red fish, and the next day even more. The fish were swimming upstream from the lake, in small schools of a dozen or so; within a week there were so many of them in the pool that it became uncomfortable to bathe; the fish had become so thick that they were forever brushing against my body, tickling me so much that I could not stand to be in the water. The pool is roughly circular and only four yards wide, yet I estimated that it contained over ten thousand fish, packed into a tight shoal, forever circling around and around the pool. As the fish were so numerous, and had come from the lake, it had by now become clear to me that they could only be the lake minnows, but that they must have undergone some kind of transformation. But how, and to what end?

Although I could no longer bathe in its waters, I continued to visit the pool each evening, both to smoke my evening pipe, and to observe the fish. One morning, some ten days after I had noticed the first red fish, I arrived at the pool to find that all the fish had gone. Not a single fish remained anywhere in the pool, and it seemed that why they had come, and why they had returned to the lake, would remain a mystery. Though I was disappointed that my natural history investigation had come to such an abrupt end, it was with much relief that I reclaimed the pool for my daily ritual. As I lay back in the warm water, my head resting on a rounded rock at the water's edge, my pipe in hand, I felt once again that complete contentment that only a bath can bring. Above the soft splashing of the waterfall, I could hear the music of the sargassum birds, which had recently resumed their daily chorus, drift over the island. The thread of smoke from my pipe rose unbroken into the still air. As my gaze followed the smoke upwards to a blue sky, unbroken by the smallest cloud, I noticed, out of the corner of my eye, above the waterfall and about fifty yards upstream, a large patch of red. I stared at it more closely. The patch completely covered the rocks, yet in my dreamy state it took me several moments to realise what it was. It could only be the fish.

Almost leaping from the pool, I hastily pulled on shoes and trousers and began a careful climb up the side of the waterfall. It was indeed the fish, thousands of them spread like a living blanket over the rocks, still moving slowly upstream. They were using their pelvic fins (which are fleshy and placed forward on the belly, just below the pectoral fins) as suckers, with which they managed to cling effectively to even a vertical rock, provided it were wet and smooth. The way they moved up the rocks was simple but effective. A few hundred fish having attached themselves to the rock at the edge of a pool, others would wriggle over and between them, then more fish would wriggle between them, and so on, each row helping the next gain further height. When all had left the pool, it would be the turn of the fish in the bottom row to move to the front. It was slow work, but in the twenty-four hours since I had last seen them in the bottom pool they had already gained fifty yards, and they had only another fifty to go before they would be over the falls and into the stream above. I was curiously impressed by this teamwork, but what I found even more impressive was that the fish were moving over rocks and through water that was too hot to touch, water which I knew was hot enough to cook a normal fish.

* * *

I have since discovered that my small galaxiids are able to tolerate temperatures almost up to boiling point, and that they ascend the stream to its very source. For it is here, among the thick beds of green alga, that the fish lay their eggs. Each male fish (recognisable by its slimmer form compared with the relative rotundity of the females) tunnels into the weed at the edge of the stream, making thus an elongated nest, the bed of which it decorates with small stones, each stone being carried to the nest in the fish's mouth. The nest being completed to its own satisfaction, the male returns to the main stream in search of a mate, which it persuades, by much wriggling and pushing, to enter its tunnel. If the female is also satisfied with the nest, she sheds her eggs (of which there are several hundred) within, where they attach to the stones by some intrinsic adhesive property. The male, who has remained outside the tunnel during this procedure, then drives the female away from the nest by biting her tail, and himself enters the nest to shed his milt over the eggs. The females all appear to die after spawning; the males remain within the tunnel for a day or two until the fry hatch, then they too die. From my observations, the fish exhibit neither polygyny nor polyandry.

When they hatch from the eggs, the fry are also bright red. They feed on the green alga for several weeks, gradually work their way downstream, eating the alga as they go. At the end of this period, the countless thousands of young fish have grown to between one and two inches in length, and have consumed almost all of the alga in the stream, which temporarily loses its green appearance. It is at this time that the seasonal rains begin. The sudden influx of freshwater not only greatly increases the flow of the stream, but also lowers its temperature, apparently giving the signal for the fish to head downstream. Within a day of the first heavy rain, every single fish has disappeared over the falls and into the lake.

It is a great puzzle to me how these minnows can live in water that would cook any other fish. That it is a principle found only in the living animal is attested by the fact that the fish are themselves cooked when they die. When the adult fish die after spawning, they are carried over the falls to the pool in which I bathe; for several days this becomes almost choked with their bodies, which have now lost their bright red colour and become milky white, the flesh taking on exactly the colour, appearance (and taste) of any other cooked fish. Yet while the fish are alive, the cooking process is somehow prevented. In North America, salmon also turn red when entering their natal rivers, though I have not heard that they ascend into hot streams. Many years ago I met a man in Australia who said he had been to the South Pole,[34] and maintained that there is a fish living beneath the ice which is colder than the ice itself, a fact proved when several were caught and immediately put alive into a bucket of freshwater, which immediately froze around them. Whether or not these fish were red, I do not recall, nor can I guess what the chemical principle behind such a prophylactic may be. As to why any fish should make such an arduous journey when they might remain safe at home in the lake, I suppose one should ask an eel or a salmon, but I surmise that the alga is a rich and plentiful source of food, while no doubt the hot water of the stream offers an almost perfect protection against the fish's enemies at such a vulnerable stage. The dead fish are eventually washed down into the lake, where they are gathered up by flocks of noddies, which appear at the lake as if by magic, plucking the fish from the surface of the water to take back to their nestlings in the *Pisonia* forest.

I have named the species *Galaxias borealis*. I find it puzzling that Galaxiid fishes should be found on my island. I had previously included them among that group of animals having

[34] HMS *Erebus*, under the command of Captain James Clark Ross, made three expeditions to the Antarctic from 1841 to 1843 though none of the expeditions went far inland, and none reached the South Pole.

an exclusively southern distribution (they are also found in Australia, New Zealand and Patagonia), which supported my theory that the southern continents were once joined.

Chapter 13

THE MOUNTAIN COMES AND goes. Sometimes it disappears for days at a time behind a wreath of low cloud, at other times it is the major part of every view. But cloudy or clear, night or day, I feel its presence always, and our fates have become indivisible. When the first rains came, a few months after I arrived on the island, I could not see the mountain for several weeks. Then one night in late January, while I slept, the clouds were blown away and I awoke to a sky so clear that the mountain appeared to have taken advantage of its recent cover to move a mile or two towards me. I could see every tree, every bush, every rock, and high in the blue sky above it, I saw the storks.

My island has few seasonal visitors. The swallows and swifts are always with me, the cuckoos seem to call all year round, but the storks reside here for only a short time. They are lovely birds, graceful in flight and dignified on the ground. I think they may be the same species as that commonly seen in other parts of the East; they have white bodies and a black head, with black edges to their white wings, and their beaks and their legs are bright red. Every year after the rains they come gliding in from the south, heading for the island. They come in their thousands; for two or three weeks the island seems full of nothing but storks. Then one day they are gone, and when they leave the island seems even emptier than before they came; but while they are here it is a wonderful time, and wonderful things happen.

In the waters around my island I have found several varieties of tripang, the large holothurian common in most tropical seas, which the Moluccans, who are the great fishermen of the area, hook out with long poles, then boil and smoke to sell to the Chinese for food. These 'sea cucumbers', as they are generally known, come in several sizes and colours, but during my first rainy season on the island, I noticed that one variety had become particularly common. About the size and shape of a Lancashire sausage, though of a dull green colour, they seemed to almost fill the shallow waters around the eastern end of the island. All along the shore I found pairs of these animals, always end to end; it was clear that they had assembled in the shallow water to mate.

With slow manoeuvring, two animals approach each other; each then turns around so that one end (which end was head and which tail, I could not determine) is almost touching the other's, and each extends its intromittent organ. These long flexible organs enter a corresponding orifice on the opposite animal and are then pulled tight, drawing the two together in a tight embrace. With the pair thus conjoined, a wave of contraction starts at the end of one of the animals. The wave passes slowly down its body, and when it reaches the point at which the animals are joined, passes across to the other and flows along its body; another wave begins, in the opposite direction. After many minutes of this slow pulsing back and forth, both animals suddenly shudder in unison, as if with the deepest satisfaction, and the whole process is repeated. So they remain, pulsing and shuddering, for several days.

It is thus that fertilisation takes place. These holothuria do not shed their eggs and spermatozoa into the water to combine, as with most of their kind. Fertilisation takes place internally, and I later discovered by dissection that the holothuria are among those fortunate animals which 'can either sex assume, or both'. They are hermaphroditic, each possessing the sexual apparatus of both a male and a female (do such creatures get twice the pleasure of we simple dioecics?). After mating, the animals disjoin, but remain close to each other, resting in the shallows. It is at this time that the storks arrive.

There is nothing that a hungry stork appreciates more after a tiring journey than a fat, pregnant holothurian. The storks arrive from the south in small flocks. After flying two or three circles over the island, they land beside the sea and soon thousands of storks can be found along the northern shoreline, picking up and swallowing holothurians like Dutchmen swallowing herrings. After taking their fill, the storks, now heavy with food, begin to scramble and flap their way up the mountain; for the island is no more than a short port of call, and it is from the highest point on the island that they will continue their journey. It takes the storks some hours to reach the summit. By the time they arrive they are in need of a rest, and the trees and bare rocks around the caldera provide a convenient roost. After much squawking and squabbling, they eventually settle down to sleep.

In the morning, the sun begins to heat the rocks. The rocks then heat the air, which starts to rise. By ten o'clock this rising air has gained such a force that the branches of the trees at the summit are blown about by it. One by one, the storks open their broad wings and launch themselves off the mountain. Upwards they climb, circling round and around until they are the smallest of black specks against the blue. Then they break from the circle and glide away towards the north. But before they leave the island they have one last task to perform; in order to fly, they have first to rid themselves of excess ballast. As each stork bends its legs prior to leaping off the mountain, it lets go a muddy stream of excrement. It is thus that the young holothurians enter the world.

You may have seen a cheese skipper, the little *Piophila* maggot which jumps out from an old cheese, bending round to grab its tail with its mouth, then releasing it so suddenly that it springs into the air. So it is with these young cucumbers. From each deposit left by the storks leap hundreds of little bright green gherkins, each no bigger than a grain of rice. There are tens of thousands of storks. Thus, each year, millions of these young 'land cucumbers' are deposited on the top of the mountain.

I have not yet fully described the vegetation of my island. The flat land is mostly covered with forests of what I take to be typical trees of the region, *Pisonia*, *Ficus*, etc. Around the many swamps and ponds in this flat land are various sedges and rushes, which are again unremarkable, while the coastal dunes are clad with coarse grass, mostly *Spinifex*, and with a few low shrubs. The cocoa-nut tree is found both along the coast and inland. There is a clear change in vegetation as one moves up the mountain. The lower slopes are covered with grasses of various kinds, but higher up this grassland gives way to a sparse forest, composed largely of a kind of tree cactus or dildoe.[35] These plants greatly resemble *Opuntias* (similar, I imagine, to those you saw in Patagonia, my dear Bobby),[36] though this species is without thorns and may be closer to the *Euphorbia* tribe. The dildoe forest extends right to the top of the mountain, and it is here that the young land cucumbers find both food and shelter.

By much laborious investigation, I have discovered that land cucumbers feed on the dildoe trees, or should I rather say, feed *in* them. The young skippers, having leaped from their natal pile, head off down the mountain. As soon as they come to rest near a dildoe tree, they immediately begin to burrow into the ground. Here the little animals somehow find their way to a root, bore their way inside, and begin to feed on the soft tissue within. During the next few months, they eat their way up the root, through the main stem, and finally into the branches. By the time they have reached the outer branches they are some

[35] A word formerly used, primarily by sailors, to describe the large cactus-like trees of several oceanic islands, primarily *Cereus* spp.

[36] Darwin noted several plants of this genus during his voyage on the *Beagle*, one of which, from Patagonia, was named *Opuntia Darwinii* after him by his friend Professor Henslow.

six inches long and fully grown. It is now time for them to leave the tree and return to the sea whence they came.

Like other holothurians, land cucumbers have no legs or wings or other aids to locomotion, but they have an ability which, I think, is found nowhere else in the animal kingdom. After the first rains of January, the animals eat their way out of the branches inside which they have been feeding; at this time hundreds can be found hanging by a short sticky thread from the branches of each dildoe tree, looking like nothing so much as the vegetable after which they are named. They are now ready for the next stage of their journey. Each cucumber slowly contracts its body so that rather than looking like a cucumber, it more resembles an apple. This contraction produces so great an internal pressure that at this stage the animal resembles a ball of green gutta-percha. It then releases its hold on the branch and falls to the ground, but it is so elastic that, instead of remaining where it lands, it bounces. And because the dildoe trees are growing at the top of a mountain, it bounces downhill, down towards the sea. Should one of the animals find its progress halted by a rock or plant, it once more takes its previous form, wriggles clear of the obstacle, and flings itself once more into the air. Here, it immediately resumes its spherical shape, and bounces off again. I have now twice witnessed the migration of the land cucumbers, and the whole mountain seems alive with bouncing balls. It is a most wondrous sight. I have called this animal *Cocumis ciconius*.

I saw many wondrous sights on my voyage south on the *Sarah Rose*. My cabin on the poop deck had been well set up with my books and instruments, and the captain and cabin boy proved most accommodating company. But I took my greatest pleasure in observing the natural history of the voyage, much of which was completely new to me. I remember my first sight of phosphorescence at night (which my seine revealed to be caused by a small *Pyrosoma*), my fascination at the antics of flying fish (one of which I witnessed with my own eyes fly clear over the foredeck, a height of at least fourteen feet), and my chagrin on first seeing that most fascinating creature, the *Physalia*. I had known of this creature from books, where it usually went by its more romantic name of 'Portuguese man-o'-war'. Having never seen one *in vivo*, I had assumed that it must be a huge creature, at least half a yard long. I was disappointed to find that most are less than the length of my little finger. I was also slightly disappointed in the power of its sting, which I had read could kill a man but found, when I was myself stung while rummaging in a bucket of plankton, that its effects were hardly greater than that of a common nettle. What with my daily discoveries in marine natural history and my nightly dalliances with the captain and the cabin boy, my voyage to Cape Town passed quickly, but by the time we touched land I decided that I had had enough of life at sea. I decided not to continue to New South Wales on the *Sarah Rose*; instead, with the money from Bobby's father and uncle still in my pocket, I disembarked at the Cape, intending to investigate the country about, perhaps collect some beetles, and, in general, to enjoy myself.

I did indeed collect several hundred beetles, and I did indeed enjoy myself, to the price of about a thousand pounds over the two years I stayed in Africa. The Cape was then known as the place where the flowers have no scent, the birds no song, and the women no morals. I soon discovered this to be untrue. Several of the birds had a passingly pleasant song, many of the flowers were sweetly scented, and lack of morality was by no means the sole prerogative of women. Though I spent most of my time in Cape Town itself, which I found to be a gay and lively place, I also made several expeditions northwards, well beyond the Limpopo. These I have described in another journal.[37]

---

[37] No other reference is made to this journal in the present manuscript. Its fate is unknown.

Chapter 14

In May of 1834 I left Cape Town on board the *Pegasus*. After two years in the Cape I had spent almost all of my ready money, and was delighted to find, on arriving in Port Jackson in June of that year, eight hundred pounds waiting for me at the bank as promised. This would equip me to set up house in Sydney as a gentleman of means. I had just turned twenty-five years old, and had seen enough of the world to understand something of how it worked. Knowing that impressions can be just as important as substance, I rented a fine house at No. 26, George Street, bought a carriage and two fine horses for my stable, and set up a brass plate on the front gate with the two magical letters 'Dr' in front of my name. Thus established, I sat back to see what fortune would bring me.

My lack of genuine qualifications was little hindrance to my soon being recognised and accepted as a physician of the first rank. There were few enough medical men in the colony at the time, and my medical studies at Edinburgh and Cambridge, though curtailed by circumstance, had equipped me well enough for most of the consultations I was called upon to perform. Though one or two patients may have been disadvantaged by the treatments I prescribed, this was no more than was the average for that time and place. If I did recognise a serious case, I borrowed a trick that Philos told me his father used. He would refer it on to some other practitioner, who was usually so flattered to be asked to take the case that he failed to notice when more than the usual number of them proved fatal.

What with making a place for myself in the professional world, and in what passed for society in those early days of the colony, it was some time before I found the opportunity to begin a thorough investigation of the natural world. For my first expedition into the bush, I chose a fine, sunny day in early December. Packing only my net and vasculum, a loaf of bread and a brace of beer bottles, I directed my horse east through the city and out towards the South Head. Once out of town, I found the country was not unlike that I had come across in parts of the Cape, comprising sandy heaths with soft sandstone outcrops. The vegetation, too, bore many similarities to the *fynbos* of that region, with the native honeysuckles reminding me of African proteas. By simply sweeping the bushes beside the road from my saddle, I was able to quickly obtain a number of interesting beetles, which I found were also similar to those of the Cape. I was slightly disappointed at this similarity, and remember wishing that, like Cook and Banks (and later you, Bobby), I had come westwards around the globe, so that the botanical and zoological productions of New South Wales would be all the more strange and new. But this feeling soon passed, and by the time I reached the Heads, and had stopped to transfer some fine *Stigmodera* and *Paropsis* from my net to my jars, I was already becoming entranced by the natural history of my new home. It was then that I espied the dragonfly.

The magnificent insect was hovering in the air directly in front of me, not three yards from my face. Occasionally it darted off to harry some other insect, but always returned to hover in the same spot, from where it watched me with its enormous eyes. Though my knowledge of the Odonata is not extensive, I have always admired the insects for their beauty; this one was indeed a beauty. It was not particularly large, but it was most wonderfully coloured, its body being a rich vermilion, while its wings were boldly tipped with black, reminding me of a species I had often seen in the Cape, but had never been able to capture. This one would surely be mine. Holding my net low by my right leg, I gave my horse a slight tap with my heels to ease her gently forward. My plan was to get close enough to sweep my net up and over the dragonfly. I slowly approached, and to my delight the dragonfly stayed hovering in the same spot. Up came my net; the prize was mine.

I must have had a full half-second in which to savour my triumph, before I felt myself rising suddenly and unexpectedly into the air. I had foolishly neglected to inform my horse of my entomological manoeuvre, and the sight of a large white object sweeping upwards an inch or two from her right eye was thus completely unexpected. She reacted in the same way that most horses would have reacted; with a sound that was more scream than snort, she reared up on her hind legs, then bolted. What goes up must come down, and it was thus that when Bobby arrived at Port Jackson one clear January morning in 1836, I was still walking on crutches, a bandage around my ankle.

I could not say what surprised my friend more, the sight of my bandages, or of me. I had given my word to his uncle and father that in exchange for their money, I would not contact Emma nor Bobby. After I had left England I could see little point in corresponding with Emma, but I had second thoughts about Bobby. Suspecting this, his father had taken the precaution in an early letter of telling him of the circumstances in which his boyhood friend had been forced to flee England. I learned the story in a letter from Philos. Inveterate gambler that I was, I had come unstuck in a shady Newmarket scheme, a warrant of civil outlawry had been issued against me and I had thought it best to flee abroad. Bobby had no reason not to believe the story; it was unthinkable that his own father should lie to him. Although my immediate reaction on hearing of this deception was to refute it, I soon realised on reflection that there was no point. No-one, not Emma nor Jos, nor even Philos, would support my version of the events that had caused me to leave England. My best course of action was to remain silent on the subject, even though I knew that my silence would be taken as

141

corroboration. When I wrote to Bobby in Rio, where I knew a letter would eventually find him, I received a short reply admonishing me for causing my own demise. Was it not my own greed which had led to my downfall, he asked, and I almost laughed at this, from one who had never wanted for anything, not money, not friends, not family, not love. But perhaps you were right, Bobby; perhaps it was greed which led to my being in Australia. I have always been greedy.

Though Bobby and I had exchanged no more letters during his voyage, I had kept up a regular correspondence with Philos. I think Philos had been more amused than appalled by my affair with his cousin Emma, for whom he had no great affection, and had declared himself most impressed with the sum I had extracted from his father, with whom he always seemed to be in dispute about one or other of his London accounts, and who was always badgering him to be married. Now here was the same man paying me handsomely *not* to be married. But Philos had been loath to see me leave, and we had already exchanged several letters while I was in Africa. It was from Philos that I heard the details of Bobby's travels, of Rio de Janeiro and Montevideo, of Fitzroy and Covington (and all about Donna Clara, Bobby). I had recently received a letter from Philos saying that his brother was about to leave South America for the Galapagos, and should be arriving in Australia in the new year. I was determined to see him.

I remember the morning exactly. I had just begun examining a young woman who had been brought to me by her mother, complaining of 'palpitations'. My examination immediately confirmed my suspicions. As is common in these cases, the girl was pregnant, and I was debating in my mind whether to tell the daughter alone or both women together, when word arrived that the *Beagle* had been seen passing through the Heads. Pleading an emergency, I instructed my patient to come again by herself on the morrow, hobbled from my house as fast as my crutches would allow, and hailed a cab

to Circular Quay. My estrangement from Bobby was about to
end, our silence to be broken. But how would he greet me? As
far as Bobby knew I had been disgraced at home, flown the
country and taken up self-exile in a penal colony at the ends
of the earth. It had been four years since he had last seen
me. Would his heart have turned against me? Would he have
forgotten me? Would he even recognise me? When the ship
finally arrived at the quay my heart was in my mouth and my
mouth too dry to swallow it. The gangplank was dropped and
two men walked down it, both hidden behind the long hair and
beards of an extended sea voyage. But I recognised Bobby; the
nose that poked out above the whiskers could belong to no other.
And he recognised me. At the sight of me standing there on my
crutches he stopped dead on the gangplank, then my trepidation
turned to joy to see that familiar smile appear from beneath his
beard and my old friend opening his arms towards me.

There is but a single species of dragonfly on this island,
somewhat resembling the English *Aeshna* in general form,
though with the rounded hindwings of an *Anax*. The male is
a large and handsome insect, in size and colouration not unlike
the Norfolk Darter though with pigmented, rather than hyaline,
wings. The female, however, is quite different. Not only is she
considerably smaller than the male, with much reduced head
and legs, she is completely wingless.
   The first time I saw a pair of these insects, I did not
immediately recognise them as belonging to the Odonata. I
at first imagined the object I saw skimming across the lake
to be some bird of the swallow tribe, and it was not until
I had seen several such creatures, and been puzzled by the
apparent iridescence of the wings, that I realised that what I
was seeing was not a bird, but an insect, or rather, a pair of
insects. For, though the female has no wings, this is not to say
that she does not fly. Whenever she wants to take to the air,
she simply summons the assistance of a male.

Both sexes begin their lives much as other dragonflies, as minuscule larvae living in the waters of whatever pond or lake the female has chosen to lay her eggs in. The larvae presumably feed on small worms and other water creatures, having the projectile labium common to their order. The metamorphosis of the male larva is normal. It lives in water throughout its early life, eventually reaching a couple of inches in length, a size at which it must effect considerable predation on tadpoles and young minnows. For its final moult, it climbs out of the water a short way up a reed (I have found the males' exuviae only at the base of a stem, never at the top), casts off its larval skin, and, as soon as its wings have expanded and dried, takes flight. The male has the normal form of Odonata, with a head largely comprising two enormous eyes of a bluish colour and a pair of stout, toothed mandibles. Its thorax is equipped with long, hairy legs and two pairs of exceptionally large blue wings (but which shine iridescent green and gold in sunlight). Its abdomen is mostly black in colour though with blue spots along the flanks, tapering down to a pair of long claspers on the penultimate segment. The growth of the female is, at first, similar to that of the male, but at the fourth or fifth instar, the female larvae, which are now recognisable by their less gracile form, leave the water to take up a terrestrial existence among the reeds and grasses on the lake shore. Whether or not the females feed during this time I cannot say, but I have found them to be fairly active, and think it likely that they catch and eat smaller insects. Just before their final ecdysis, the females return briefly to the water, from where, like the males, they climb to the top of one of the reeds to moult, and assume their final form. This is not the usual one for a dragonfly, adult females resembling more the larval shape. The head is much reduced, compound eyes are absent, though the ocelli are slightly enlarged, and the mouthparts are also small, but functional. The thorax, too, is much reduced, and completely without wings, while the legs are so small and flimsy that it is

144

only with some difficulty that the creature can grasp the reed up which it has climbed. The abdomen is depressed, with the genitalia alone recognisably those of an adult. This final moult always takes place at night, after which the female clings closely to the reed, where her colour, which is dark green rather than the brown of the larva, makes her almost invisible by day.

Try though I might, I have never been able to capture a male dragonfly on the wing. Their vision is much too sharp to allow them to be stalked, and they are too fast and adroit in flight to be taken by the chase. I have occasionally chanced across one at night by the light of my lantern, resting on a low bush, often a considerable distance from the lake. One night, not far from my house, I found a mating pair. The male was perched vertically on the branch of a thorn bush, using its abdominal claspers to grasp the female just behind the head (as is usual with dragonflies); the female was simply hanging down below the male. This coupling could clearly not have occurred in flight, which I believe is usual among dragonflies, as the female is wingless. Exactly how the insects conjoin, I have only recently discovered.

I was sitting by the lake one early morning last July. The day had started cool. Thin clouds of vapour still swirled over the surface of the lake, but there must have been a few small gnats and midges about, as numbers of both swallows and dragonflies were already hawking low over the water. Judging by the number of exuviae I had recently seen on the reeds, this was high season for dragonfly emergence. The males were easy to see, swooping low over the water or hovering over the reeds. Sometimes a pair of males would meet, and, with a clearly audible clatter of wings, engage in brief combat. While I was watching one such battle I noticed a bright blue flash coming from one of the reeds nearby. It was over so quickly that at first I did not have time to locate it, but when it flashed again, I could see that it was coming from the tip of a reed only five yards from where I sat. No sooner had I fixed the spot than a male dragonfly darted towards it, hovered for a second, then darted away. As the insect flew off I could see that something was dangling from the end of its abdomen. It must surely be a female dragonfly. A little more investigation soon revealed the full story.

On emergence from her larval skin, the female dragonfly, flattened close against a stem, head–down, is indistinguishable from the reed. But as soon as she sees a male close by, she quickly lifts her abdomen away from the reed, curling it over her head to reveal its underside. Though the underside of the female's abdomen is the same drab colour as the rest of the animal, when it is stretched by this exercise, the membranes linking the segments, usually hidden beneath the sternites, are revealed. They are bright blue. On seeing this blue flash, the male dives down towards the female. He grasps her behind the head with his abdominal claspers and flies away with her in tow.

From further observations I have made of mating among this species, it appears to proceed in the manner typical of the Odonata. The male, before flying off in search of a mate, has first inserted a packet of sperm from his genital opening at the rear of his abdomen into the receptacle on the underside of his third abdominal segment. On being grasped by a male and carried aloft, the female bends her own abdomen underneath, reaching forward to take the sperm packet into her own genital tract. In this species the male does not release the female after mating, but, as is the case with some Zygoptera, keeps hold of her while she lays her eggs. I have never seen the pairs landing to deposit the eggs, like *Aeshna*, nor dipping like *Libellula*. The female appears to simply drop them at random while being carried over the lake. I have named this species *Anoptera cyanogaster*.

It is probable that the dragonflies remain *in copulo* for all of their adult lives, though I admit that my evidence for this assertion is circumstantial. There is no doubt that the female's lack of wings and weak legs and jaws make it difficult, if not impossible, for her to catch her own prey, yet I have identified fragments of midges and other small insects in the guts of the few females that I have dissected. This could be explained by the insects remaining paired, the male passing on to the female some of the food that he catches. I believe this to be unique among the Odonata, but that a similar situation obtains among some of the Mecoptera.

Chapter 15

How MY HEART REJOICED to see my old friend, and to feel his embrace. It was as if the past four years had been a dream from which I had just awoken, and now that Bobby and I were back together there seemed nothing to prevent us continuing with our friendship from where it had been left. After greeting me, Bobby briefly introduced me to his companion. He was the captain of the *Beagle*, an Irishman, but after the usual formalities we soon bid him farewell and the two of us set off into town. I was delighted to hear that the ship would be in port for at least three weeks. This was time enough for Bobby to see the sights, but the first sight I wanted to see was my friend's face. My barber was happy to oblige me, and as Bobby's hair and whiskers were shorn away I could see that some things, at least, had certainly changed. The young man whom I had last seen at the Bristol dockside four years ago was no more. The brown hair, which used to flop down over his forehead and touch his eyebrows, had retreated. The forehead itself bore lines where none had been before, as did his eyes. Bobby's eyes were always deeply set, but now seemed to have withdrawn even further beneath his brow. Yet the old smile and voice remained the same, and my friend readily accepted my offer of accommodation during his time in Sydney. This was on the condition, he added with some seriousness, that the staircase I had clearly fallen down not long ago had been well mended. I told Bobby how I had broken my ankle in falling from my horse while catching a dragonfly, a story which both

149

amused and impressed him, and soon we were back at my house and I was showing him my new specimens, including the insect which had caused my injuries and was now paying for its sport by decorating my cabinet.

'So, my friend,' said Bobby, after admiring my specimens, 'I can see that your net and collecting jar have not been idle, but what else have you been up to?'

Until that very moment I had thought in the back of my mind to tell Bobby everything. It was time that he knew the true story behind my leaving England, about Emma and about his father's deceit, and surely I could make him believe it. But now that the opportunity was in my grasp, I let it fall.

'This and that,' was all I said. 'Perhaps you could say I've just been looking for more beetles.'

'But not just beetles, surely,' said Bobby. 'It seems to me you must have collected a few stories to tell.'

I agreed that I had, that my time in Australia and my two years at the Cape on my way there had not been uneventful.

'You must tell me all about it,' said Bobby, and as I began to recount of one of my African adventures I realised that the past, no less than the future, is what we make of it, and we can make of it what we will. The need to set things straight for Bobby, to reveal the truth, to change the story, no longer seemed to matter. It was enough that Bobby was sitting before me with that old smile on his face.

'Now, enough of past glories,' I said, 'we need a new challenge, "in fresh fields and pastures new". What say you to a small collecting trip here in the colony?'

I was apprehensive that my friend, after four years of travelling, would prefer to spend his shore leave in more metropolitan explorations, but I need not have worried.

'A capital idea,' he said. 'Where shall we go?'

I had long entertained the idea of a short trip over the Blue Mountains, which, though I viewed them in the distance every day from my bedroom window, I had not yet visited.

'What about Bathurst?' I said. 'We'll hire you a horse, and be there and back within a week.'

'Bathurst it is,' said Bobby, adding with a laugh, 'I take it there are beetles in Bathurst?'

Three days later we said farewell to Fitzroy and the *Beagle*, and to Sydney, and rode off westwards. Those few days in New South Wales with you, dear Bobby, are still among the happiest of my life.

It was mid-January, but the year had not yet been so hot that the vegetation had lost its freshness, nor so dry that the roads were full of that choking dust that can make riding such a torment in the Australian summer. Our first day's journey took us west through Parramatta towards Emu Ferry, where I had arranged to spend the night. I rode my usual mare, while Bobby, delighted at the thought of being back on horseback after so long a sea-journey from South America, insisted upon hiring a lively young colt which he said reminded him of Flight.[38] Our first day's journey was leisurely enough, Bobby being content to question me about every aspect of the country we were passing through, and I being content to answer. Though we both carried nets and jars, and I was keen to collect from any likely-looking tree or bush, it was soon clear that Bobby was more interested in the geology of the area than its fauna. He was particularly impressed with the clear stratification of the sandstone, which even in those relatively flat areas was visible in small riverbeds and cuttings, and which intrigued him greatly. I also remember him remarking, after we had been riding for some time, on the uniformity, in colour and form, of the vegetation, a feature of Australia which seems to strike most visitors from Europe, though one to which the old chum and native-born are alike oblivious. Having spent time in both Australia and Europe, and in Africa besides, I

---

[38] No horse of this name is known from Darwin's own records; it may have been a horse which he had ridden on his extensive inland journeys in South America.

suggested that it is surely England whose flora is the more impoverished.

'At home there are perhaps two thousand species of plants, here there are twenty thousand.'

Bobby would have none of it.

'But they are so similar,' he said. 'A hundred banksias, a hundred acacias, two hundred eucalypts. And all the same drab green.'

'Yes, I am sure that in England all plants are twice as green,' I said. 'But as far as my memory goes, it is for only half the year.'

As Bobby laughed at my small joke, we spied before us a group of the local Gurinjai natives. This was Bobby's first contact with the original inhabitants of Australia, and he was keen to make the most of the encounter. My language skills were inadequate to translate all the questions my friend bid me ask them, though I did manage, with the aid of a silver coin, to persuade three of the men to amuse my friend with a display of spear-throwing, Bobby's hat bearing permanent testimony to their skills (I hasten to add that it was not on his head at the time, but pinned to the trunk of a tree).

Thanks to Major Mitchell's new road, which skirts cliffs and valleys with almost magical ease, our second day's journey up into the Blue Mountains was as easy as the first had been across the coastal plain. We stopped at midday at the Weatherboard Inn, where we had our first view of the magnificent scenery for which the area is so famous, though Bobby was again more excited by the geology than the aesthetic. On our walk back to the inn, he was full of speculations about the agents which had formed the cliffs and chasms, and the similarities between these elevated features and present coastal formations. We reached the Blackheath in the late afternoon, and after Bobby had satisfied himself that our horses were well cared for, we still had time to take a glass before our dinner.

So far it seemed that I had been the one telling the stories; about my time in New South Wales and my previous adventures in Africa. When we stopped that first night in the mountains, it seemed as if Bobby felt that it was at last his turn. I was eager to hear all that my friend could tell, from when he left England in 1831, to when he arrived at Circular Quay those few days before. I wanted to know about the people he had seen, and above all the natural history of the many lands he had visited; the pumas and guanacos, the ostriches and armadillos, and especially the beetles. Sitting on the bench outside the inn, a pot of beer in one hand, the fingers of his other scratching the ears of the old slut who, having barked at us in a most unfriendly manner on our arrival, had now abandoned her pups and lain her head blissfully on his lap, Bobby began his tale.

Adventurous as my own recent life sometimes seemed, how I would have liked to have been on that voyage of the *Beagle* to South America, to have witnessed volcanoes and earthquakes, to have seen the gauchos and the strange naked Fuegans. How I would have loved to have seen the American *Lampyris* and *Elater* (and how I regretted that Bobby had already sent all his specimens home to England). It was while I was listening to my friend's account of the unusual birds that he had come across on the Galapagos that once again the idea of evolution came into my mind. Bobby had been telling me about the hawk and the dove and the flycatchers that he had found on the islands, but the strangest, he said, were the finches.

'In what way strange?'

'Well,' he said. 'As I just told you, there are five species,[39] and they are all so alike yet so different. Alike in colour, alike in size, yet their beaks show an almost perfect gradation in size. One species has a beak as large as that of a hawfinch, one as small as a chaffinch. One even has a beak like a parrot.'

'Transmutation,' I replied, 'evolution.'

---

[39] Darwin thought he had collected five species. When he gave his specimens to the London ornithologist John Gould to identify and describe, Gould recognised thirteen species.

'You still agree with my grandfather, I see.'

'I do indeed,' I said. 'And to some extent with Buffon, and Saint-Hilaire, and Lamarck. Do you still not? Are you still where you were at Cambridge?'

From a few of the things that he had already told me, it had seemed to me that Bobby had been giving this matter some thought during his voyage, and I was therefore disappointed, and somewhat surprised, at his immediate reply.

'I remain with the word of God, if that is what you mean,' he said, which words immediately recalled to my mind his cousin Fox. But could I detect just a trace of uncertainty in his voice?

'Ah yes,' said I, 'the word of God. Then let us look at the word of God. Do you have it with you, your Bible?'

The only book Bobby was carrying was his well-thumbed copy of Lyell, but I managed to procure a Bible from the innkeeper (who insisted that while he 'didn't hold with 'ligion himself', he felt it necessary to keep a Bible on hand for gamblers to swear their debts on). I opened the book and ran my finger down the first page.

'Ah yes, here we are,' I said, looking up to make sure that I had my friend's full attention. '"And God created every winged fowl after its kind, including some unusual black finches which he thoughtfully placed on a small group of islands five hundred miles west of South America where nobody could see them, and God saw that it was good."'

Though my weak parody made him smile, Bobby was silent.

'Are you really satisfied with that, Bobby? Surely you can see that your Galapagos finches were not individually created, that they must have all descended from a common ancestor? How else do you account for their similarities?'

My friend again made no reply.

'You say', I continued, 'that your finches have different beaks. Now, are these beaks not perfectly modified for the food on which the birds subsist?'

'I suppose one could argue so,' Bobby replied warily. 'Are you suggesting, then, that from an original paucity of birds on the archipelago, one species has been taken and modified for different ends?'

'That is exactly what I am suggesting,' I said. 'Is it not the same here in Australia with the honeyeaters, or the parrots?'

We had seen vast flocks of white cockatoos on our way up to the Blue Mountains, and many beautiful parroquets and lories besides, all of which Bobby had remarked upon.

'Why are there so many honeyeaters and parrots in Australia, and none in England?' I said. 'How does your God explain that?'

Bobby was looking intently at the ground. I followed his gaze to where an ant was heading towards a group of small conical pits in the dust near the veranda post. The ant avoided the first two pits, slipped half way into another but managed to scramble out, then tumbled headlong into the fourth. In a flash two small jaws appeared from the bottom of the pit and the struggling ant was jerked beneath the dust. The ant-lion larva had got its supper.

'Despite some similarities,' he said, turning to me with a half-hearted smile, 'it has recently occurred to me that perhaps two different creators were at work.'

'Perhaps,' I replied slowly. 'Or perhaps the two countries are so far apart, and have been so long separated, that two different faunas have evolved. Although your geological investigations may suggest that Australia is of considerably greater age than the Galapagos, it is just as much an island.'

I could see that Bobby was interested in my idea. Despite his desperate attempt to cling on to Christian doctrine, he had already begun to look beyond appearance. I had first suspected this when we first viewed the great chasms of the Blue Mountains, and Bobby had wondered aloud whether they were the result of erosion by freshwater, or had they been carved out by waves at a time when the great Cumberland Plain was covered by the sea. If Lyell had already convinced him that the earth was of considerable age, and that the geologist need look no further than recent or even present events to explain the past, could I not use the same argument to explain evolution?

'You have told me', I said, 'that in South America, you have seen the land rising up before your very eyes.'

'Yes, the earthquake in Valdivia. It is the strangest feeling, to feel the earth, the very emblem of solidity, moving beneath your feet.'

'But if the earth is indeed as old as Lyell suggests, such events will have occurred countless times in countless places.'

'A hundred earthquakes to make a mountain rise up from the sea, a million drops of rain to wash it back again.'

'Yes, Bobby, and could it not be the same for living things?'

'How do you mean?'

I gestured towards the old slut, who had now crawled under the bench and was again suckling her puppies.

'In each litter of puppies, in each nest of birds, we witness small variations before our very eyes. Could a thousand variations not similarly accumulate to form different species?'

'But species breed true. Cats breed cats, dogs breed dogs. It is all very well to say that similar species have evolved from a common ancestor, but we can see that, in nature, this does not happen.'

'How then', I said, 'do you account for all the different breeds of dogs? This animal, if I am not mistaken, is what is known here as a kangaroo dog.'

The dog seemed to know that I was talking about her and wagged her tail in the dust.

'A combination of greyhound and mastiff, specially bred for chasing and bringing down kangaroos. Greyhound for speed, mastiff for strength. Already, in fifty years, man in Australia has produced a new breed of dog to suit his requirements.'

'But you are simply saying this dog is a cross. She is not purebred. She will not breed true. Look at her puppies.'

The puppies were indeed a mix. A couple seemed to have the characteristics of the mother, but the others varied from almost pure greyhound to one which had the sandy coat and white-tipped tail of the native dog.

'Then how', I asked, 'does man create a new breed?'

'Originally by crossing, perhaps, but then by generations of selective inbreeding. It is not a quick process. You should know, you and your pigeons.'

I was pleased that Bobby had remembered my pigeons. When I began my breeding experiments in Edinburgh he had shown little interest, though he was surprised, I recall, at the number and extent of varieties, the pouters, tumblers, carriers and runts, barbs and fantails, turbits, Jacobins, trumpeters and laughers.

'Yes, Bobby, exactly so. If we want to create a new breed, we choose those animals nearest to our desired end, and breed only from them. If I wanted to create a new variety of long-tailed pigeons, I would breed together my two longest-tailed pigeons, and after several generations of repeating this procedure, I would have a new breed of long-tails. Not all of each new brood would be exactly like their parents, but by selecting those which were, and breeding again from them, the line would eventually breed true. That is how varieties are created, as well you know.' (I did not mention that things were never quite as simple as this. Try as I might, I never did manage to breed that pigeon with both small beak and normal-sized feet; it appears that small feet is the price you have to pay for a small beak, no matter how you mix your stock.)

'For my new breed of kangaroo dog, I would take those two,' I said, pointing my empty mug to the two puppies most like their mother, 'and drown the rest. Now, if man can create and maintain new varieties by artificial selection, might not nature do the same?'

Calling for another beer, then another, I carefully explained to Bobby, as I had explained to Fox, my theory of evolution by 'natural' selection. And I watched the early light of comprehension dawning in his eyes.

Chapter 16

How was it that similar species, which must have shared ancestry in the relatively recent past, were sometimes found not as neighbours, but existing on different continents? How could there have been time enough for the gradual accumulation of differences which distinguish present species, it being clear from present experience that nature does not make great leaps. How could I explain the presence in some species of organs which appeared to serve no function? What happened to the intermediate forms between evolving species, which are not present now nor apparent in the fossil record?

I have always been a thinker. I cannot rest with the mere appearance of a thing; I need to touch its substance, uncover the reasons behind its existence. Since those days at Edinburgh and Cambridge, I had been giving much thought to the idea of the transmutation of species, and the new plants and animals I had come across in my travels had only served to reinforce my initial speculations. How could it not be so that similar species were descended from a common ancestor? By the time Bobby arrived in Australia, the problems which had so troubled me in Cambridge had largely been resolved. It was my beetles which gave me the answer to how similar species, which must have shared ancestry in the relatively recent past, were sometimes found not as neighbours, but existing on separate continents. The explanation must be that the continents have not always been separate, but were once joined together. The disjunction of distribution that we see today must be a result of their subsequent separation. My second problem was explained by the uniformitarianism doctrine of Bobby's great hero, Lyell. If there had been time enough since the world began for sediments to accumulate several miles in thickness, that was time enough for the gradual accumulation of small changes needed to form separate species. As to what had happened to the intermediate forms between evolving species, which are not apparent in the fossil record, there need be no mystery. The chance of any animal being fossilised after death must be minuscule, the chance of it then being found again almost infinitesimal. Absence from the fossil record was evidence for nothing. As to the mechanism which produced this result, we need look no further than our own clumsy attempts at creating new varieties among our domesticated breeds to see a perfect analogy. With aeons at her disposal, nature selects with an infinitely surer and nicer touch than we humans.

After leaving the Blackheath, we spent the following night with Ian Henry, a Scotchman of my slight acquaintance, who unsuccessfully endeavoured to entertain us with some kangaroo hunting over rough country, then continued westward to Bathurst. Our journey to Bathurst was unremarkable save for the heat. Though just over one mile elevated from the coastal plains, the road along which we travelled seemed then a thousand miles closer to the sun. The vegetation was parched and brown, the Macquarie River, which in its season is the source of the most impetuous floods, was reduced to a chain of disconnected ponds. I had arranged for us to stay at Bathurst with another acquaintance, Richard Chetwode, in whose company we remained the following day and night, which we mostly occupied in drinking ale and playing two-up, which, when game-shooting has gone off, is the only amusement in which the inhabitants of that town appear to indulge. We returned from Bathurst via Lockyer's Line, but on our arrival back at the Weatherboard Inn, Bobby was struck down with an enteric attack, which necessitated us resting up for a couple of days. As the weather had now closed in, not an infrequent occurrence in the mountains, I was myself unable to get out and we had even more time for talking over events past and present. Much of it was spent in discussing the Theory, with its details and shortcomings. On no occasion did Bobby mention the reason that I had left England, and on no occasion did I.

Our eventual return to Sydney was punctuated by an overnight stay with Captain King, who had previously captained the *Beagle* and whose acquaintance Bobby had made in England before departing on his own voyage. The captain was eager to hear about my friend's recent adventures on his old ship, and as I had already heard these accounts, I amused myself for a few hours with young Master Philip, King's son. He was a good-looking boy. The following morning we all rode down to the Vineyard to lunch with King's brother-in-law, Hannibal M'Arthur. I was most interested to discover that M'Arthur had been experimenting with some ancon sheep which he had acquired, apparently at much difficulty and expense, from a cousin in Massachusetts. It was believed by many in the colony at the time that these peculiar short-legged sports, whose length of leg made them unable to run or to jump over fences, might be suitable for open pasturing in Australia. M'Arthur told us that in breeding trials at Parramatta, he had found that although putting an ancon ram to an ancon ewe always produced ancon lambs, putting an ancon to a normal sheep gave one of two results. Either all offspring were normal, or half were ancon and half normal. I found this information of great interest. Could it be, I wondered, that there was a mathematical basis to this heredity? It was this question which, after Bobby left, gave me the impetus to continue my own experiments.

*   *   *

161

Instead of sheep or pigeons, I chose shell parrots[40] as my subject, which were easily available in Sydney and which I soon found to be almost as easy to breed as pigeons. If all the varieties of pigeons had originated from wild rock-pigeons, might I not produce similar results from my wild Australian birds? I had long known that variation is, so to speak, the fuel that drives the engine of natural selection, but what is the source of this fuel? For the great Lamarck, it was 'besoins', and much as men have argued as to the meaning of that simple word, to me it only served to replace darkness with fog. I was sure that the answer was to be found not in philosophical speculation (which is why Lamarck, and others, had failed to find it), but in practical experimentation. This was why I had started breeding pigeons in Edinburgh, and why I was now beginning breeding trials with parrots.

Though the natural colour of shell parrots is green, I early managed to acquire from a bird dealer an unusual variation, a female with blue wings; this bird became the basis for my experiments. By controlled crossing within and between generations, and by keeping careful records, I found that, after several generations, I could usually predict with some certainty which colour combinations would appear in a brood, and in what proportions. If I crossed a wild green with a wild green, the offspring would all be green. If I crossed a blue-wing with a blue-wing, all the offspring would be blue-winged. If I crossed a wild green with a bred green which had blue-wing in its ancestry, the offspring were also green. If I crossed a bred green with a bred green, the offspring varied; sometimes all would be green, sometimes a few would be blue-winged, though overall more were green than blue-winged. By thus creating, I began to understand the principles of creation.

I have previously mentioned the gambling game, commonly played in Australia, called two-up. Two pennies are thrown

---

[40] Now more commonly called the budgerigar *Melopsittacus undulatus*.

in the air, the spectators making bets on how they will land. Two pennies can, of course, land in four ways; heads-heads, heads-tails, tails-heads, and tails-tails. As the odds of getting heads or tails with any throw of a true coin are even, each combination will occur in equal proportion. But now let us say that heads are worth more than tails; if you throw at least one head, you win, and only when you have no heads at all do you lose. You will then win three times out of four; heads-heads, heads-tails, tails-heads. With my shell parrots, crossing blue-winged with bred green gave greens in exactly this proportion, three times out of four. Could it be that green was 'worth more' in hereditary terms than blue-wing, the birds only needing one green parent to be green, but two blues to be blue? This would explain my results.

I soon found that the problem was considerably more complex than I imagined. For instance, just as certain characters always seem to go together in pigeons (such as small beak with small feet), so it is with shell parrots. And certain traits are found only, or mainly, in one particular sex. Since arriving on the island I have planted some of the dried peas which I brought with me for food, and have begun experimenting with them. The colours of the flowers and form of the seeds appear to conform with similar mathematical rules, and, if the mountain gives me time enough, I believe I will soon have the complete answer to the puzzle.

Four days after Bobby and I arrived back in Sydney, the *Beagle* sailed away. I was an exile once more, and though I would not have exchanged those few weeks with Bobby for anything, when he left Sydney I quickly sank into a deep melancholy. I was alone, I was friendless, and more than all these things, I was dissatisfied. I missed my friend, I missed Philos, I missed England; for the first time in four years I even found myself thinking about Emma. My life seemed empty, a void which even my busy medical practice could not fill. Bobby had observed to me before departing that in New South Wales a man could easily make treble the interest on his capital he could make in England, and with the least amount of care was almost sure to grow rich. I decided to give up medicine, and devote myself instead to the serious accumulation of wealth.

There are a number of species of both parrots and pigeons on my island, some of which, I think, are not found elsewhere. Of the pigeons, one is much smaller than is usual for the tribe, being less than the size of a common sparrow, with a beak not unlike that of a finch. It is bright green in colour, feeds mainly on grass seeds, and occurs in large flocks, comprising several thousand birds. The flocks may be seen at all times of year except April and May, when the birds separate into much smaller groups. This is the time they choose to moult.

Feathers are surely one of the most mysterious of nature's productions. Though mostly composed, like our own hair, of non-living matter, and being similarly produced from a follicle within the skin, they develop into the most wonderful array of sizes, shapes, colours and patterns. The soft down of the eiderduck and the stiff quill of the eagle's wing, the humble brown plumage of the sparrow and the extravagance of the peacock's tail, are each in their own way a miracle of form and function. But no matter how intricate in form, or how well oiled and preened they may be by their owner, each feather is bound to deteriorate over time, and all birds replace their feathers at regular, usually annual, intervals. For many birds this is a continuous process, the old feathers dropping out one by one to be replaced by a new one. Others have a distinct season for moulting; the black swans for which Australia is so famous lose their wing feathers at one go. For several weeks they cannot fly, and are forced to keep themselves safe from dingoes and other predators by floating on a lake far from shore. The little shell pigeon on my island takes this process one step further. It does not simply lose all its wing feathers at once, but every feather on its body.

I was first alerted to this phenomenon by the appearance of numbers of small green feathers appearing in spiders' webs around my house. Over several days their numbers grew. The lightest puff of wind carried with it a further small load of the feathers, so that they soon appeared not only in the spiders' webs, but caught up in every bush and tuft of grass. The pond near my house became infected with green spots, which wafted across its surface when a breeze blew to form, on the leeward side, green drifts. I assumed that these feathers must have come from the shell pigeons, and that they must be moulting, but when I saw my first completely naked bird, I could not make out what it was.

There is small enough resemblance between a barnyard fowl, strutting around in its shiny brown coat, and the limp pink thing on the poulterer's hook: there was even less between the little green pigeons, with their long tails and delicately patterned plumage, and the weird creatures I found clambering among the grass stems on the open ground between the ponds and the lake. It was only when I picked one up and studied it closely that I could see that its head terminated in a beak rather than a muzzle, and that the final part of the forelimb was tucked up against the middle part, thus freeing the small claw, which many birds possess, to act as a terminal digit. I could also see that the animal's hind legs were distinctly avian, with three forward-pointing and one backward-pointing toes. The little animal was most dexterous, climbing over my hand with great skill and speed. When I returned it to the ground it immediately climbed to the top of a grass stem and began pecking at the seed-head. I have named this bird *Columbina muscula*.

As the island has its dwarf pigeon, it also has its giant. This bird is unusual not only from its size, which is about that of an

Aylesbury duck, but from the fact that it has lost the ability to fly (in both attributes, somewhat resembling the extinct dodo of Mauritius, of which, my dear Bobby, you may still recall that comically stuffed example in the Fitz). The giant pigeon lives chiefly in the forest, where it subsists on all manner of fruits and seeds, swallowing them whole in the manner of its kind. Small groups of this bird are often to be found beneath the fig trees which grow in the centre of the island, and whose fruit are in season year-round. They are also fond of a kind of nutmeg which grows in the central forest. In its season, the ground beneath the nutmeg trees, which are of a considerable size, is strewn with their fruits, consisting of a large woody seed enclosed within a thin fleshy rind. Though these fruit are as large as a pippin, the birds have no trouble in swallowing them, their beaks being not only wide to begin with, but possessing the ability to dislocate at the mandibular condyles. The sight of one of these birds swallowing a fruit as large as its own head is in equal parts amusing and bizarre.

The fruits of the nutmeg tree are produced in such quantities that only a small part can be eaten by the pigeons. Most of them remain beneath their parent tree, where the fleshy rind soon rots away to reveal the nut within. These nuts may remain beneath the tree for years, for they do not appear to germinate, forming a layer several deep. Away from the parent tree, seedlings are not uncommon, and it has occurred to me that this may be connected with the giant pigeons. It is not improbable that some process within the gut of the pigeon is necessary to initiate germination in this species. If this were to be the case, it is interesting to speculate that the extinction of the pigeon would eventually lead, perhaps some centuries later, to the extinction of the nutmeg tree. The giant pigeon is a shy bird, more often heard than seen, its voice being a deep and mournful 'Woo', not unlike that of a large owl. From the fact that it is heard as often by night as by day, I take it that this species is at least partly nocturnal. I have named it *Phaps nyctibrychus*.

Chapter 17

AFTER BOBBY LEFT AUSTRALIA we began a regular correspondence. It was thus I heard, three years after his return to England in 1836, of his inevitable marriage to Emma, then of his Uncle Jos's death and, in 1848, of the death of his father. I took some satisfaction at this news. By this time I had no thoughts of returning to England, but I still bore some resentment towards both men, especially Bobby's father, for my exile. Then, only weeks after I had heard from Bobby, I received, out of the blue, a letter from Philos. What he told me forced me to rethink not only my attitude to the doctor and Jos, but my whole life. While sorting through his father's papers and diaries, Philos had discovered the true story of the doctor, Jos and my mysterious Trustees.

It is strange to me now that, up until that time, I had felt so little curiosity about this matter. For my first twenty years and more, the Trustees had controlled my life. They had paid for my fostering, dictated my move to Shrewsbury, then supported my medical studies in Edinburgh and Cambridge. When I had discovered that the doctor and Uncle Jos were somehow part of this mysterious entity, that I was a beneficiary of their charity, my curiosity had been greatly heightened, but at that time other matters were more pressing. Now I was to discover the truth.

It all went back to grandfather Erasmus. Philos had long ago told me that his grandfather, despite his fame as doctor and poet, was not the paragon of propriety which his younger son, the doctor, later tried to set him up as. The image of grandfather Erasmus as the great polymath, which became generally accepted both within and without the family, was only half the picture. The other half was shrouded in mystery, and stained by death. Firstly, there was the death of Erasmus's first wife from an overdose of laudanum that had been prescribed by her own husband. Though the death was accepted as accidental, Erasmus's subsequent fathering of two daughters by his mistress, Mrs Parker, fuelled much dark rumour and speculation. Then there was the mystery surrounding the death of his eldest son, also named Erasmus but generally known as Ras. Philos knew that his Uncle Ras had drowned himself in middle age, but although there was talk among the servants of sexual scandals, nobody seemed to know the truth behind it. The papers revealed all.

Philos and Bobby's father, Robert, was thirty-three when his brother died. Philos had not yet been born, but Robert was already making a name and fortune for himself in Shrewsbury as physician and financier. His brother's death obliged him to take on a financial undertaking that brought him no returns. Mrs Parker, their father's mistress, had died long ago, but the daughters he had by her had grown up into two young beauties. The two girls lived together, under their mother's name but father's provision, in a town just over the Welsh border, where their parentage, and patronage, were unknown. Yet as they grew, the fame of their beauty soon spread into the neighbouring English counties, and many of Shropshire's finest young bachelors found an excuse to ride over into Wales to view and woo the two young women. Among them was a Lichfield man, a quiet, sober man, the son of a doctor and brother of a doctor, though himself a solicitor. It is not known how young Ras first met the two women, but it was he who won the heart of the elder sister, and it was he who made her with child. Ras was not a dishonourable man. He was honest of heart, and he loved the elder sister most truly. He was overjoyed at the thought of being both father and husband, and though he did not expect that his own father, the elder Erasmus, would rejoice at the match, he had no reason to expect him to forbid it. But that is what happened. Erasmus told his son unequivocally that such a marriage was impossible. He did not say, as Ras had anticipated, that it was impossible for reasons of social etiquette, or moral nicety. His father told him that the marriage was impossible because the woman to whom he was betrothed was his sister. The news that the only woman he had ever loved was the illegitimate child of his own father was clearly more than his sensitive nature could bear. The day after he received this news, Ras's body was fished from the River Severn.

Robert was distraught at the death of his beloved brother, and soon discovered the truth of what lay behind it. From that day on, he exchanged not a single word with his own father, taking it upon himself to support his half-sister and the child she had conceived (no, it was not me. It turned out to be a girl, and anyway, all this happened a long time before I appeared). Robert thought it best that his brother's natural wife, and the daughter whom she soon bore, should move back to Shropshire. His brother-in-law had recently bought a large property not far from Shrewsbury and, when Robert took him into his confidence, offered to have mother and child occupy the pretty little white gatehouse on the estate. Here they continued to live for many years in peace and happiness, supported by the benevolent purse of the doctor, under the benevolent eye of his brother-in-law. But what of the other daughter? She was also a beauty, and, with her older sister gone and to nobody's great surprise, was immediately married to a handsome young naval lieutenant, of good birth but little wealth, and moved down to Chatham. The lieutenant soon rose to become captain of his own ship, but, not being as prudent as he was handsome, failed to return from a short trip to Trafalgar. It was natural that the young widow should herself return to Shropshire and move in with her sister, and it was thus that Robert gained another stipendiary, and the gatehouse another occupant.

Now although Robert's brother-in-law (whom you will by now have realised, Bobby, was none other than your Uncle Jos) had found no difficulty in keeping a benevolent eye on the young mother and child in the gatehouse, he soon discovered that he had other eyes for the younger sister, and, what is more, she for him. Not long after his own wife had been delivered of her eighth child, this mutual admiration found its inevitable physical form, and on the 13th of February, 1809, another child was born, its mother unfortunately, but somewhat conveniently, dying in childbirth. The elder sister was all for keeping her new nephew, and Jos would have agreed to the adoption, but his wife had other ideas. She had soon discovered (as women will) what had been going on while she had been busy nursing her newest daughter. She insisted that the 'little bastard' (as she accurately but somewhat unfeelingly referred to the innocent child) be sent away, fostered out somewhere where she would never have to set eyes on it. You have recognised your Uncle Jos, Bobby, and no doubt your Aunt Bess, and that her eighth child was your cousin Emma. Have you also recognised the little bastard?

Yes, this is how I came into the world, and it explained much. It explained why I always felt so close to Bobby (being twice cousins, did that not make us almost brothers?). It explains why Jos and the doctor provided for me so generously through the Trustees all those years. It explained the comment of Doctor Butler about a family resemblance. And it explained why they were so adamant in refusing to allow me to marry Emma. It was not simply because I was poor, nor because they were keeping Emma for Bobby. It was because Emma, dear Emma, was my sister.

When Bobby wrote to me soon after his marriage to Emma, I remember his telling me how pleased Emma had been with the fine silver forficula I had sent them as a wedding gift (do you still use it to serve the asparagus at Down, Bobby?). There is, as far as I have discovered, but one species of *Forficula* on the island, which I have named *Forficula socius*. I remember my delight as a child in discovering a female *Forficula auricularia* guarding her eggs in a small hollow beneath a stone. Alone among the common insects, the mother earwig guards and tends her hatchlings, caring for them until they are old enough to fend for themselves.[41] In this regard, the earwig here is no exception, though she does so in a way not found in others of her kind.

The earwigs on my island are small insects, hardly larger than the common black ants of England. As well as size, they share another trait with ants, for the earwigs here are sociable creatures, living together in large nests beneath the ground, in which may be found many thousand individuals, each existing as much as part of the whole colony as an individual. The society that the earwigs have developed, while similar to other sociable insects like ants and termites, differs in several respects. By carving away the side of a nest near my house, and inserting a small piece of window glass which I then covered with a piece of cloth, I have been able to observe the economy of these insects in some detail.

Each earwig nest is home not just to a single queen, as with the hymenopterous species, but many hundred breeding females. Each female lays her brood of eggs in a large chamber at the centre of the nest, but instead of remaining with her eggs until they hatch, she leaves them in the care of a group of twenty or so 'nursemaid' earwigs, which can easily be distinguished from others by their large size, almost that of a common wasp. The nursemaids further resemble wasps in that their wings do not fold beneath the wing-case, as is usual among earwigs, but when at rest are folded lengthways along the back. The nursemaids spend all their time caring for the eggs, licking

[41] The author seems to be ignoring the social insects (Isoptera and Apocrita); egg guarding and larval care are also found among certain Coleoptera, Embioptera, Pentatomidae and Symphyta.

171

and turning them, and using their large wings to fan them. They appear never to leave the nest, being fed by the mothers of their charges, who return at intervals with food, which they offer to their helpers. The young earwigs, which are pure white but otherwise miniature versions of their parents, are in turn fed by the nursemaids, but not on regular rations. They are fed with milky liquid exudations from the underside of their nursemaids' abdomens. This method of feeding continues for about two weeks, after which the young earwigs have reached the size and colour of the adults and leave the nursery.

I have not yet mentioned the guard earwigs. Each nest has a single entrance, a round hole about the size of a percussion cap. This hole is constantly monitored by a single large earwig, about the size of the nursemaids but different in form. The guard earwig's head is greatly enlarged, of a size to fit exactly the entrance to the nest. By simply removing and replacing its head in the hole, like a bung in a barrel, it controls ingress and egress. The guard's abdomen is armed with formidable forfeces, of such sharpness and strength as to deter even a potential invader as large as myself. Adult earwigs, be they guards, nursemaids or mothers, are highly specialised in their diet, appearing to feed almost exclusively on young aphids. At first, I assumed that the earwigs simply gathered the aphids from the surrounding vegetation, but further investigation showed this not to be the case; my sociable earwigs are not hunters, but farmers.

There are certain species of ant, both in England and Australia, which tend aphids and various other hemipterous insects[42] and drink the honeydew exuded by them. My island earwigs farm their aphids not for milk, but for meat. Associated with each nest are half a dozen or so smaller burrows, each excavated beneath a clump of grass and connected to the nest by an underground passage, but each also having its own

---

[42] Some aphids and coccids excrete excess sugar from the sap they suck as a sweet liquid, which is eagerly sought by various species of ants. The ants discourage potential predators from the plants on which their sap-suckers feed.

entrance, monitored by a single guard earwig. The burrows open into large underground chambers, networked with living roots, which provide food and home for thousands of aphids. I have observed earwigs deliberately translocating aphids from the grass stems to the roots, but the earwigs choose only the wingless female aphids which, when they are settled and have inserted their stylet into the grass root to feed on the sap, soon begin to reproduce, giving birth, as is common in their kind, to live young. It is these that the earwigs harvest, thus obtaining a constant supply of fresh meat, conveniently located near the nest.

From my regular observations of my little colony for over a year now, I have found that the nursemaids and guards are not born as such, but as normal females. When a member of these special castes starts showing signs of senescence, one of the breeding females will, by some signal invisible to my eye, cease laying eggs and remain in the nest, where she is fed by the other mothers. In the course of a few weeks, and after two or three additional moults, she grows to the size and form required by the colony, and takes up her new role as nursemaid or guard. Males are produced in similar fashion. Like bees, the males of this species are not required to perform any duties within the nest, their only role being in the act of procreation. But whereas male bees are kept within the hive all their lives, leading a useless and indolent life until the time for mating comes, the earwig colony simply creates males to order. Soon after the beginning of the rainy season, several of the females stop their usual activity and enter a kind of torpidity. After about ten days, they begin to become more active and moult; microscopic examination reveals that they have now acquired the primary and secondary sexual characteristics of males. The male insects fly from the nest after the next good rain, though what happens to them then I know not. I have never found one by day, though I have occasionally found one among the insects flying around my lantern at night. Though at some time they presumably find and mate with a female, they otherwise lead a solitary existence. I have named the species *Forficula dolorosus*.

Though in Australia I led a solitary existence after Bobby had left, after a time I found that my melancholy lifted. Both the climate and society of my new home were more to my taste than that which I had experienced in the Cape, or in England, and Bobby's observation that Australia was an easy place to grow rich was fully justified. After he left in '36, I applied myself to that very end and, mostly through quiet speculation in land around Sydney and Newcastle, within five years I had increased my capital twentyfold. I began to enjoy my money. Though I lived alone, yet many would have considered me quite the sybarite. I was frequently to be seen at Government House and Vaucluse, and any visitor of note to Sydney was sure to receive an invitation to my table, and to hear enough about my hospitality to accept it. In 1847, I gave such a party for the officers of HMS *Rattlesnake* that for weeks afterwards not a bottle of champagne was to be had throughout the city. It was at this time my interest in natural history was rekindled. Young Huxley had arrived as surgeon on the *Rattlesnake* and became, during his frequent visits to Sydney, a regular at my house. No conversation could be dull if Tom was taking part, and such conversation was my greatest delight, though I often found that it was thinking women who provided the better conversation and company. I indulged as never before in the pleasures of the flesh. The tricks I had learned to ensnare the hearts of my schoolmates in Shrewsbury and my teachers at college had not deserted me, and I found no difficulty in gaining access to many a fine bed and boudoir. Yet as I approached forty I found that even this pleasure palled. One alone remained, the pleasure of gaining wealth.

It was then that I began to apply myself to trade. The principle was the same as speculating in land; buy low, sell high. But it was faster, and so for me the pleasure was greater.

In '53, when gold was discovered in Victoria, I was in cash and ready. I had no need to dig for the stuff. As soon as the news from Ballarat reached Sydney, I bought all the shovels I could lay my hands on. Before taking ship down to Melbourne, I placed binding orders for more. Within weeks, men were pouring into Australia from every corner of the globe, eager to dig for the yellow metal. English, Irish, Californian or Chinese, one thing they all had in common was the need for a shovel. I sold my original stock in weeks. When my new shipments started coming in from England and America, for a few weeks in early '54 I almost cornered the market, and made over four thousand pounds profit. As new fields were discovered and more men arrived, I continued to trade shovels for gold, then gold for shovels, and shovels for more gold. Within a year, simply from selling shovels, I had made more money than I knew how to spend.

Chapter 18

As some men were hooked on gold, so had I become hooked on trade. It was not the money now which fired me, it was the buying and the selling, the bargaining and bartering. Australia became too small for me. I branched out, chartering ships to take my gold to Liverpool or Nankeen, returning laden with tools and blankets, or spices and Chinamen. I also began trading in the East Indies. Singapore, Malacca, Batavia, the Pedir Coast, Kuching, Macassar, there was good business to be done all through the area. And feeling the urge once more to travel, I started going on my ships myself as supercargo.

The tropics reinvigorated my interest in natural history. The giant apes of Borneo, the dragons of Komodo, the paradise birds of New Guinea, and beetles everywhere. And all the time a guinea to be made by trading gold for spice, spice for silk, then silk for double the gold. But in the Indies I soon discovered that trade was conducted differently from what I had known in Australia. I had the gold, and I knew that the merchants had what I wanted, the silks and spices for the rich men of Sydney, the cotton and rice for the poor men. But how could I judge the value of things? Was my golden guinea in Batavia worth one sack of nutmeg, or ten? How many silver florins should I pay for this bolt of silk in Singapore, and how much for that? And I was greedy (have I not admitted as much before?). If I wanted to make money on a transaction, another must lose. I bargained hard, but no matter how clever a deal I thought I had made, no matter how much I had driven down the prices, I found in the final reckoning that I barely covered my costs. I had the excuses – a turndown in the market, a glut of the commodity, a change in popular taste. The truth was that by any standards other than Australian, I was a bad trader, for I had never learned the most important lesson. The man who taught it to me was See Ko Suan.

See Ko Suan ran his business from a old wooden godown on the dockside in Singapore town, a building so decrepit it appeared to have been not so much deliberately made as left behind by the tide. But on sunny days See Ko Suan would always be sitting in the shade of a large paper umbrella at a desk outside its door, and on rainy days you could always find him just inside. To enter the godown of See Ko Suan was to enter a magical place. It was a place of smell rather than sight. No matter how bright the sun was shining outside, inside was always twilight. Only dimly could you see the crates and barrels, the sacks and baskets, but you could smell everything. Just as we can see a hundred colours in a glance, a single sniff inside the godown of See Ko Suan was enough to identify a hundred 'Sabean odours from the spicy shore of Araby the Blest'. The smells of food were the clearest; cinnamon, cloves and nutmeg, dried fish and tripang, dried figs, dates, apricots and tamarind. Woven among these were the heavier smells of whale oil, coconut oil, Macassar oil and castor oil, while overlaying them all were the perfumes of sandalwood and rosewood, and, unmistakable to the nose of an Australian, the scent of eucalyptus. You could smell Persian carpets and bolts of Manchester cotton, even smell the iron from a barrel of nails. Then there were the boxes and barrels themselves; the sharp smell of pine, the thin oak smell of new barrels, the tarry smell of old ones, gunny and hemp smelling like old hay. The godown was full of almost every conceivable merchandise, and if See Ko Suan did not have what you wanted, he would know where to find it.

See Ko Suan knew everyone, and everyone knew See Ko Suan. He seemed to be at the heart of every deal, and when in Singapore I always found myself visiting him at his place of business, where I would be shown to a seat and offered a cup of tea or coffee, or the milk from a freshly opened cocoa-nut, sipped through a thin bamboo straw. Although this ritual was very much part of the etiquette of trade, See Ko Suan was a naturally hospitable man, always keen to encourage conversation along with the bargaining. Though I think he never travelled, he had a great interest in the world, and, unusual among orientals, especially in the natural world. During my several visits we came to enjoy each other's company, and I would seek out See Ko Suan whenever I visited Singapore, bringing him news of my travels and of the plants and animals I had seen. I remembered him being particularly interested in my description of the song displays of the birds of paradise of New Guinea, and of the Australian lyrebird, with its magnificent tail feathers and peerless mimicry; on a subsequent visit I brought him some of the feathers I had described. I also brought him a piping crow[43] in a cage, which I had picked up on the quayside the day I left Sydney, and whose singing I thought he would enjoy. I was surprised to see my friend quite clearly upset with this gift. He told me as kindly as he could that he would arrange for the bird to be taken back to Australia on the next ship, and released there, and that he wanted no more such gifts. I think it was partly in recompense for this rejection that he extended me an invitation to visit him at his house, and perhaps also it explains why he decided to tell me the real secret of trade.

See Ko Suan did not appear to be a wealthy man. He was not excessively fat, like many Chinese merchants, and he dressed modestly in typical Cantonese style of plain cotton tunic and

---

[43] An earlier name for the Australian Magpie, *Gymnorhina tibicen*.

trousers, though he wore his hair short, rather than in a
pigtail. The food and drink he offered his guests, and of
which he himself partook, was good but simple. The only
sign of wealth he showed was the gold in his teeth, of which
he had much, though this was not unusual for Chinese of even
modest wealth. When he invited me to his house I assumed that
it would be as unpretentious as his business premises. Instead,
I found a palace.

Much gold has passed through my hands over the years
I have been a trader. It has been my currency of exchange,
both in Australia and overseas, and I have seen more and
accumulated more than most men. In all my trading, I have
not seen a tenth of what I saw in See Ko Suan's house. The
door to the house was in a narrow laneway no more than a
hundred yards from the wharf. The door was not large; though
carved in a most intricate style, it was old and weathered and
gave little clue to what lay behind it. See Ko Suan himself
pushed open the door (I remember being surprised that it was
not locked), and gestured me through the narrow doorway into
a courtyard. The first thing I noticed was the marble. Pure
white marble completely covered the floor and the walls of the
courtyard; in each corner, a marble fountain played; marble
urns stood against the walls, each containing a large tree of
dark foliage (fruit trees of one form or another; mango, fig,
citrus of various kinds). The second thing I noticed was the
gold. Each urn was intricately decorated with engraved script
inlaid with gold. There was more golden script and decoration
carved around the walls of the courtyard, and also around the
windows and door of the house, which stood at the far end.
The two steps which led up to the house appeared to be made
of solid gold. Leaving our shoes on this priceless threshold, we
entered the house.

The entrance hall was dominated by a life-sized statue of the
Buddha, seated on a low plinth, and completely covered with
gold leaf; sticks of incense burned before the statue in golden

stands. Down long wide corridors, I could see other rooms similarly filled with golden statues and golden ornaments. See Ko Suan ushered me into the nearest of these rooms and bid me to be seated. As I sank down on to some cushions at a low table, tea arrived, fragrant with the scent of flowers, served by a small dignified woman whom See Ko Suan introduced as his Number One Wife. The cups and pot were the finest porcelain, the cups decorated with a band of gold around the rim. Some small sweet cakes nestled in a basket of golden filigree, carried on a golden salver. Wherever I looked around me, there was more gold; smaller golden Buddas in little alcoves around the room, golden thread in the rich silk hangings. I could not help but remark on this opulence.

'But did you not know,' said See Ko Suan, raising his thin eyebrows in enquiry, 'that gold brings good luck? In my country, we believe that the more gold a man has, the more luck he will have.'

'It is different in my country,' I said. 'We believe that the more luck we have, the more gold we will get.'

See Ko Suan lowered his eyebrows in a thoughtful frown. 'Really?' he said. 'How very strange.' I saw the faintest trace of a smile on his lips.

As I say, See Ko Suan seemed to be at the heart of most of the trade in Singapore, and whenever I had sat talking with him in his godown, men would be always calling in to discuss this deal or that. Most of these transactions were very short, contrasting greatly with the transactions in which I took part, not only with See Ko Suan but with other traders, which always seemed to go on for hours. As his wife broke into our friendly silence by offering more tea, I told See Ko Suan of my observation.

'What you say is quite right, my friend,' he replied. 'But have you not also observed that the shorter the transaction, the better the trade?'

I confessed that I had not, and that I was slightly surprised by his claim. How could this be so? The essence of trade was surely bargaining. It took time to deal and haggle, to push down prices and so increase profits. See Ko Suan smiled.

'Then can you tell me, my friend, why am I a rich man, and you are not?'

He spoke the truth. For all my travelling, for all my trading between different markets, for all the time and effort I put into every deal, my wealth did not approach that of See Ko Suan. I was not a poor man, but compared to his golden palace, my own houses in Sydney and Melbourne were hardly more than hovels.

See Ko Suan looked at me for a few moments, his round face full of friendly concern.

'May I tell you something, my dear friend,' he said, 'which may be of some help to you?'

He put down his cup.

'Perhaps the essence of trade is not as you imagine. You say that a trader has to get the best price, in order to get the best profit. It seems to me that what you are saying is that in order for you to win, someone else must lose.'

I nodded. That was exactly what I thought.

'But that is not the essence of trade,' said my host. 'That is the essence of war.'

Again See Ko Suan looked at me in silence for a moment, then got to his feet and took a few steps towards the window.

'You have often told me that you enjoy the singing of birds,' he continued. 'The lyrebird of Australia, the mavis and the merle of England. And you know that I, too, love the song of birds. It is a peaceful sound, telling that all is right with the world. Indeed I sometimes think that the song of birds creates peace, rather than simply reflecting it.'

He had spoken this last sentence as if to himself, not looking towards me as he said it, but out into the courtyard.

'The local people here, you know, they trap birds and keep

them in little bamboo cages to sing. They imagine that some are better singers than others, and pay high prices for a good bird. They hang the birds in cages outside their houses, and feed them on special rice. The people believe that the birds will then feel they are free, and this will make them sing. But the birds never live long. In their tiny cages, they usually die in a few weeks, a few months at most.'

See Ko Suan took from the basket one of the small sweet cakes, broke off a small piece and tossed it on to the window sill. A shadow immediately appeared across the opening, and a small brown bird landed on the sill and hopped towards the food. Though completely plain of plumage, with its bright eye and small, neat beak, it looked something like an English robin. The bird picked up the crumb, and quickly swallowed it. It then began to sing.

'Sweet bird, that shun'st the noise of folly, most musical, most melancholy.' I have wondered since if perhaps it was the silence within that house that made the bird's voice sound so. Or perhaps it was the soft sounds coming in through the window; the splash of fountains and the rustling of leaves, perhaps it was their accompaniment that made the bird's simple song sound so beautiful. Or was there something about the shape of the room, or the tranquil mood I was in, or perhaps it was the tea (for I have heard that occidentals sometimes react strangely to Chinese tea)? How could the simple whistles and warbles of a small brown bird make a human heart first soften, then melt? How could song of a bird cause a man to cry? As the bird sang, I felt tears well from my eyes and run down my cheeks. All the tender thoughts that I ever had came flooding into my mind; of pink clouds and summer evenings beside the Severn, of England and Australia, Home and home, of Philos and Emma, and you, dear Bobby. Yet there was no nostalgia, no feeling of loss. As I looked over at See Ko Suan, I felt only perfect peace. My friend's eyes were closed as if in sleep, but such was the expression on his face that I knew he was in his own place of peace. Like the sweetest human voice, like a violin perfectly made and perfectly played, the bird continued to pour forth its own pure music.

When finally the song stopped and the bird flew away, it was as though I had just awakened after a long sleep to a sunny morning. I opened my eyes to a new world; what I had thought was beautiful, was now sublime, what I had thought attractive, was now perfect. I looked at See Ko Suan. He too had opened his eyes, and from them shone forth such love and kindness, such acceptance, that it was as if I had never really been known by a human being before.

'Now you see,' he said with a smile. 'A crumb, or a song, which is worth more? Trade is not a fight. In good trade, there are no losers.'

It is difficult to explain exactly how See Ko Suan's lesson changed things for me, but from then on I found my business becoming more and more successful. Before, I had been tormented by the need to discover the true value of everything. How much was my gold coin worth, one sack of nutmeg or a hundred? Which was worth more, this piece of silk or that one? Now I saw things differently. In good trade, there are no losers. By letting go of the need to win every exchange, I became a winner. I benefited from the simple knowledge that, in any transaction, my fellow traders could also benefit. My dealing became much shorter. I began to recognise those men who also had this knowledge (perhaps they too had listened to See Ko Suan's bird, though I would never ask), and found that rather than treating and being treated as a rival, we treated each other as partners, sometimes even friends. I began to see that trade is part of the process of creating wealth, just as surely as is digging gold from the ground; it need not be gained at the expense of others. Though I sold the silk and spice in Australia at a profit, my Chinese and Malayan counterparts exchanged the gold to their countrymen at a profit. All gained from the transaction. And as my profits rose, so did my satisfaction. I often returned to Singapore, and was often a visitor at the house of See Ko Suan.

Chapter 19

SINCE BOBBY'S DEPARTURE FROM Australia in 1836, he had
kept me informed of his own life in England; of his return,
his marriage, of his move to the country. I rejoiced with him at
the birth of each child, and when his little Annie died I shared
his grief. The death of his favourite daughter in 1851 affected
Bobby deeply. Up until then he had taken some care to keep
me up-to-date on developments in evolutionary theory. On the
continent, von Buch was creating a following, and I followed the
English debate about the *Vestiges*[44] with much interest (though
I remember pointing out in one of my own letters that the
mechanism of evolution proposed by these writers was little
improvement on that of Bobby's old favourite, Lamarck). The
seed I had sown in my friend's mind when he came to visit
me in New South Wales those few years ago had clearly
taken root in the fertile soil of his mind. Despite Bobby's
grave doubts about the religious implications of evolution (I
remember him telling me that even harbouring thoughts of
evolution felt like blasphemy), he had already begun amassing
the evidence needed to support the Theory. I was pleased to
hear that this included my own observations on the breeding
of pigeons and other domestic beasts, and that he had finally
read Malthus and seen the connection between competition and
natural selection. When Bobby told me that he had discussed
the Theory with Philos and with several of his other friends, I

---

[44] *The Vestiges of Creation* was published anonymously in 1844, and engendered as much
debate about its authorship as about the evolutionary theory it espoused.

was sure that, despite his misgivings, he would be the one to publish it, that he would be the one to reap the rewards. As I had realised the gift which See Ko Suan had given me, so my gift to Bobby would at last be realised. After Annie died I heard nothing more of such plans.

I have to thank See Ko Suan not only for introducing me to the secret of trade; it was in his godown that I first tasted the milk of the cocoa-nut, a drink which is as refreshing as it is delicious. Cocoa-nuts trees grow abundantly on my island, offering me not only food and drink, but building materials. The house I have built myself is both walled and roofed in the *atap* fashion, using the enormous fronds of the cocoa-nut palm, which are split along the midrib and cut to size when green, then tied to the frame of the house, overlapping like shingles. The frame is made of the long stems of fallen bamboo, which, having no knife larger than a sailor's clasp-knife, I was able to make into length by placing them over a fire. It was a source of some frustration, after Charley had died, to find that both leaves and fruit of the cocoa-nut were unavailable to me. The fruits of cocoa-nut trees fall only when old and past their prime as foodstuff; the fronds fall only when brown and dry, when they are almost impossible to bend or to split with a knife. To obtain either in the green state, I would either have to climb one of the enormous cocoa-nut trees (a feat at which Charley had been as adept as any native, but one which is far beyond the capacity of this old man), or cut one down (an achievement beyond the capability of my clasp-knife).

When Charley and I had first arrived on the island our shelter consisted of a simple canvas sail strung across a rope between two trees. This served against both sun and rain, for we arrived just as the little rains began, and rainfall was an almost daily occurrence. After Charley died, I conceived the plan to construct for myself a more substantial dwelling, but was frustrated from doing so by the lack of suitable materials.

One day on my morning walk, I came across a freshly fallen cocoa-nut tree. Here, at one go, were leaves for my shelter and food for my stomach. But as I approached the tree more closely, what I saw nearly stopped my heart. All around the stump I could see sawdust; the tree had not simply fallen, it had been felled. The stump itself was clearly stepped, showing that it had been sawn through by experts, first from one side, then the other. In all the months I had now been on the island, I had neither seen, heard nor smelled a single trace of another human being, nor did I wish to do so. Yet here was clear evidence that I was no longer alone. I hurried down to the shore. No ship was in the lagoon, no boats were pulled up on the beach. I returned to the tree, carefully examining the sand for tracks. The only footprints were my own.

Although the trunk of the tree was completely surrounded by an even carpet of sawdust, yet a most careful examination still revealed no sign of footprints other than my own, nor were there any in the soft sand around. That the tree had been sawn through I had no doubt, but now I noticed another unusual feature. The natural place to cut through a tree is at about waist height, or higher if the tree is of a kind which flares sharply at the base. This one had been cut down at ground level. I went to see if any fruit were on the crown; there were none. They, too, had been sawn from their stems and were now nowhere to be seen. I confessed myself completely mystified, but my mystification did not prevent me from seeing that here was the opportunity I had long hoped for. I immediately began removing the green fronds from the tree, and within half a day had enough material for my house. Over the next few days I spent most of my time gathering bamboo for the frame of my house and preparing and fixing the *atap*, all the while keeping a close lookout for any signs of human activity. I saw none, and though I was still uneasy, I was forced to let the matter rest. About three months later, I was awoken in the middle of the night by a sudden crash. A cocoa-nut tree had fallen down just outside my new house.

The first thought that came to my mind was to rush outside, but then came reason. If I had heard the sound of a tree falling, perhaps it, too, had been felled. The men who did the work might still be out there. I arose quietly from my hammock, and peered through the door. A quiet wind was stirring the treetops, and the moon was full. I strained both my eyes and my ears; I hallooed, but received no reply. After hallooing once more, and remaining still at my door for some minutes without hearing or seeing anything unusual, I struck a light to my lantern and went outside. The moon was bright enough to cast dark shadows beneath the trees; the sound of the wind in the leaves mingled with the chirps of the crickets and the squeaks of the bats. Shining white in the moonlight, I could see the cut stem of a tree.

It was one of the very cocoa-nut trees to which I had first hung my hammock on arriving at the island, and just like the first tree, it had been sawn through cleanly at ground level. As I drew nearer I could see sawdust also showing up white against the slightly darker sand. There was no trace of the sawyers and, once more, though I shone my lantern low to the ground, no trace of footprints on the sand. I looked along the trunk towards the crown of the tree, now lying on the ground some twenty yards distant, and my heart leaped into my mouth. Something large and white was moving along it. For several seconds, I stood transfixed. The thing was about the size of a pillowslip, and was moving up the tree in a fluid motion, like a wet cloth sliding on glass. I had no conception of what it might be. There were no visible legs, the thing just flowed slowly up the trunk. Holding my lantern aloft, I walked through the darkness towards it.

It was not until I was within a few feet of the white thing that I finally saw that it was not a single creature, but a large number of small ones. It was a tightly packed swarm of small crabs, moving as one up the tree. My fear dissolved. Finding that the creatures were not disturbed by my lantern, I was able to examine them closely. The crabs were of two kinds, each about the size of a sovereign, somewhat flattened. One type had their left claws greatly enlarged, like those of the signal crabs found in tropical mangroves; the second type had claws of equal size and were of otherwise unremarkable shape. They moved slowly along the trunk of the fallen cocoa-nut tree in perfect phalanx. On reaching the crown of the tree, they began to separate into pairs, comprising one of each type, which I then took to be the male and female of the species. Presumably the one with the large claw was the male. Each pair clambered around the base of the crown until they found a cocoa-nut. While the small-clawed one stood guard on the stem, blocking the path to any other roving pair, the other began to cut away at the side of the fruit with its enlarged claw. It did this by snipping away minute fragment by minute fragment with the very tip of the claw, until it had cut a deep slit in the outer fibrous layer surrounding the nut, right through to the shell. When, after several trials, it was satisfied that this was of a size sufficient to just admit its body, it climbed to the top of the nut and began snipping away, piece by piece, at the thin stem which was anchoring it to the tree. At this point its partner abandoned its position as guard to scramble on to the fruit. After a few more snips, the cocoa-nut, with both crabs onboard, tumbled to the ground.

Similar pairs of crabs were at work all over the tree. In each case a female was standing watch, while a male did the work of first making a slit in the nut, then cutting it from the tree. Within an hour, all the nuts had been removed, and it was now that the real work of the females could begin. The fallen nuts were each still accompanied by its pair of crabs, none of them the worse for the fall. I was at first surprised to find that there had been no injuries, until I examined some of the animals and found that their carapaces were unusually thick, strong enough to resist having even a cocoa-nut roll on them. The next stage in the procedure was to bury the nut. This the female did by busily digging beneath it and scooping away the sand with her small claws. She worked with surprising strength and speed, so that within another hour the nut was already three-quarters buried beneath the surface of the sand. The female crabs were remarkably skilled at their task; no matter which way up the cocoa-nut had landed on the sand, they managed by fine judgment to so manoeuvre its descent that the slit, which the male had cut while the nut was still on the tree, remained at the top. The males, meanwhile, were kept busy fighting off rivals, for there were many more crabs than there were cocoa-nuts. The combat was mostly bravado, the crabs being usually content with waving their large claws at each other, with only the occasional half-hearted grappling. It was only when the cocoa-nut was almost completely buried that the male ceased his defence, and quickly ran towards the slit near the top of the cocoa-nut, into which he fitted himself head-first. Within a short time, he and the cocoa-nut had disappeared beneath the sand.

Not all the nuts which the crabs had harvested had fallen on to the sand, several had become more or less entangled in the leaves of the tree. The crabs did not abandon these nuts; the females usually managed, by pushing from underneath, to free them from the foliage. In the case of a particularly entangled fruit, the male would help by snipping away leaves and stems with his claw. By the time dawn arrived, every one of the nuts had been removed from the tree and buried.

The burying behaviour of the crabs reminded me strongly of our sexton beetles; just as the common *Necrophorus* buries any dead animal it finds, so the crabs buried cocoa-nuts. This led me to the assumption that, like the beetles, the crabs might use the buried booty as food for their young. The following day I returned to the fallen tree and dug up one of the cocoa-nuts (which by this time was buried some few inches beneath the surface of the sand). I found that the slit which the male crab had made had been enlarged, being now of sufficient size to admit both male and female to the interior of the nut, where they appeared to be feeding on the soft flesh inside. To investigate the complete history of the species, I would need to take some nuts to my house for regular observation.

The crabs fed inside the coconut for about twenty days, during which time the female fattened considerably, passing through two moults in as many weeks. The male did not moult, and appeared to feed little, using his large claw to garner food for the female. Soon after her second moult, the female laid her eggs, which were duly fertilised by the male. This was done, as is usual in Crustacea, underwater, or rather 'under milk', there being still a large quantity of this liquid within the fruit. The female then stopped feeding, remaining at rest within her vegetable home with her eggs, or coral, firmly attached to the underside of her abdomen. The eggs were large and few in number, and hatched in about nine days, the larvae being released into the cocoa-nut milk, where they quickly passed through the post-larval stage (the *nauplius* stage usually found in this order being completely absent). Within ten days the young had achieved the adult form, though at this time they were not much larger than common money spiders.

I have since been able to investigate the habits of free-living animals, and have discovered that at this point the male crab digs a tunnel out of the cocoa-nut to the surface. About forty days after the cocoa-nut was first buried, the father crab leads his progeny out into the world. The female, who has grown too large to pass through the slit in the cocoa-nut, dies within it.

Having observed the cocoa-nut crabs remove and bury the fruit, it occurred to me that it might be the very same crabs who were responsible for felling the trees in the first place, though how they did so I could not imagine. Since that time, however, I have been able to observe the procedure on several occasions.

It happens always on a full moon. The crabs usually live in small burrows on the beach, just above the high tide mark, coming out by day or night to feed on detritus washed up on the sand. They are usually solitary animals, but a full moon and a spring tide is the signal for them to leave their burrows and 'wander forth like sons of Belial' to assemble in groups of several hundred at the top of the beach. Each group then heads towards a nearby cocoa-nut tree to begin the seemingly impossible task of cutting through the trunk. They do this in the same way that they cut the stems and husks of the cocoa-nut fruit, which is to say, little by little. Once again, it is the males, with their enlarged claws, who do the cutting. About thirty or forty of them line up around one side of a tree, and begin snipping away the bark and wood. The wood of cocoa-nut trees is tough rather than hard, and the crab's sharp, scissor-like claws are able to cut through the fibres one by one, gradually making a groove about half an inch deep in the trunk. The groove greatly resembles that made by a cross-cut saw, and as it is extended further and further into the tree, the small pieces which are removed are scattered about, exactly resembling sawdust. The males, of which there are several hundred in any group, work in a kind of relay, so that as one tires another takes its place, working their way deeper into the trunk until they have reached a point slightly over half way through it. At some invisible signal, the cutting ceases; the crabs then go around to the other side of the tree, and begin a second cut.

The animals never appear to select a tree which is growing straight, but always one which is leaning, and the first cut is always made on the leaning side. Thus, the second cut is made on the side away from that where the tree will eventually fall. As the sand on this side is almost always slightly higher, so is the cut. The crabs continue cutting through the far side of the tree until the two cuts overlap, at which point the tree inevitably topples to the ground. The whole process takes the crabs no more than six hours. Two questions I have yet to discover,

194

which are how the crabs measure the depth of the first cut, and when to stop, and how the buried cocoa-nuts stay fresh, which they inevitably do, even when breached by the crabs, many of them indeed sprouting. It is interesting to note that because the crabs always choose the night of a full moon for burying their cocoa-nuts, by the time the young are ready to leave their 'nest' some six weeks later, the night of their emergence will always be dark. I have named the species *Uca cococoptus*. It is a remarkable animal, and I am sorry that Charley did not live long enough to share with me in its discovery.

Chapter 20

BOTH OF US ARE old now, the mountain and I, and all lives must end. I should write quickly, says the mountain, and it is time to tell of Charley Allen; of how we met, of how we parted and met again, and of Charley's fearful fate. It was Charley who brought me to this island, and it is because of Charley that I cannot leave.

In the April of 1855 I was again in Singapore, having arrived on the *Cormorant* from Western Australia with a load of sandalwood, for which there is always a ready market in the east. I had intended on the way to visit Christmas Island, whose natural history I much wanted to investigate, but had instead been forced by a cyclone to put into Port Essington for over a week, an expensive delay; when we arrived in Singapore the *Cormorant* was so riddled with shipworm that substantial repairs were required. With the help of my friend See Ko Suan I had little difficulty selling my cargo, and I now found that I had several weeks in which I might do as I pleased. 1855 was the year when the rage for cananga, or Macassar oil, had suddenly re-erupted. Every would-be beau from Scotland to Sydney demanded this matchless hair tonic, and the price of cananga had risen twenty-fold within months. It was clear that anyone who could get his hands on a good supply before the bubble burst might almost name his own price. See Ko Suan helped me charter a local junk in Singapore and gave me a letter of introduction to a merchant he knew in Macassar, the son of the local sultan, who might be able to provide me with a quantity of cananga at favourable terms (such a letter from See Ko Suan was itself worth as much as a treasury bill).

'And I have something else that you might be interested to hear,' my friend added, as we sat outside his godown, sipping the cool milk from a cocoa-nut. 'A few months ago an English naturalist turned up here, a collector of birds and butterflies, a trader too, in his way. He told me that it was his intention to spend some time hereabouts, and the last I heard he had taken ship to the Celebes. It is not unlikely that you will meet him in Macassar.'

My voyage eastwards was occupied as much by speculations on the identity and character of this man as on the quantity and cost of the oil I hoped to buy. Though European traders were plentiful enough in the East, European naturalists were not. As usual, my friend's intelligence was correct; not only did I negotiate with the sultan's son an excellent price for two hundred barrels of oil, I was assured by him that the English naturalist had indeed been in Macassar. He had arrived the previous month, and although he and his young assistant were presently on a short collecting expedition in the interior, they were expected back within the week. As the shipment that I had contracted for had not yet all arrived, it seemed likely that we would indeed meet.

Whenever I was in port for more than a day or two, it was my habit to stay ashore rather than onboard ship. In Macassar, the sultan's son offered me accommodation in his palace, and while awaiting the arrival of my goods, I kept myself occupied in conversation with my host, and in losing judicious amounts of silver at cribbage to his favourite catamite. After spending four pleasant days and more than a few florins thus engaged, there came word that the boats carrying my cargo had been seen upriver. I hurried down to the wharf, where I found a flotilla of canoes about to tie up, laden high with barrels. My oil was not the only cargo the boats had brought down from upcountry. Sitting upright on one of the barrels was a tall figure in European garb, his bearded face shaded by a large hat and covered in a net. His face was further shaded by a black umbrella, held over him by a bare-chested Malay. Seated on a barrel in a second boat was another hatted figure, also clearly European, though his face, too, was obscured by a dark fly net. It could only be the English naturalist and his assistant.

As the boats approached the wharf, I hailed the two men. The second, who appeared to be the younger, waved back, and when the boats pulled up I greeted them in English and extended my hand to help them, one after the other, ashore. First to take my hand was the young man, who thanked me with a flash of smiling teeth behind the veil, but the elder refused it.

'Thank you, sir,' said the English naturalist, 'I manage quite well by myself.'

Despite this small rebuff I introduced myself, saying how pleased I was to meet up with two fellow-Englishmen, especially fellow-naturalists, in this part of the world.

'I trust that your expedition has been a success,' I said.

The naturalist lifted the net from his face and, giving me a look between suspicion and disdain, replied that as far as collecting went, the trip had been disappointing.

'But what about the birdwings?' came the voice of his young companion, his accent immediately betraying a West Country origin. 'Are they not the finest we've seen?'

His employer looked at him coldly.

'A few of the specimens are adequate,' he said. 'Now come, Charley, you have work to do.'

With these words the elder man turned his back on me and began to direct the unloading of his things. It was clear that our conversation was at an end.

As I returned to the sultan's palace, I puzzled deeply over this man's behaviour. I had been greatly looking forward to meeting a fellow-naturalist in such an interesting and out-of-the-way place, and a fellow Englishman at that, yet it was clear that my sentiments were not reciprocated. Though we had never met, I had the feeling that the man had already formed some judgment about me. But he, too, had accepted the hospitality of the sultan's son and, having left his assistant to supervise the porters, the naturalist soon arrived at the palace, where I was already sitting down to lunch. As the servant showed him into the room I gestured for him to join me. He sat down at my table, though with clear reluctance.

'I am sorry to hear that your expedition met with less success than you had hoped,' I said, 'though I must tell you how much I have been looking forward to meeting another Englishman in such a place. I trust that at least your journey was a comfortable one.'

'Hardly comfortable, sir,' replied the naturalist, 'unless you find comfort in sitting under a tropical sun for two days on a barrel of stinking oil.'

'Perhaps, then, it was at least of some consolation that my boats were available.'

'Yes, I had assumed that they might be your boats,' said the naturalist, adding, with some coolness, 'You are in trade, I see.'

'That is indeed my business here,' I replied. 'But a friend in Singapore told me that you had come to the East in search of natural history specimens. This is a subject which is also close to my heart.'

'Then you have come to the wrong place, sir,' said the naturalist. 'I have never known a tropic country so poor in fauna.'

'You surprise me,' I said. 'I must confess to a particular liking for beetles, and though I have not been here a week, I have already found several score of beetles, some of great beauty.'

'I prefer butterflies,' said the naturalist. 'I find that most men of taste prefer butterflies.'

'Do I understand, then, that you do not just collect for your own cabinet?'

'I have clients, sir, among the most distinguished families in England.'

'So,' I said with a smile. 'It seems that we are both in trade.'

'No sir,' said the naturalist, 'not trade. I am a collector.'

'But do you not sell and exchange the specimens you collect?'

The English naturalist's nose rose an inch or two in the air. 'An artist may sell or exchange his paintings, but that does not mean he is in trade.'

There is a time to protest such a comment, and a time to ignore it. Judging this to be one of the latter occasions, I turned the conversation to other topics. It was heavy work, and by the end of our meal the Englishman had revealed himself as not only a snob, but of small mind and rather a bore. Even his knowledge of natural history was limited. 'Deep versed in books and shallow in himself', the man had a prodigious memory for names and events, but little intelligence. It had been some time since I had enjoyed a proper conversation in English. I persevered, making several attempts to engage in more philosophical discussion. The Englishman showed no interest in the theoretical aspects of even his own subject. Like too many self-styled naturalists, he knew the names of things but cared little for their relationships. I remember his being completely sceptical of my observation that the fauna of Australia and South America, though separated by the Pacific Ocean, do not differ as much as those of Australia and Asia, separated only by a narrow strait, and quietly poo-pooing my theory that there is a clear line dividing the Australian and Asiatic types, which runs between the Celebes and Borneo, and down past Lombok and Bali: no many how many examples I gave him, he would have none of it. When I tentatively assayed his thoughts on evolution, he could not have cared less. Though I would not have called him a religious man, his own theories and observations were both mistaken and misinformed. I soon found myself tiring of his pontifications, and was relieved to notice, as we were finishing our meal, the arrival of his assistant. On entering the room the young man pulled the hat and veil from his head, and my feelings of relief were replaced by slow astonishment. There was no doubt that he was by far the most beautiful boy I had ever seen.

'In naked beauty more adorn'd, more lovely than Pandora', Charley Allen must have been about seventeen at the time, though he was so fair of face and soft of voice that he seemed quite three years younger. Of fine build, but not overly short, with dark hair and complexion, he was a regular Ganymede. His eyes were of the palest grey, so arrestingly pale, indeed, that they gave him an almost unearthly look. Add to these eyes a fringe of long, dark lashes, and, though there was nothing feminine in him, he was more beautiful than any woman. But there was also something about Charley, the tilt of his nose or the way his hair flopped down over his forehead, that reminded me of a face I had first seen some thirty-five summers before, in a patch of green asparagus in an English garden. The effect on me was as immediate as it was profound.

The young man sat down at the table and immediately began talking to me in the most friendly manner. What was my name, where had I come from, what was I doing in Macassar? When, in the course of our conversation, I discovered that Charley had acquired from his employer a keen interest in natural history, I found myself even more attracted to him. That night, as I lay awake in my room watching the chit-chats stalking small moths around the lamp, all I could think about was Charley Allen. My head felt light, my throat tight, my heart as if it had outgrown its enprisoning ribs. I was experiencing a feeling I had never known before.

After a night of little sleep, I arose early and went out on to the lower balcony to watch the loading of the cananga which had arrived the previous day into my chartered vessel. The sultan's

202

son was already on the balcony, a pot of coffee on the table by his side. He gestured for me to join him, and himself poured me a cup. As he did so I saw a taller figure appear among the labourers below, hatless and clad in a loose white robe. It was Charley.

'Yes, my friend, I see what you see,' said the sultan's son as he handed me the cup. He looked down at the activity below, then spoke again. 'And I see that your ship is getting full. The bar across the harbour is shallow and the tide is low.' He looked up at me with a smile. 'Next week the moon will be full. I think it might be wise if you waited, just a week, for a higher tide.'

That evening, soon after dinner, the English naturalist came down with a sudden attack of recurrent fever and was forced to retire to his bed. It was as if providence herself was playing my hand.

Almost every moment of the following week I spent with Charley. I found him not only beautiful to look at but excellent company. His good humour was endless, his wit an irresistible mixture of the clever and the absurd, his enthusiasm delightful. I found myself telling him all about my early life in England, and all about Bobby and my exile in Australia. Charley was himself the most excellent storyteller, keeping me both entertained and amused with many a story about his recent travels and his own boyhood. Like me, Charley had never known his parents. Born in a small village in Somerset (whose name I now forget), raised in an orphanage, then apprenticed to a Bristol silversmith, he had run away to London when he was fourteen. Though at core no more than a provincial urchin, he soon discovered how to live well on his wits and good looks. He quickly ascended into higher and higher circles, where his manner and appearance eventually made him a great favourite of the Duchess of Bedford's younger son. It was at her house in Mayfair that Charley met the English naturalist, who had recently returned from South America. It seems that on the voyage home the naturalist had been shipwrecked, losing in the process most of his collection, which he had been hoping to sell for a considerable sum. After recuperating from his disaster at Bredely Hall (and, Charley told me, only just escaping another disaster with a certain young woman and her brother), he had arrived in London with a plan to recoup his fortune by a collecting trip to the East Indies. When Charley learned that he was looking for an assistant, he put himself forward. The naturalist, having as keen an eye for a boy as a butterfly, immediately recruited Charley as collector and companion. When I met up with them in Macassar, the two had already spent over a year travelling together around the Malay archipelago, though Charley admitted that he had been growing tired of his inferior position, as well as the English naturalist's growing obsession with what he termed the 'Other World', one aspect of his character that I had so far been spared. The Englishman was given to lecturing his assistant on the limitations of past and present religious and scientific dogmas, and urging him to look forward to the dawning of a new age of human enlightenment.

'I do sometimes get tired of listenin' to him goin' on all day about his social this and his spiritual that,' Charley told me. 'I'll tell you what, sometimes I think he could bore the eye out of a cocoa-nut.'

Even so, it was clear that during their year together each had, in his own way, become quite fond of the other, and the naturalist had taught Charley much about natural history. Charley had become especially adept at catching and setting insects, of which he had begun his own collection. Despite his employer's prejudices, he had an impressive display of beetles (a preference which endeared him to me yet further), ranging in size from smaller than a grain of rice to as big as a mouse. In form and colour the insects were just as varied; elegant longhorns and stocky ladybirds, jewel beetles all the colours of the rainbow, goliath beetles black as jet. Pride of Charley's collection was a specimen which he told me that he had not captured himself, but had bought from a one-eyed sailor, not long before I had arrived, in the very port where we were now staying. Charley kept the beetle in a small box, nicely carved and inlaid in the local fashion, which, he said with some pride, had cost him as dear as the beetle itself. He allowed me to open the box.

Inside was a scarab, a dung-beetle in lowlier terminology, with the squat body and strong legs typical of its kind, the front pair splayed and curved to enable it to form its ball of dung. The beetle was about an inch and a half in length, with a smooth carapace, and appeared to be totally without eyes. The gena were completely smooth, while the vertex contained no trace of even the simplest ocellus. But what was most remarkable about the beetle was its colour. It was purest, brightest, shiniest gold.

There is a butterfly in Australia commonly called the crow (I presume from its colour, though it is not totally black, but black and white), plentiful enough in certain years around Sydney. The imago itself is unremarkable, as is the caterpillar, but the intermediate stage, the chrysalis, is one of the most beautiful natural objects I have ever seen. In shape it resembles others of its tribe, being somewhat lozenge-shaped, with the form of the head and legs of the adult insect visible beneath the skin. Its beauty comes not from its form but its colour, for the chrysalis of the common crow is pure silver. There are many insects which have a metallic sheen to them, beetles especially, but none compares with the perfection of this silver chrysalis. It is not a dull silver, not a silvery sheen, but the perfect silver of a highly polished mirror. The chrysalis of the common crow does not seem to belong to the natural world, and neither did the scarab which was now before me.

That it was a real beetle, I had no doubt. Charley had pinned it through the right wing case into a piece of some coarse vegetable pith lining the base of the little box. He allowed me to pull the pin from this makeshift cork and examine the insect minutely with my lens. Each leg, each plate on the body, each segment of each antenna reflected all around it in miniature perfection. The scarab was more like the finest example of a jeweller's art than a real insect, and it was a surprise to find that it weighed so little. As I held it in my hand, I saw in my mind's eye another beetle being held in another hand, now so long ago and far away. There was nothing in the whole world I wanted more than a specimen of the golden scarab.

Chapter 21

DESPITE MY ADMIRATION OF all things coleopteran, I have long sought a way to rid my island garden of the small weevil of the *Apion* genus, whose larvae are such a pest on the ripening seeds of peas, which I grow to provide me both with food and subjects for my experiments on inheritance. At the start of my experiments I was compelled to remain constantly vigilant, inspecting each plant every morning, and removing any weevil I found. As any gardener will know, this is a tedious task, and not necessarily effective; despite my daily endeavours, I would often find, on breaking open a ripe pod, that it was already infested with the weevil's grubs. Though I recalled that an extract from the roots of some papilionaceous plants, used by the Malays as fish poison, is known to deter, and even kill, some insects, my botanical knowledge is such that I would be unable to identify such species even were they to grow here. That I eventually found help in my horticultural pursuits was due to observation rather than learning.

Though not perhaps as rich in species as an English down, the grassy areas of my island have their share of commensal plants. Among the tussocks can be found the spreading leaves of several small Compositae and Papilionaceae, and a small decumbent *Acacia*; its leaves, when crushed, having the scent of melons. I was one day walking between two of the well-marked gadzock paths that criss-cross the island, both forest and plain. As my feet brushed against the low herbage I could hear a rapid clicking noise, which I took to be made by some insect, possibly an orthopteran of some sort. Intrigued by the sound, I bent down to see whether I could spot its source. Sheltering beneath a tangle of vegetation was a large grasshopper, but as I reached to pick it up, my hand brushed against the seed-head of a small plant. I heard more clicks, and saw several tiny puffs of what looked like yellow smoke. When I brushed my hand over the plant, a small vetch of rambling habit with thin stems and narrow leaves, there were more clicks and puffs. It was not the insect which had caused the phenomenon, it was the plant.

You may be familiar with the common furze of England, whose pods spring open in late summer at the smallest touch, to fling their seeds far and wide. The seeds of the vetch rely on a similar mechanism. Its flowers appear in heads not unlike a clover, and ripen into a cluster of elongated pods, each about two inches long. When the seeds within are ripe, the two halves of the pod become under such tension that the lightest touch will trigger them to spring apart. The source of the puffs, of what I had taken to be yellow smoke, is a powder which is also contained within the pod. As I traced the plant along the ground with my hand, it released more seeds and powder. At the same time, I noticed several other insects, mostly cockroaches, sheltering beneath the plant, but when I went to pick them up I found that they were not sheltering. They, and the large grasshopper I had first noticed, were dead.

Death is not uncommon in the world. In every generation more die than live, so why is it that our world is not one gigantic morgue, littered knee-deep with the corpses of dead animals? It is surely because that same process of natural selection which had given us such numberless variety of species has given us an army of sextons, whose lives are devoted to the dead. As soon as any animal, or plant, dies, it immediately attracts the attention of a footman of that ghoulish army, and the process of dematerialisation begins. Sometimes the body is swallowed whole, sometimes it is dismembered and interred, sometimes it is eaten away *in situ*, by creatures ranging from the size of a bacterium to a vulture. Few corpses remain in their pristine form for more than a day. So how could I explain the presence near my crackling vetch of such an array of small cadavers? They must surely have only recently died, and the ghoulish army had not yet had time to find them. In which case, a further question immediately presented itself. How had they met their deaths? The answer to this conundrum was staring me in the face, but I took no little time to recognise it.

It is my firm opinion that water is scarcely kinder to cloth than it is to skin, but since arriving on the island I have, when I have noticed them getting a little stiff for comfort, occasionally washed my clothes. My preferred method is simply to immerse myself fully clothed in my bathing pool, then remove my clothes and rub them together in the water a few times; it is surprising how much extraneous matter then floats away. I was thus engaged one evening, soon after my discovery of the crackling vetch, when I noticed that the water beetles, which were such a pleasant feature of my bathing pool, appeared to be distressed. Rather than skating in circles around the surface of the pool, they remained floating in one place, hardly moving. Could the cause of their distress be something that I had introduced into the water, possibly from my clothes? It took only seconds for the connection to be made between the beetles and the dead insects I had found the previous day. The connection must surely be the yellow powder, some of which must still have been attached to my clothes. Once the hypothesis had been established, the proof was simple. The yellow powder from the vetch pods is indeed a powerful toxin against all insects and their tribe. I have tested it to good effect on several species, and by filling a small cloth with the pods I am now able to dust my pea plants with enough of this clever poison to kill off all weevils. It has occurred to me that the effects of the dust are necessarily of benefit to the crackling vetch itself, by ridding its surroundings of insects which might prove injurious to its seeds or seedlings. I have named the plant *Vicia curculiolus*.

In the course of our days together I would often open Charley's carved wooden box and feast my eyes on the golden scarab within, and the more I looked at it, the more I coveted it.

'Well you can't have this one,' said Charley with a laugh, 'but I'll find you another.'

After promising to send a message to his sailor friend, from whom he had procured his own specimen, he suggested that we make some natural history investigations together.

'We might even find one of them beetles by ourselves, and you'll have saved yourself a packet.'

Over the next week we made several short trips into the hinterland, which gave us much time both for collecting (much of which was done through intermediaries in the form of the local Dyaks or Toala, who were singularly adept at capturing live animals), and for conversation. Charley had a quick mind and was a keen student, particularly eager to learn as much as he could about the class of insects for which the English naturalist showed such disdain, but were his chief interest, and about the more theoretical aspects of natural history.

'Why,' mused Charley one afternoon after we had returned to Macassar and were sitting on the palace balcony, I checking my manifest, he pinning out his beetles, 'why are some species so similar, others so different?' He held up a specimen which he had recently collected and pinned, its legs still waving slowly in the air (I had already noticed that Charley was curiously indifferent to the suffering of animals, and was far from thorough in his use of the killing jar).

'Here now, here I have a new beetle.' He held it close to his eye. 'It belongs to the genus *Hyperchorion*, if I'm not mistaken,' he added proudly, carefully emphasising the aitch. It was a magnificent green-bronze longhorn, its wing cases iridescent in the sunlight. 'Beauty, ain't it?'

He then held up a second beetle.

'And this one here you've already told me is another *Hyperchorion*. This one I got last year up in Penang. Two different species, from different ends of this archipelago, yet so alike that you can only tell 'em apart usin' a glass.'

The beetles did indeed look identical, though I was confident in Charley's diagnosis. Charley then held up two more beetles, fat and round like large ladybirds, one black with a red edge to the wing case, one pale green, and only half the size.

'Now look at these two,' he said. 'They're different, ain't they, but accordin' to the books, both belong to the same genus, *Chrysomelus*. Why?'

I had already explained to Charley a little about the Theory, and I knew that he had no need of a creator in the argument. But I wanted to see if he could think this problem through for himself.

'Might it not simply be,' I said, 'that the men who named them thus used different criteria? One concentrated on colour, perhaps, and one on form. Had uniform criteria been applied, your second two beetles would have been put into different genera, and your confusion would not have arisen.'

Charley thought a bit, but then said, 'All right then, but now answer me this. Even if what you say is right, still some groups, and it don't matter what you call them, genera or families or orders or what you will, have more species in them than others. Why are there more beetles than butterflies, why are there more birds than bats?'

I had the answer, of course, the Theory explained it all, but I continued my Socratic game.

'Could it not be that men's minds are again at the root of your dilemma? What are the intrinsic similarities which cause us to group things together, be they animate or inanimate? Are they not simply subjective judgments?'

With eyes narrowed and lips pursed, Charley waited for me to continue.

'According to the Bible,' I said, 'Jonah was swallowed by a big fish. We modern naturalists say that he was swallowed by a whale, and class this creature not as a fish but a mammal. But is this not purely subjective? If we define all animals with fins as fish, the whale is a fish. If we define all animals which suckle their young as mammals, the whale is a mammal. Both follow logically from the definition, and who is to say which is right?'

'So you mean that such groupin's together are not real, that they're not in nature itself?'

I nodded, and Charley stared silently at his beetles.

'But I don't think that's true,' he said eventually. 'I think it's more than that. What if there's some sort of reality behind it all?'

'What do you mean?'

'Look,' he said, holding up the beetles once more. 'These two beetles. Mightn't they be similar in the same way that two brothers are similar?'

'But your beetles are of different species; brothers are not of different species.'

'Well, not brothers, then, but cousins, say, very distant cousins.'

Charley was beginning to see it.

'So you are suggesting that although the beetles are now separate species, they are descended from a single species?'

'Yes, that's it,' he said, getting up and walking to the rail. When he turned back towards me, his eyes were bright with excitement.

'And think,' he said. 'This would explain everythin'. Like some human families are large and others small.'

'Yes, Charley, it explains some things, but it does not explain everything. Your idea is not new. The idea that similar plants and animals are related, have evolved from common ancestors, has often been suggested. As you say, it explains similarity, and it may even explain diversity. But it raises more questions. How do your two lines diverge, Charley? Are you a different species from your cousin? No, you are the same. Lines, even divergent lines, breed true.'

Charley fell silent again, and it was not until the next day, again in that quiet time we spent each afternoon in preparing the new specimens we had collected, that he returned to the subject.

'I've been thinkin' about what we talked about,' he began, 'about the problem of species. I know what you say is right. Animals do breed true. But you can change them, can't you? And what about people? You can change people.'

'How do you mean?'

'Well,' he said, 'look at them Dyaks, there. They ain't like us, are they? They're little, and dark; made for the jungle, you might say. Even their faces look different. It's the same with the Chinese, and the Malays. They're all different, ain't they? But when a white man gets together with a Malay woman, say, then the children won't all be the same. I mean, some of them might look half-and-half, but some might look all Malay, and some might look almost white.'

I could see that he was getting on to the wrong track. Perhaps a little guidance would help.

'But Charley,' I said, 'have you ever thought about how it came to be that we are all different colours to start with? If Adam and Eve were white, how is it that some of us are black, or brown, or yellow?'

'I don't know,' he said.

'Well,' I said, 'let us use the same rules we apply to animals to humans. Let us suppose that Adam and Eve, or anyway our distant ancestors, were indeed white. Even among the white races, have you not noticed that there is much variation? Hair colour, eye colour, even skin colour to some extent.'

'I know that. Red-headed Irish, black-haired Welsh, fair-haired English. I think I might be Welsh.'

'Yes, I suppose you might. But even in the same family,

though all the children resemble their parents to some extent, one child may have red hair, one black hair, one fair hair. One may be tall, one may be short, one thin, one fat. It's just the same as your white man and your Malay. Is this not so?'

'But that don't really matter, does it? It don't matter what colour your hair is.'

'Doesn't it, Charley? Take these Dyaks, the Toala; as you say, they might be made for the jungle. It surely matters to them what colour their hair is, what colour their skin is, how tall they are. What would happen to a Toala with fair skin and yellow hair? When he was out hunting in the forest, would he be able to hide in the shadows? If he were tall, would he be able to slip through the bushes and creepers? Such a man would not last long in the world the Toala inhabit.'

'I can see that, how did they get that way?'

'By the same mechanism that they stay that way, by what we've been talking about, by natural selection. Even though, as you say, species tend to breed true, there is still much variation. Just as we Englishmen may be born with different hair and eyes and skin, so are the Toala. But a Toala child who is born with lighter skin will be at a disadvantage compared to his brothers. Out there in the forest, he will be more visible to both prey and predator. He is the one that in hard times will starve, he is the one that will get eaten by a leopard. But because such children die before they have children, any disadvantage which they carry is not passed on. Nature is continually selecting those individuals best suited to the situation into which they are born.'

'Ah, now I see it,' said Charley, and he began thinking up other examples. It soon became clear to me that he had grasped the essential concept of natural selection, and that the Theory was as obvious to him as it was to me. In my pride, I marvelled at Charley's brain almost as much as I did at his beauty.

The reason that Charley understood the Theory so quickly was partly from his intelligence and innate curiosity, and partly from the absence within him of any competing religious dogma. Though he had been given large and regular doses of religion as a child, the medicine had failed to cure his chronic atheism. This was also manifest in his peculiar insensitivity to the suffering of animals. Charley did not seem to think of animals as living things. To him they were simply specimens, and his first thought was how to kill so as to best preserve an animal, be it bird or beetle. His favoured method of killing birds and small mammals was simply to hold them in his hands and squeeze them until they suffocated. 'Like a snake,' he would say. Sometimes he would squeeze them almost to the point of death, then relax his grip to allow them to recover. He would then repeat the process, and became very expert at being able to so judge the state of asphyxiation that he could bring an animal to within a whisker of death several times in succession. This had nothing to do with preserving the specimen; Charley did it simply for pleasure, a fact which, when I questioned him on it, he did not deny.

'Why, it's harmless enough fun, and it's only an animal,' he said, with a smile. 'How many animals have you killed yourself? You're killin' animals all the time for your collections, not to mention your food. Don't you like it that I get a little fun from it?'

'But Charley,' I protested, 'when I kill for food, then I am killing out of necessity. We men are among the animals which eat meat. We must kill for our food, just as the lion must kill, and the wolf.'

'And what about all those things you kill and skin, or put away in bottles? You ain't eatin' them.'

'No less than we men must eat meat, so we also must seek knowledge. We are born that way; it is our blessing and our curse. None of our present knowledge of natural history could have come about without collecting and dissecting. You're a naturalist now, Charley, you must know this. But we are careful not to cause undue suffering when we kill.'

215

Charley listened to me in silence until I had finished my short oration, then spoke again.

'Why?' he said.

'Why? What do you mean why?'

'Why everythin'?' Charley smiled at me. 'Why must we kill to eat? Are there not men who eat no meat, and live long by it? Why must we seek knowledge? Are there not men and women who live happily in ignorance? And why, my clever friend, why must we not cause sufferin', if sufferin' we do cause? Is it because we will be punished? By who? By God? But you say you do not believe in God. By men? Why should any man punish those who cause him no harm?'

What Charley said was true. If I so abhorred killing, why did I myself kill? I had often heard of vegetivorous people, and whole vegetivorous races, who, it is said, live long and healthy lives. To what real purpose was the scientific knowledge which I, or anyone, accumulated by our collecting and dissecting? Was I any happier in my world of science, any worthier, than a Dyak with his own world of myth and legend? And if, as I had frequently claimed, I had no God, what was my premise for not causing other creatures to suffer, and for exhorting others to do the same? Yet, though I had no words to explain it, I knew that I was right about this, just as, as a child, I knew that I had been right about there being no God.

Chapter 22

BEAUTY IS SURELY AS much subjective as objective, as much in the mind of the observer as in the body of the observed. As we grow from childhood, our awareness of things beautiful also grows, even though, brought up as we are with objects at our own scale, it can be difficult to see the beauty of things enormous or things minute. An appreciation of landscape, of the sublime or the picturesque, is seldom found in children; rather it is something that comes with age (or perhaps simply with reading Gilpin).[45] Conversely many children, as they grow into adults, lose the appreciation of beauty at a smaller scale. Among the fortunate few who acquire the former while retaining the latter is often to be found the naturalist. Should that naturalist possess a microscope, then world upon world of new beauty is his to discover.

My investigations of the natural history of this island have not been confined to those creatures visible only to the naked eye. Fascinating though I have found the trees and the spiders, the birds and the beetles, my Coddington has revealed creatures of equal wonder and beauty, though their entire lives may be spent in a teaspoonful of soil, or in a few drops of water caught between the leaves of a plant. There is a whole system of creatures which I have discovered here which are born, live and die within a drop of dew.

The fall of dew is not as uncommon on my tropic island as

---

[45] Presumably William Gilpin (1724–1804), English writer on aesthetics.

might be supposed. It is my understanding that the phenomenon is rather a result of condensation than precipitation, and is dependent more on relative temperature than absolute. No matter how hot the climate, if the difference between daytime and nighttime temperature is sufficiently great, then dew will form. Though nights here are never cold by any European measure, if the day has been dull and the night clear, dawn will reveal a million dewdrops sparkling like shattered glass on the grass outside my house. How long the drops last depends on the subsequent weather. On a sunny day they will all have disappeared within an hour after daybreak, but this short time is enough for a whole system of life to pass from infancy, to adulthood, to dotage and to death.

My discovery of the dew creatures was due to no great scientific endeavour, but to simple curiosity. Ever since Robert Grant had shown me in Edinburgh how every drop of water, in open sea or darkest sewer, contains its own collection of minuscule vitality, I had often amused myself by inspecting through my microscope samples of water from any novel source that I came across. Rotifers wheeling across pondwater, tardigrades lumbering among the thread-like roots of damp moss, nematodes eeling their way between grains of soil, can be a source of as much wonderment and delight as any bright parrot or dancing dragonfly. Towards the end of the long rainy season, several stormy days and nights were followed by an evening when the clouds disappeared to a clear, calm night. I slept more soundly that night than I had for many weeks, and awoke at dawn to see dewdrops glistening on the grass outside my house. The thought occurred to me to look within one. Taking a glass slide from my box, I captured a single drop, laying on either side of it a hair from my own head, and covering it with another slide. These I placed on the stage of my microscope, my fingers turned the focusing wheel until I saw the top of the glass slide, small specks of dust clearly visible on its surface, and I dived through the glass and into the hair-thin layer of water. Suddenly I was swimming in a drop of dew; nor was I the only swimmer. Small clumps of animated green needles jittered about the bottom. Formless, translucent shapes dashed past in a blur of protoplasm. I saw the dark creeping shape of what looked like jointed legs, though their owner remained tantalisingly outside my field of view. But gradually, over the next hour, I was able to form a complete picture from these individual glimpses. It was as remarkable as anything I had yet discovered on my island.

Distilled from the very air, containing nothing but water, the essence of dew is purity. How, then, can life exist within a dewdrop? The answer is that dew does not float free in the air from which it precipitates, but coalesces on some earthly object. Our microscopes show us that earthly objects will always mix together to some degree. The blade of grass which to our naked eye may appear pristine and immaculate, beneath the lens of the microscope is littered with detritus. We see that its surface is no more than a dust trap, a spiked palisade to capture every passing mote. Should a drop of dew form on the leaf, the debris on its surface becomes incorporated within the drop, and to something as small as a bacillus living within a dewdrop, a single piece of such dust provides more than enough food to grow and grow.

There were many such bacilli within the drop of dew I had placed beneath my microscope. They were the green needles I had previously seen, though why they should be green I could not at first conjecture. It was only when I saw a clump of them enveloped by an amoeba, and watched as their tiny bodies dissolved within it, that I noticed that the green pigment was contained within small cells or granula. They reminded me strongly of the tiny spheres which contain the chlorophyll within plant cells, and suggested to me that perhaps the bacilli, like plants, were using the light from the sun to transmute water, together with the dissolved air and minerals from dust trapped within the dewdrop, into the very stuff of which they were made. Further evidence for this conjecture came when, later in my investigations, I examined a dewdrop *in situ*.

It was delicate work, transferring the dewdrop still intact on its blade of grass to my microscope, but despite my years, I have a steady hand, and I soon had my instrument focused on to some green bacilli within the drop. I was puzzled to find that they were not at the base of the drop (where, due to the simple effects of gravity, there was the greatest accumulation of detritus), but swimming at its very centre, like a shoal of flickering green fish. As usual, I had been illuminating my specimen by shining sunlight on to it from a mirror, when a cloud passed over the sun and the drop that I was observing became shaded. The bacilli immediately spread out within it, and it took me some time to deduce the cause of the reaction. It is at the centre of the dewdrop that the light from the sun is at its most concentrated, magnified by the convexity of the dewdrop's surface. For creatures that, in effect, feed on light, this is the most advantageous position. When clouds diffuse the sunlight, the bacilli leave their rich pasture to scavenge among the surrounding wasteland. That creatures of such minuscule size should have the ability, not only to move within a drop of dew according to more than the laws of chance, but also, in effect, to see, were marvels indeed. I have lately considered that Herr Haeckel, invaluable ally though he has been in understanding and propagating the Theory, has taken too simplistic a view of the organisation of the animal kingdom, especially the minuscule. There are many more creatures, both in number of species and number of basic forms, than can be subsumed under his simple category of *infusoria*. I propose that my photophilic bacilli should be described as the type species[46] of a completely new phylum, which I name *Photophilia*.

Although the bacilli were too small for me to observe their

[46] The author is under a taxonomic misapprehension. Although under the original Linnaean system a type species is needed to establish a new genus or family, this does not apply to higher levels of nomenclature, including phyla.

reproductive strategy, I observed a noticeable increase in their numbers even within the space of a quarter of an hour. To a dew-bacillus, whose life can last no longer than the drop of dew into which it hatched, fifteen minutes may be half a lifetime. But though the life of such creatures seems simple enough, swimming with their companions through the nourishing medium of a dewdrop, basking in the sunlight and continually reproducing, just as the sheep has the wolf, the bacilli have their own enemy. Within each dewdrop are found amoebae.

I had first observed these animalcules within the thin layer of water I had trapped between two glass slides, when they flowed over its surface engulfing any bacillus in their path. I discovered that, in their natural state within the intact drop, they are not so fearsome a foe. For the amoebae, possessing neither flagellum or cilia, are unable to swim, but are forced to crawl over the bottom surface of the drop, where few bacilli are to be found. They compensate for this disability by being able to extend their bodies in the most remarkable way. You may have yourself seen a rat-tailed maggot, the larva of the large drone fly and a common enough inhabitant of slowly moving or stagnant water, whether it be stream or muck-pond. Though basically maggot-like in form, this animal can extend its posterior segments to ten times the length of its body, so forming a thin tube to the surface of the water, through which it breathes. The dewdrop amoeba has a similar ability. Though condemned to crawl across the bottom of a dewdrop, it can project outwards and upwards from its body a long tendril, reaching up into the centre of the liquid. This forms a kind of tentacle, which it does not use to breathe, but to capture bacilli, drawing them down to its main body to be absorbed and digested.

Fearsome foes though they prove to bacilli, the amoebae themselves have a predator, a monster of such awful strength and ferocity that it can shake the very walls of a dewdrop, and such gigantic size that it may be almost seen with the naked eye. Equipped with eight strong legs for walking or swimming, its head armed with a coronet of six large eyes for spotting prey, and a beak as sharp and strong as a Scotch dagger, this terrible creature is an acarus or mite, and, like others of its ilk, it feeds by spearing and sucking the juices from its chosen food. Almost every dewdrop contains a mite, though there is never more than one. This lord of the sphere roams at will throughout its tiny fiefdom, constantly on the lookout for another meal. As well as its all-seeing eyes, its pedipalps are extremely elongated and are constantly being whipped through the water. Should they come in contact with an amoeba, it is immediately pounced upon, stabbed by the sharp proboscis, and its inner contents sucked away. But the mite never kills its prey. Once the mite has reduced an amoeba to about half its original size it is discarded. The amoeba soon recovers from this assault, and once more resumes its own predation on the bacilli.

We are used to distinguishing between predators and parasites. Predators are fierce creatures which capture their prey by strength or stealth, while parasites feed on their hosts without killing them. The dewdrop mite falls into both categories, which serves to remind us that the line between predator and parasite is not always clear. In the Cape there are tribes of cattle-herders who, while keen to hunt and eat the wild animals that surround them, seldom kill and eat the domesticated beasts that they so jealously accumulate, preferring to take their nourishment by drinking a mixture of milk and blood, which they tap from veins in the cattle's necks. Thus humans are both predators and parasites in one, and it is so with the mites that live within the dewdrops on my island. I have named the mite *Acarus eosmilus*.

Chapter 23

I LOOKED FORWARD TO my imminent departure from Macassar with a mixture of feelings. I would be leaving Charley, and though I had secured a valuable cargo of cananga at favourable conditions, I still had no golden scarab; our own collecting around Macassar had yielded not a single specimen. On the morning before I was due to leave Macassar I reminded Charley of his promise. He assured me that his sailor would by now have acquired another and left immediately for the town. He returned towards evening with disappointing news. His one-eyed sailor had disappeared; Charley had spent the whole day trying to find him, or to find another specimen, to no avail. It was with bitter heart that I accepted this news.

It was natural that talking with Charley about the Theory had brought back to me memories of Bobby. It had seemed from the last letter I had received from him before I had left Sydney, that he was no closer to publishing the Theory than when we had first discussed it in Sydney. It was his now, but little good would it do him if it were never published. I suspected that he was still being held back by his deference to religious dogma. Prevarication led to procrastination, doubt to delay. But perhaps there was something I could do to assuage his fears. I had now been away from England for twenty-three years. The woman who had been the cause of my exile was now happily married to my best friend; the men who had engineered my disgrace were both long dead; I had made enough money in Australia over the years to keep me in modest comfort for the rest of my days.

'Why don't you come home with me, Charley?' I suddenly asked him.

'Come where?'

'Back home, back to England,' I said.

'And what would I do there? I have little enough money,' said Charley.

'You'll have the five hundred pounds I give you for your golden scarab,' I said.

Charley grinned at me.

'Can I have that in writing?' he said.

Is it so in every life, that each great disappointment seems to be worse than the last? On that May morning in 1855 came a blow that was almost more than I could bear. Instead of Charley coming aboard with the golden scarab, there came a native boy with a note. Charley could not come with me, it read, as he was no longer in a position to fulfil his side of our bargain. It seemed that the English naturalist, on hearing of Charley's plans, had informed him that if he broke his contract, not only would his wages of the last year be forfeit, so would his specimens, including his beetles. His employer claimed that as all of them, including the golden scarab, were collected while in his service, they belonged to him. This was a bitter blow indeed. Not only had my heart been lost to Charley, it had become so set on the wonderful scarab that I had regarded it as already in my possession. Now that the English naturalist had trumped my ace with his dubious wild card, I felt both cheated and betrayed. Yet the tide would not wait for Charley, and nor could I. I had no choice but to return to Singapore without my Charley Allen, and without my prize.

Never before had I felt such grief. I now knew that my sadness on seeing Bobby depart on the *Beagle*, first from Bristol, then four years later from Sydney, was just that; sadness. Looking back, my forced separation from Emma had had more excitement about it than dejection. It was only now that I truly knew grief, for I knew what it felt like to suffer a broken heart. I, who had always thought my early deprivation had made me immune to love, was now as much a victim of its loss as a swooning maid. Yet all the while, there was a part of me standing back from even my own suffering. Was I grieving more over losing Charley, or over losing the golden scarab? Around each I had woven different futures. Charley was going to be my boon companion, would fill a space in my life that I had never before known the existence of, but could never again be denied. The golden scarab had gradually developed its own unbidden future. In my mind was a picture of another hand holding the prize, of two friends estranged but now united. The golden scarab was going to take me back into the past; it would be the key that would unlock the door that had been so firmly bolted against me when I left England. Now both images had been torn from me, and I could not see to the bottom of my despair.

The only balm was the one I knew of old, to throw myself back into business. See Ko Suan had been right about the Macassar oil. I sold my cargo on the dockside at Singapore to a Liverpool merchant for twelve times what I had paid for it, and was immediately on the lookout for another venture. The repairs on the *Cormorant* were not yet finished, and I spent much time with my old friend, See Ko Suan, both at his house and his place of work. I learned that his network of informants had reported early signs of trouble brewing in America.

'There is talk of war,' he said, 'of the worst kind. I have little doubt that some of the states are already arming.'

'You are suggesting that I join this trade?' I said.

'No, no, my friend, I value your life too highly. Guns do not kill only the people they are aimed at.'

See Ko Suan reminded me that, as much as an army needs guns and ammunition, it needs cloth.

'Every soldier needs a uniform, does he not?'

Although the Americans had mills aplenty for spinning and weaving, they were finding it difficult to buy wool from their usual sources in Europe. The English had already seen which way the wind was blowing and would only sell cloth ready woven, as well as making it difficult for the Americans to buy supplies of raw wool from Europe and South America. Australia had wool aplenty, but English merchants controlled most of the trade, shipping it home around the Cape. My friend suggested that if I could buy Australian wool and ship it straight to America, east around the Horn, I should find an eager market.

Armed with this intelligence and with the profits from my Macassar venture ready at hand, I returned to Australia, where I chartered two lumbering barques out of Newcastle, stuffed them to the gunwales with bales of wool, and in late 1855, with 'sails filled, and streamers waving', set sail for America.

The money I made on my very first cargo made my previous attempts at trade seem insignificant. I returned to Sydney with a chest full of American gold and orders for as much wool as I could carry. Within two years, American mills from Boston to Wilmington were being supplied by sheep from Goulburn and the Darling Downs. During this time I heard nothing from Charley Allen, and as the months turned into years, though I thought of him often, the pain of recollection grew less.

But as profits from my American trade grew, my interest in them diminished. I found my mind turning more and more towards the North. It was not gold that increasingly dominated my thoughts, but the golden scarab. I became impatient to return to the Indies. I knew that Charley's specimen had been bought from a one-eyed sailor, probably one of the Bugi pirates who infested that part of the Celebes. Perhaps the man could still be found. Even if this were not possible, why should I not, as Charley had once suggested, find the source of the specimen myself? It took some time to make the decision to resume the search, and more time to properly arrange my affairs. I knew not how long the search would take; rather than chartering a ship for the venture, I thought it best to buy one; rather than relying on a local agent to take care of my properties, I thought it best to sell them. Eventually I was ready. I had chosen the 15th of May, 1860, as the day of my departure, and as it grew nearer my spirits rose. I had spared no expense in fitting out the ship, nor on her crew. This would one of the best-equipped expeditions ever mounted. Success was sure to be mine.

On the 10th of April, I had just finished my breakfast and was about to leave my house to attend to some final business, when I received two packets by mail. I recognised the hand on the first packet. It was from Philos. Inside were a letter and a book:

The Origin of Species by Means of Natural Selection
or
The Preservation of Favoured Races in the Struggle for Life

At last, though to my great surprise, Bobby had published the Theory. I thumbed eagerly through the pages; it was all there in the chapter headings, all that we had talked about; the origin of domestic varieties (ancon sheep, pigeons and all), the struggle for life, the evidence of the geological record. The account of the difficulties associated with the evolution of organs of extreme perfection, which Bobby and I had discussed in some detail when we were laid up at the Weatherboard Inn, was particularly persuasive. I delved further, almost crying out with pleasure at each new discovery. The Theory was explained with such clarity and effect that only a dunce or a zealot would not be convinced. I was slightly disappointed not to find my own name mentioned in the text, but assumed that, as with my absence from Bobby's book on his travels on the *Beagle*, this was because my friend did not wish to draw the attention of certain legal parties to my move to Australia. But perhaps I would find my name in the introduction. I turned back, but as I read through those first few pages of the book my joy turned to horror. I could scarcely believe what I was reading. Someone else had come up with exactly the same theory. A certain Alfred Russel Wallace, 'now studying the natural history of the Malay archipelago', had sent Bobby a copy of his memoir on the theory of natural selection, ingenuously asking for his advice on publication. Wallace claimed to have suddenly come up with the idea early in 1858, while in bed, sick with fever, in the Moluccas. Bobby's hand had been forced, and he had been compelled to give a joint presentation of the Theory to the Linnaean Society, to share the acclaim. What should have been his alone had to be shared with another, a simple journeyman collector of butterflies, a man I knew to have as much interest in biological theories as I had in his wretched spiritualism. Alfred Wallace, the very man whom I had met in Macassar, who knew and cared less about the theory of evolution than his own untutored assistant, had been given equal credit for one of the greatest scientific theories of the age.

I turned to Philos's letter. From it I learned that Bobby had only reluctantly been persuaded by his friends to publish the Theory, and while it had already proved immensely popular, it had also met with much opposition, some of which Philos described to me. I was delighted to learn that my dear friend was now famous, and equally pleased that Tom Huxley, the young man whom I had got to know so well during his stay in Sydney after Bobby had left, had taken up the title of the Theory's defender, and was holding it against all comers. Despite Bobby's misgivings about publishing the Theory, its popularity was surely vindication of its importance, and even though Wallace had tried to trump his ace, it was Bobby who appeared to have the game.

I turned to the second packet which had arrived in the same mail. Again, I recognised the handwriting. It was from the famous man himself, it was from Bobby, but the letter was not what I expected. It contained no words of malice nor of incivility. If it had, perhaps I would have found it easier to bear.

The letter began by stating that I knew Bobby had not wanted to publish the Theory. While unpublished, it had been safe, though Bobby had long found it a heavy burden to carry, more especially since the death of his daughter. It was true that at one time he been excited by its audacity, but recent events had made it clear to him that there are some things which should not be challenged. Since Annie died, he had come to realise, with the loving help of his dear wife, that foremost among these was the word of God. But now he had been forced to publish, and who had acted the part of Satan's agent? Poor Wallace was not to blame, for it was stretching the bounds of credulity to believe that Wallace could have come up with the same theory, couched in the same language, by himself. It could only have been me who told Wallace of the Theory, and I must have done so knowing that Wallace would himself seek publication. Bobby had then no alternative to publishing the Theory himself. He had been forced to allow the genie from the bottle, and now he could only pray that the genie would not cause as much mischief as he feared. The letter ended by saying that Bobby had no alternative but to hold me responsible for ruining his life, and that, futile though regret might be, he regretted having ever met me. Enclosed with the letter, tied up with string in a bundle, was every letter that I had ever written to my friend; also enclosed was a small cardboard pill box. At first I did not recognise it. I had not seen it since that December day in Portsmouth in 1831 when I stood at the dockside bidding my friend farewell. It was the gift I had given him then, the beetle for which we had spent so many Cambridge days together searching in vain, the *Copris lunaris*.

Chapter 24

I STILL HAVE OUR letters, mine to Bobby and his to me. I have them with me now on my island, and I had them with me when, on the 16th May, 1860, I left Sydney for Macassar. For I did not cancel my departure. It had all been a misunderstanding. I had not wanted Wallace to publish the Theory; when I met him he had shown not the least interest in doing so. I had not wanted to force my friend's hand. I was sure that I could explain this, and explain it I would, in person. I would return to England and I would bring a gift. Had not Bobby told me that he would rather have that golden scarab I had showed him in Cambridge than all the paintings in the Fitz? Had he not said that it was the most exquisite thing he had ever seen? I left on my search for the golden scarab as planned, but now, instead of wishing to possess it, I wished to give it away.

On the long voyage from Sydney I puzzled much over why Wallace had written to Bobby. Wallace was a collector; he had never made any claims to be a theorist. I was sure that what Bobby had said was true, that it was my Theory which Wallace had claimed as his own, but how had he got hold of it, and why had he then written to Bobby? I arrived in Macassar to a warm greeting from the sultan's son, who was surprised to hear me asking about Charley Allen. Had he not left with me those four years previously? He had certainly left at the same time, and everyone was sure he had left with me, including the English naturalist. I told the sultan's son about the plans we had made, then told him about the note on the morning we were to leave. He could neither explain it nor understand it. Neither could he find for me the one-eyed sailor. I left Macassar with more questions in my mind than when I had arrived. What did this mean, and was it connected with Wallace and the Theory? Finding Charley was becoming almost as important to me as finding the golden scarab.

I sailed on to Singapore; surely See Ko Suan, with all his contacts, could help me with my search. But I found that my old friend had retired from business; soon after I had last seen him he had sold everything he owned and returned to the land of his ancestors. No-one else in Singapore knew about the golden scarab or about Charley Allen, and though the English naturalist was thought to be still somewhere in the Indies, no one could tell me exactly where. This second failure, though disappointing, only served to increase my desire to find them both.

I shall not tell here of each port and country I visited, each league I travelled, of each person I asked the same questions, 'Have you seen the English naturalist?', 'Have you seen Charley Allen?' and, more importantly as the months and years passed, 'Have you seen a golden scarab?' Many said they had seen one or another, but when I went to where they told me I would find them, I was always disappointed. Yet each disappointment was a spur. It was as if up until then my life had been a shadow-play, and now that its real purpose had been revealed to me I could no more have given up my quest for the golden scarab than could Sir Galahad have stopped searching for the holy grail. I ranged further, my travels taking me from Madagascar in the west to Japan in the east, yet nowhere could I find what I sought. Eventually I heard that the English naturalist had left the Indies and returned home, but still there was the golden scarab. Had I not seen it with my own eyes? All I needed was a little more time, a little more time.

Sixteen long years I searched, all for a single beetle. Was I mad then? Perhaps I was, though some might understand

232

my madness. But in time enough every storm will blow itself out. When my storm abated and I finally returned to Sydney without my prize, it was the year 1876. I was an old man, and a changed man. I no longer felt comfortable with 'towered cities, and the busy hum of men'. Abandoning all thoughts of returning to England, I bought a small house in Surrey Hills and retired into solitude.

My years abroad had not been completely wasted. I may not have found the golden scarab, but I had not neglected my other collecting. On my various travels I had acquired a good number of other beetles, and back in Sydney I developed a new routine; my days at the Australian museum, naming, arranging and collating the new species, an early supper at the club, and my nights at home, writing out the journal of my recent voyages.[47] It was a peaceful but productive life, and over those next three years, I think I almost put out of my mind all thoughts of evolution, of Charley and the golden scarab. Then one June morning in 1879, as I was walking down College Street on my way to the museum, my madness returned.

'Pardon me,' said a voice in my ear as I stood waiting to cross the road, 'are you still lookin' for a golden scarab?' With a mixture of surprise and contentment, pleasure and fear, I recognised the owner of that voice. It was Charley Allen.

The years had been kind to Charley. The most beautiful boy I had ever seen had become a handsome man, and a rich one too, judging by the cut of his clothes. Though his face was now that of a man rather than a youth, it had retained its boyish charm, and as I once again looked into those pale, long-lashed eyes, I felt my heart give an old, familiar lurch. When I had recovered from my surprise, I took Charley's arm and directed him across the park to my club. Where had he been, I wanted to know, and what had he been doing? And where, I finally managed to ask, as we sat down at my

---

[47] The whereabouts of this journal has not been discovered.

usual table with a bottle of Madeira before us, where was the golden scarab?

'Didn't you hear?' said Charley, taking a sip of wine. 'I sold it to the Chinee.'

'The Chinaman? Not See Ko Suan?'

'Yes, that's him.'

'But how did you get to Singapore? What about coming to Australia? What happened with the English naturalist?'

Question followed question.

'Oh, you didn't hear then?'

'Hear what, Charley, what happened?'

'Well, no harm in me tellin' you now, I suppose,' said Charley.

He pushed back his chair.

'Let's see now. Well, that night in Macassar, the night before we were going to leave, I got to thinkin'. I liked you well enough, you know that, but did I really want to go with you, and did I really want to give you that beetle?'

'You mean sell it to me,' I protested.

'Well, yes, but how did I know what was a fair price?'

Charley gave a small smile.

'So I changed my mind.'

'But why didn't you tell me so,' I said. 'Why the note?'

'Keepin' my options open, I suppose,' said Charley.

If it had simply been more money that Charley had wanted, I would have happily paid him. But Charley had been a young man, and perhaps the idea of exchanging one older man for another had not been as attractive as I had hoped.

'But still, you'd given me an idea,' Charley said, 'and the more I gets to thinkin' about it, the better it seems. A couple of weeks later I writes old Wallace a note too, sayin' that I've gone off to find you. Then I hops on a ship for Singapore, not forgettin' of course, to take the golden scarab with me. I'd remembered what you'd told me about your Chinaman and all his gold, see, and him being interested in natural history and all. Now there's a man who'd give a good price for a golden beetle, thinks I, and off I goes to find him.'

'See Ko Suan, he was still there?'

'He was there, all right, and I found his place easy enough, and we sits down outside his shed, and he gives me a cup o' tea, just like you said. Then I shows him my boxes of beetles and asks him if he's interested, but I keeps the one box closed. What's in there? says he. Oh, that's not for sale, says I, that's my good luck charm. Well now, he don't say anything, but I can see he's interested, so after he's had a good look through the other boxes I asks him if he'd like to take a squizz. He says he wouldn't mind. I tells him again it ain't for sale, and I opens the box. "Name your price," he says.'

Charley laughed.

'So I did. Easy as that, it was.'

But what happened then, I wanted to know.

'Well, set me up, that did, I was a man o' means. I decided to stay around the peninsula for a while, do a bit o' collectin', a bit o' tradin', just like you, old friend.'

I called for another bottle of wine, and Charley told me a little more of what had happened during that year. After he had sold the golden scarab to See Ko Suan, he had stayed on in Singapore. He felt sure that 'somethin' would turn up', and so it did, in the form of the Raja of Sarawak, Sir James Brooke. Brooke immediately took a fancy to Charley, inviting him to Kuching, where he soon became a great favourite; by Charley's own account, Brooke indulged him most shamelessly. He stayed with the Raja through many an adventure (from some of what Charley told me, old 'Blood-money Brooke' well deserved his alternative title). Charley had eventually returned to England with Brooke in 1857 ('first-class, mind') with several thousand pounds, both from the sale of the golden scarab and his subsequent service with Brooke. He invested in a small glassworks, the very one where he had been apprenticed. For some reason which I do not now remember, he had decided to set it up to manufacture laboratory glassware, and had done very nicely from it. He had even tried his hand at marriage, to the daughter of the former owner of the factory, though she had since died.

I naturally wished to know what had brought Charley to Australia. Had he grown tired enough, or rich enough, to retire from business? Charley told me that he was indeed a wealthy man, but although he had not regretted selling his golden scarab to See Ko Suan, the memory of it had been haunting him over the years, much as it had me. He had finally decided that he, too, would try to find the source of the wonderful insect, but before going on his own search he thought he might have a look at the Australia I had told him so much about. He had already spent two months in Tasmania and ten days in New South Wales, and had been surprised to find me still here.

'And what are you up to these days, old friend?' he asked.

I told him about my own life since we had last met, and my own search for the elusive beetle.

'You didn't find one?'

I shook my head. Charley leaned forward towards me over the table.

'There's a ship leaving for Batavia next week,' he said.

Six days later Charley and I were standing on the deck of the *Jane Darkely*, watching the Sydney Heads fade into the distance as we sailed north.

Chapter 25

DESPITE ALL THAT HAS happened since, I bless the fate, 'that power, which erring men call chance', which brought Charley back to me, then brought me here. To encounter a new world and to name its inhabitants is a gift such as few men are given. That I am old now makes it doubly sweet, for, as my own end approaches, each day increases its value. This morning I was awoken by the mountain. I felt the very ground beneath me shake, as if in anger, or in fear. But we are good friends now, the mountain and I. I understand it well, and I shall not desert it.

Our departure on the *Jane Darkely* had been somewhat hurried. Charley and I spent much of the time on our voyage from Australia in planning how best to execute our search for the golden scarab. Though Charley had discovered to his dismay that the banker's draft which he had arranged to be forwarded to Sydney had not arrived before our departure, I had brought gold enough to cover all the costs for the equipment we might need, and which I was sure we could acquire in Batavia. We had already agreed that we would need to charter a vessel, and I suggested that I call on some of my previous Dutch contacts; I was sure we would have no difficulty in chartering a Dutch ship. Charley was adamant that we hire a local Javanese prau and crew for our search. Though I expressed my unease about trusting ourselves to unknown hands, Charley would have no argument on the subject.

'One thing I learned from the old Raja was this. You don't want men who know you, you want men who know the place.'

Charley then told me a story of how Brooke had a long history of trouble with rival traders. They were mostly Chinamen, though they had been living and trading in Sarawak long before Brooke's arrival in 1839. When this brash Englishman turned up and became so sweet with the sultan, they did not think too highly of it. Brooke and his fellow traders had been at each others' throats ever since, but despite some dirty deeds on both sides and a few outright skirmishes, things had simmered on without any major confrontation. Then Brooke saw that he might have a chance to get the upper hand.

'He was always clever at playin' the political card,' said Charley. 'In forty-eight he had to go back to London to see to some business matters, and while he's there he tells a few friends about these "Chinese pirates" who are posin' such a threat to British interests in the area, at the same time hintin' that the Dutch Company was almost certainly behind the whole thing. He's scarcely back home in Kuching when a Portuguese merchantman slips into port with a small consignment for him from Her Majesty's Government. "Sign here, no charge," says the captain, and old Jim finds himself with enough ordnance to clean up the Crimea.'

I had heard a little on my previous travels about the ruthless private campaign that Raja Brooke had waged against the 'Chinese pirates', and about the British parliamentary inquiry that had ensued. Though Brooke had been formally exonerated and had continued his trading, he was no longer able to rely on the unconditional support of the British government. During the early 1850s a slow war of attrition was being fought in Sarawak, and it was during the final stages of this war that Charley arrived in Kuching.

'Jim had more cannons, and howitzers, and mortars, and small arms than all the armies in the East. When I met him in Singapore he was not there for arms, but information. On the way back to Kuching he asks me whether I'd noticed the other passengers. The only ones I'd noticed were a couple o' Chinamen. "That's them," he says. "Worth their weight in gold."'

Charley found out that the two Chinamen were themselves traders from Kabong, from where Brooke's rivals were planning an organised assault on his stronghold in Kuching. Some internecine dispute had forced the two men to leave Sarawak, and they hoped that by allying themselves with Brooke they would end up on the winning side. Their part in the alliance was to provide information on the strengths and weaknesses of the opposition.

'Jim was quite right,' said Charley. 'It worked. Without them we would never have got out of Kuching when the big attack came, and we would never have retaken it so soon after. They *were* worth their weight in gold. That's what I mean, you see. We don't want men we know, we want men who know the place.'

Charley was ever a good storyteller. By the time we arrived in Batavia, he had won the argument; I agreed to his choice of vessel and crew, though I took care to supervise the provisioning. We left Batavia in a Javanese prau with a Javanese crew, and after a calm passage, our little party reached Macassar on the 15th of August, 1879.

The sultan's son was now sultan. Though he was old and of wandering mind, he made us welcome and once again allowed us the use of what was now his second palace. The town had changed little. The same dingy godowns lined the wharf, the same untidy piles of barrels and boxes, the same smell of wood, fish, tar and filth. Charley thought he might still recognise the tavern where he had bought the golden scarab those four and twenty years ago. He remembered enough of his Malay to question the porters who were idling on the wharf, and after a few words, we set off with one of them down one of the narrow streets. We were led through ever more narrow streets and alleys, finally stopping before the doorway of a small, decrepit shack. Old bits of wood, nailed and tied together anyhow, formed its walls, and it was roofed in similar fashion. There were no windows to this hovel, but drifting through its curtained entrance came a soft murmur of voices, and a sweet and unmistakable smell.

'Here,' said Charley. Pushing open the tattered curtain with one arm and beckoning me to follow, he stepped inside.

When Charley let go the curtain I had to pause for several moments to allow my eyes to accustom themselves to the dim light. Low benches lined the walls of the room, on each a recumbent figure. In the corner lay an old man in ragged clothes, a small pipe held loosely in his hand. A tallow candle spluttered and smoked on the floor in front of him, reflected in the vacant stare of his single, dark eye.

'And here's our man,' said Charley.

It was indeed the sailor who had sold Charley the golden scarab, but years of opium-smoking had destroyed the old man's body, and his mind. Though we had brought gold and other gifts, he seemed to have little awareness of our questions, sometimes even of our presence. It was only when Charley paid the owner of the opium den to withhold the drug that, returning some hours later, we eventually got the old man to speak. Yes, he remembered the golden scarab, but no, he had no others. And no, he could not remember from where he had got the first one. We pressed him further. Surely he could remember? We would be happy to pay him. I took some coins from my purse. Here, I said, as I placed a coin in his hand, was gold for as much opium as he wanted. The old sailor's one eye gleamed dimly. Struggling to an upright position, he reached inside his torn and filthy shirt to pull out a small bag tied around his neck, from which he clumsily extracted a small carved box. Charley snatched it from his hand. The sailor watched, smiling, as Charley tried in vain to open the box, then gently took it back from him and opened it with a twist.

'Mas, mas,' he said, with a toothless smile. 'Gold for gold.' And there in the box was a golden scarab.

In Australia I have become used to spectacular colouration among the Buprestidae (which there go by the general name of 'jewel beetles'), but beauty is not only found in form. Here on my island I have discovered a small beetle which could hardly be less pretty or less conspicuous, yet in its life reveals a beauty as great as any creature of more showy countenance.

One morning I had interrupted a walk in the forest to take my relief, when my idle eye was caught by the flower of an orchid, inconspicuous almost to the point of being invisible, growing on the ground not six feet away from where I squatted. There is a small orchid in Australia which goes by the common name of the greenhood. It is an unremarkable plant, but of some interest to the entomologist, in that its flowers are pollinated by a small gnat, which, on entering the flower to drink its nectar, is then held captive by a kind of valve, from which it can only escape by forcing its way past the flower's pollinia, which attach to its back and are so carried to another flower. It is a common enough thing that flowers use insects as agents of fertilisation; it is less common that the reverse should be true, but this is what the little buprestid beetle on my island has learned to do. Two of them were now resting, *in copulo*, on the withered orchid. They were, as I have said, unremarkable insects, being each about half an inch long, elongate and depressed, and mid-brown in colour. But between the unremarkable insects and the unremarkable flower I have discovered the most beautiful and intricate relationship.

The orchid is a terrestrial variety of the *Ophrys* type, putting forth a single pale yellow flower on a short stem, with small petals and sepals, and an enlarged and extended labium. This flower is sought out by the female buprestid beetle, which eagerly feeds on its nectar. But the beetle does not just use the flower as a source of food; as she is feeding, she lays several of her eggs. They are laid into a purse-shaped receptacle which is found on the tip of the flower's labium, and this action causes in the flower a curious change. Its petals and sepals begin to wither, its labium to swell and alter both in shape and colour. Within twenty-four hours the labium has assumed the form of head, thorax, and abdomen of one of the buprestid beetles whose eggs it is host to, while the withered petals and sepals resemble nothing so much as its legs and antennae. The mimicry of a female beetle is almost exact.

It is at this stage that the male beetle appears. He lands on the metamorphosed flower, but does not attempt to feed from it. Rather, he attempts to copulate with it, as he would with a female, extending his aedeagus into the egg receptacle of the flower, and ejaculating his seminal fluid. In this way he inseminates the eggs that the female has already placed there (it was almost certainly this union of beetle and flower, rather than male and female beetle, which I had originally witnessed). While he is engaged in this curious copulation, his vigorous movements trigger the style of the flower to be gently lowered on to his thorax. Its pollinia become attached there, and are carried away with him when he departs.

Within the enlarged labium of the flower, the now-fertilised beetle eggs hatch. The grubs, of which there are a score or so, immediately begin to devour their home. This takes them about a week, after which they drop to the ground. To my knowledge buprestid larvae invariably feed on the stems of woody plants, and I presume that the larvae of this species burrow into the trunk of a nearby shrub or tree, though I have been unable to confirm this.

There is no doubt that the male beetles are the agents of pollination for the orchid, but I have never come across so intricate a system of repayment, the flower providing both the agency of fertilisation of the beetle's eggs, and shelter and food for the grubs. This form of mating, where not only is fertilisation of the eggs external to the female, but the male and female do not meet, is, to my knowledge, unique among beetles, and indeed, among insects in general. I have named the beetle *Buprestis orchidaptis*. My microscope has revealed that its eggs appear to be lacking a chorionic membrane.

What is a search without discovery, what is a story without an ending? As I stood there with Charley in the opium den, the golden scarab held out before us, it was as if I too had been smoking the drug. I had found the object of my long search, and my soul was at peace. My thoughts drifted away; to home, to sunset days in some quiet retreat. Pictures of England floated across my vision; surely I could return there now, to England and to Bobby. Two old men might still go searching for beetles high up on the Sussex Downs, and perhaps one woman might be glad to see them both return. Dear Philos would surely be pleased to see his friend again, and speak the words he had for so long been forced only to write. Standing there in that dilapidated shack, I blessed Charley, and I blessed his narrow persistence which had finally rewarded our search.

My reverie was ended when Charley spoke.

'We have not quite finished our business,' he said.

Taking the box which contained the golden scarab from the sailor's hand, he held it close to the sailor's face. Where had it come from, Charley demanded.

'We have what we came for, Charley,' I said. 'We have our prize.'

Charley turned to me.

'We have one. Where there is one there is more. What good is *one* of the damned things?'

Without waiting for my answer he began questioning the old man again, in English and Malay. Where had the golden scarab come from? How far was it? Could he take us there? The old man became confused. He looked up at Charley with open mouth, then clumsily tried to take back the box from Charley's grasp. Charley's instinctive response was to push him away, and in doing so he pushed a little too hard. The old man fell back against the couch, thudding his head on the bunkpost as he did so. He rolled to the ground, moaning. Charley squatted down beside him and looked up at me in panic. He grabbed the opium pipe from the low table beside the couch and thrust it into the old man's hand. The old man tried once to grip it, then collapsed upon the floor. There would be no more answers to Charley's questions that day.

We returned to our prau through the same narrow alleys. Charley was scarcely silent for one moment, either muttering to himself or talking distractedly to me. Though still clutching the box with the golden scarab, he seemed almost oblivious to the treasure already in his possession; his passion was now engaged by the unknown number of further specimens, the untold wealth which could soon be ours.

'Don't you see?' he said. 'We are so close. We can't give up now.'

'Give up what, Charley?' I said. 'We have what we came for.'

Charley stopped walking and turned to me.

'Don't you want one too?' he said.

I had given no thought at all to who might now own the golden scarab. I had paid for it with my gold, as I had paid for the whole expedition, and I therefore considered it mine. I pointed this out to Charley.

'You seem to be forgettin'', he said, 'whose idea it was. Who found the thing?'

I had to agree that the journey and the search had been Charley's idea, and that he had led us to the scarab.

'And', Charley said, 'I did not ask you to pay for me. But don't worry, my old friend, your money will be returned to you.'

The expense of the expedition was of little concern to me. I would have gladly emptied my coffers of their last farthing to be sure of obtaining the golden scarab.

'We're so close now,' Charley reassured me. 'Surely just a few more days is a price worth payin' if we can both return home with what we want?'

Ah yes, home. How delighted my old friend Bobby would be if I were to have a golden scarab to present to him. Imagine the smile that would spread across his face as he opened the box, just as it had when I had presented him with the *Copris lunaris* in Plymouth those fifty years ago.

'Don't you worry,' said Charley. 'That old man will tell me more.'

On the fifth day Charley returned to the palace with the information that he had been seeking. *Pulau Pulau Lima*, the Five Islands. Where were the Five Islands? Charley told me that the old sailor had unfortunately died before this could be revealed. This was bad luck indeed.

We questioned everyone we could find in Macassar. Where were the Five Islands? The sultan was of little help, and despite the fact that the Macassans are great traders, who know all the waters of the archipelago, no one seemed to have heard of them, let alone know how to find them. It was only when Charley chanced on some Moluccan fishermen who had recently arrived with a cargo of tripang that we finally discovered the whereabouts of the mysterious islands.

The Five Islands are seldom visited. This is no doubt largely due both to their remoteness, some one hundred leagues from the nearest land, and to the strong and treacherous currents in that area of the Java Sea. The fact that the islands are uninhabited, and therefore of little use for trade, also gives local sailors small incentive to visit them. But the main reason that the Five Islands are avoided is because of the large and active volcano that dominates the main island, and which the coastal people invest with much spiritual significance. They tell stories of strange beasts and strange happenings, and it is only extremely brave or extremely foolhardy men who will dare to sail close to the islands, let alone make land. It was only with much difficulty, and much of my gold, that Charley persuaded two of the Moluccan fishermen to pilot us to there. Even so, there was much muttering between them and our Javanese crew when, the next day, we set sail on our voyage south on the final part of our quest for the golden scarab.

Chapter 26

OUR JOURNEY TO THE Five Islands was uneventful; the sea was calm, the crew performed their duties with efficiency and good cheer. I was gratified to observe that our Moluccan guides seemed to get on well with the rest of the men. Four days out of Macassar we first saw the volcano, with its distinctive tufts of white steam, a sight which brought both excitement and consternation. As we sailed closer we could clearly make out the main island with its surrounding necklace of four small atolls. There was no doubt that we had found our goal. The Moluccans now seemed genuinely afraid, and so clear was their consternation that the Javanese also showed some disquiet. After much talking among themselves, the Moluccans finally declared that we should turn back. Charley would have none of it. He ordered the captain to make them desist from their protestations, threatening them with the whip if they did not. This was to little avail, so that at length he was forced to order the two Moluccans to be bound and gagged, an action which caused some ill-feeling among the rest of the crew. They were Mohammedans all, and protested that their comrades would not now be able to say their prayers. I was all for conceding this point but Charley's answer was to display his English pistols, which I had to admit produced the effect desired.

As we came closer to the island, we encountered difficulties of a different kind. Sharp reefs and huge mats of pumice and floating weed compelled us to lower the sail and pole our way between the coral heads, dangerous work in such a vessel. Each time we struck or grazed against a reef a low moan would be heard from the crew. Eventually, through equal parts of luck and skill, we navigated through the reef into the lagoon and found a safe anchorage, but even though Charley tried to persuade the captain and his men that they were now safe, not even his pistols would induce them to go ashore. Leaving the captain with instructions to remain at anchor, Charley and I paddled ourselves to the beach in a small canoe.

We had gained some impression of the size of the main island when still at sea. Together with a brief reconnoitre, this convinced us that we would need at least two weeks to thoroughly explore it, which could best be done by setting up camp ashore. We found a most suitable setting where a large grove of cocoa-nut trees gave us fuel for our fire and posts for our hammocks. By the time we paddled back to the ship the captain appeared to have calmed his crew. Under our instructions they began loading the canoe with the scientific equipment I had brought with me from Sydney, the other supplies I had purchased in Batavia and enough food and water to last us several days (we had not then discovered the streams or the lake). The unloading took several hours, and as harmless reality replaced groundless superstition, the captain and his crew became more cheerful and enthusiastic. I none the less took particular care to unload my money box from the ship under full sight of the captain and crew, reasoning that where the gold was, there they would stay. When all our things were ashore, Charley returned to the prau to give instructions to the captain. The captain asked if he and the crew might fish the lagoon for tripang, to which Charley assented, giving him strict instructions not to leave the main lagoon. By the time Charley returned to our campsite in the canoe, I had lit a fire and had uncorked a bottle of brandy. With specimen jars for tumblers, I toasted his health and to the success of our search.

The tropical night was soon upon us, and as we sat around the fire watching the flickering flames light up the trunks of the cocoa-nut trees, I gazed across to where Charley sat on an upturned box, his dark hair falling over his forehead, the fire dancing in his dark eyes. He looked once again as he had when I had first seen him. He was no longer the man who had so roughly questioned the old sailor, or who with almost arrogant self-assurance had taken his pistols from his belt to threaten the crew of the prau; he was the beautiful boy sitting on the deck of the ship in the harbour at Macassar, pinning out his beetles and questioning me with such earnest fascination about natural history, and the Theory. Charley tossed back his glass and grinned.

'Here's to the enlightenment of savages,' he said, refilling his glass and mine. 'I knew they'd come round.'

'Well, Charley,' I said, 'I thank you. I have to admit that there have been times, as you know, when I was myself ready to abandon the search. But now we are here and our goal is in sight, I realise that I was wrong.'

Charley came over to where I sat and himself sat down beside me. Putting his arm affectionately around my shoulders, he raised his glass.

'Here's to success, and to friendship.'

After many another toast and more declarations of affection, we retired to our hammocks. The following morning, after the first long and peaceful sleep we had enjoyed for many days, Charley and I awoke to see the prau, with her sail raised, slipping slowly away through the outer reef.

Curse them though I might, I had little doubt that it was Charley's decision to tie up the two Moluccans that was at the root of this mutiny. The captain and crew gained little from their actions, and lost much, for they knew that along with all my money, I had taken all my equipment and my firearms with me on to the island. By leaving us marooned, they forfeited any payment or recompense. Charley, on the other hand, insisted that it was my fault.

'They saw you were soft,' he told me. 'Have you not learned by now that the only way to keep such men's respect is through fear? Keep them guessin', and keep them scared.'

It seems pointless now to retell the bitter words which were spoken then, for what could they have changed? We were marooned, and there was nothing that Charley and I could do but make the best of it. There was no saying when we would be rescued, but this seemed no reason to abandon our search for the golden scarab. We had food, water, guns and ammunition, and a variety of tools and equipment, as well as the small canoe in which we had paddled ashore. At length, I managed to persuade Charley that our best course was to begin at once the task of exploration and mapping.

By the third day Charley and I had assured ourselves that there were no other humans on the island, and had already become familiar with the gadzocks, which twice each day came down to the beach to feed, retiring at noon and nightfall to the bush and woodland of the interior. They were, as I have said, peaceable animals, who took little notice of our own comings and goings. I was already regretting having killed one on the first day, not just because its flesh was unpalatable, but because the slaughter of so innocent and trusting a beast was distasteful to my sensibilities. Charley felt no such compunction. I remembered how when I first met him he would pin out beetles while they were still moving ('Don't you worry, they'll be dead soon enough'), and seemed to take real pleasure in watching their actions gradually slowing until, at last, they stopped, though this might take several days. I also remembered how he killed the birds which our Dyak hunters brought us, by slow suffocation. On the island, I soon found that Charley's attitudes to killing had not changed over the years.

It was the third morning after our arrival, and I had been spending my time in arranging the camp, while Charley had gone off to do a little more exploring. When he had not returned by noon, I walked down the beach in the direction he had taken.

I had gone no more than a mile when my attention was drawn by a sound coming from behind one of the sand dunes. I crested the dune to find a horrific sight awaiting me. A female gadzock was lying on the ground in a hollow between two dunes, the sand around her strewn with blood. Standing next to her, also covered with blood, stood a young female calf, lowing soft and high (it was this noise which had first attracted my attention). At my approach the mother gadzock struggled to her feet and tried to climb the far side of the dune. The effort proved too much for her, and she slumped again to the ground. As she did so, I could see the cause of her distress. Her tail had been cut or bitten off at the root, and she had lost so much blood from this attack that she clearly had not long to live (already, the nose beetles had deserted their usual post). I now saw that the calf herself was uninjured, the blood with which she was covered having come from her mother. As I watched, she lay down beside her and began to gently lick her face. If her mother died, the calf would surely soon die too; even as this thought came to me, the mother gadzock's head fell heavily to the sand. Her eyes, though open, were lifeless.

For several more minutes, the calf continued to lick and nuzzle her dead mother's face. Then, getting to her feet, she resumed her high, plaintive low. I heard another sound behind me. Another gadzock, a female with heavy yellow tail and with her own calf at heel, came trotting over the dune. Passing within a yard of me, yet completely ignoring my presence, she went over to the dead mother and calf. She took no notice of the female gadzock, as if knowing her to be beyond help, but went to stand in front of the orphaned calf. The calf tried to move away, but whenever she moved, the gadzock cow moved (her own calf, meanwhile, stood a few yards away, perfectly still and taking no part). Eventually the new orphan took this hint, stopped her lowing and began to drink from the cow's udder. I returned, much mystified, to the camp.

When Charley finally reappeared later that afternoon, he was whistling a merry tune and looking very pleased with himself. In front of his face he was waving what looked like a large flywhisk, but blood still glistened at its base. Had Charley been responsible for the dying gadzock I had found? On being questioned about his trophy, Charley informed me that he had indeed removed the tail from a gadzock, then washed off its usual encrustation of salt, giving it the appearance more of a fan than a wand. If I would like one he would be pleased to provide it.

'It ain't in the least difficult,' he said. 'They stand quite still.'

My horrific suspicion was confirmed. Charley had hacked the tail from a living beast, condemning it to a slow and painful death, and all for a flywhisk. Yet when I expressed my revulsion at this brutal act, he became quite affronted.

'We have had this conversation before,' he said coldly. 'We both kill. You kill for science, I for comfort.'

Once again, how was I to explain that killing for food, or for the sake of scientific knowledge, was different from killing for such a trivial thing as a flywhisk? What *was* the difference? How could I explain to Charley that it was wrong to let a gadzock bleed to death, and risk the death of its calf by slow starvation?

'Charley,' I began, 'it is true what you say; we both kill. But I am careful not to cause undue suffering when I kill.'

Charley looked up at me.

'Sufferin' is what men feel, not animals.'

'Oh Charley, how can you doubt that animals feel pain as we do? Do they not cry out when wounded? Did not that gadzock cry out?'

'Pain ain't sufferin',' said Charley, ignoring my question. 'Pain's a reaction, a physical feeling. It's of no more consequence than any other reaction, than hunger or repletion. Sufferin's in the mind. Animals don't have minds.'

When I could think of no reply, Charley took my momentary silence for defeat.

'Anyway, old friend,' he said, with a conciliatory smile, 'even you will admit that it does make a fine flywhisk. I reckon we could sell these at a handsome price when we get away from here,' and he waved the gadzock's tail slowly to and fro in front of his face.

The next day Charley came back to the camp with more flywhisks, including some very small ones.

'Don't worry,' he said, when he saw that I was about to object. 'I promise I cut their little throats first.'

Chapter 27

FOR THE NEXT FEW days Charley and I spoke to each other but little. He would take the canoe off in the morning to explore the lagoon and outer atolls, and perhaps do a little fishing, while I made short excursions to the interior of the island. Sometimes Charley was gone all day. When I awoke one morning to find the canoe gone from its usual haul-up beneath the cocoa-nut trees, I assumed that Charley had made an early start; it was only when he had not returned by late afternoon that I became concerned. Though the lagoon was safe enough by daylight, it would soon be dark. I climbed on to one of the sand-dunes; no sign of Charley or the canoe could I see. Could he have come to some mischief? It would have been an easy matter for him to capsize the canoe while landing a fish, or to stake it on some hidden reef. I continued to peer across the rapidly darkening lagoon until all I could see was the reflection of the stars. It occurred to me that I should light a signal fire, and I hurried from the dune to gather up on the beach as many dead cocoa-nut fronds as I could find. Soon I had a bright fire burning, but still no Charley did I see.

All night I sat on the beach, feeding frond after frond into the fire. Bats flew in and out of the firelight, and once a pair of gadzocks wandered quietly by. In my imagination I saw Charley walking back along the beach, or stranded cursing on some sandbank, or even dead and drowned, but no sign of the real Charley did I see, alive or dead. Nor the next morning, though I remained on the beach until hunger and thirst forced me back to our camp. We had made a habit of keeping enough water at our camp for about three days' supply, taking it in turn every other day to walk the short distance to the nearby pond to replenish a small firkin. The firkin was usually kept in a rope sling nailed to one of the cocoa-nut trees, but when I returned to the camp, I noticed that it was gone. Also missing was an object of even greater significance. Though Charley had assumed *de facto* ownership of the golden scarab that we had obtained from the one-eyed sailor, he usually left the box which contained it hanging on the same tree as the barrel of water. I noticed that it, too, was gone, and my first thought was that both had been stolen. It took me some moments to realise what had really happened. The truth was that Charley must have taken the barrel of water, the scarab and the canoe. He had planned to escape the island, and to abandon me alone here. A more thorough search of our things left me in no doubt. Pistols, parang, compass and clothing, all were gone. This was no early-morning whim. Charley had carefully and systematically collected together all the things which might aid an escape. With no thought for me, he had crept away like a thief in the night, leaving me alone on the island.

It was Robert Grant who, in my Edinburgh days, first introduced me to the work of Spinoza. At that stage in my life I found his pure rationalism so attractive that for many months I attempted to model my own life on this philosophy. Away with sentiment and speculation, pure reason was the thing. I was particularly taken with his dismissal of regret. To succumb to feelings of regret is tantamount to trying to change the past. What use has rational man for such a pointless and unproductive endeavour? My youthful enthusiasm did not last; I soon found myself slipping comfortably back to my old ways of passion and pleasure, and I had hardly thought of the old sage since that time. When the full realisation of Charley's perfidy sank into my brain, I wished that I had learned to apply Spinoza's philosophy more successfully. Regret followed painful regret.

What a fool I had been to leave my comfortable life in Sydney and waste my little remaining time on a search I had long since decided to abandon. Why had I allowed myself to be seduced abroad by someone I had really only ever known for a week, and why had I let him choose the captain and crew? I should never have let Charley persuade me to come to this island, and could I not see that the enthusiasm of the crew was not for having arrived safely, but at the thought of being able to leave? As for Charley's love for me, it was a mirage in the desert of my life. For one day I cursed, and for the next day I cried. Then, just as my emotions and tears seemed to be exhausted, Charley returned.

On the third morning after his departure Charley came walking up the beach as if he had just been for a morning stroll in the park. He carried nothing with him, no water, no weapons, and when I questioned him about what had happened to the canoe he simply said that he had gone exploring and that the canoe was lost.

'But why take our water?' I demanded. 'Why the pistols?'

'You didn't need them here,' was his reply. 'You can fetch water in a bottle, and what are you going to shoot, old man, your precious gadzocks?'

'But if you were simply exploring, Charley, why take the golden scarab?'

Charley refused to answer this question, or any of my others which followed. He fell into a sullen silence, which continued through the following days.

Some birds are silent, others have the sweetest songs, but I have never understood why so many birds should mimic sounds; the ability seems to give them no advantage. The facility of mimicry is not uncommon among other animals, usually serving to disguise its possessor, so that it will not be seen by its enemies (how many insects are there which bear the form of leaf or stick, how many animals with the cryptic colouration of the leveret and fawn?). There is a corresponding number whose mimicry enables them to be unseen by their prey, and mimicry will often serve both purposes. Spiders, I think, have perfected this art to its highest level. I have seen spiders the colour of bark, spiders the colour of a leaf, spiders the colour of the flower on which they wait in ambush, invisible to the fly that comes to suck sweet nectar only to be pounced upon and itself sucked dry. I once came across a spider in Australia which resembled the dung of a bird, not only in appearance, but also in smell. Many reptiles also use disguise in this way. In the Cape I have watched a deadly boom-slang slither unaware along a branch not six inches from a defenceless, but motionless, camelion, and a few minutes later seen a blowfly land on the same branch, only to be snapped up by its invisible enemy. That camelions can change their colour to match that of their surroundings is well-known, though I believe there is some dispute as to whether they do so spontaneously, or if some degree of will is involved. There is a creature here on my island which can change not only its colour, but its shape.

I first stumbled upon this remarkable creature while I was investigating the habits of the orchid beetle. I was strongly desirous of finding out whether the female orchid beetle laid eggs in more than one plant, and to that end had removed a female beetle from a flower as soon as I had observed her to have laid her eggs, marking her elytra with some chalk paste that I might be better able to follow her flight by eye. This procedure seemed to inconvenience the beetle but little, and a few seconds after I had replaced her on the orchid she spread her wings and took to the air. Where she might be heading I knew not, but as she flew neither fast nor high, I was able to follow her closely. She landed on the trunk of a nearby tree, whereupon she immediately vanished.

My first thought was that the beetle had disappeared into some hole in the tree, but when I arrived there no hole was to be seen. The bark of the tree, which I now saw to be a *Ficus*, was smooth and grey. It contained nothing that my beetle could hide in or behind, nor, with the white spot on her back, could I possibly overlook her. I made the most minute examination of the tree, but no beetle could I see. It was only when, almost by chance, I ran my fingers over its trunk that I detected something unusual. Just above where the beetle had settled was a small lump, perhaps originally a scar where a branch had broken off many years ago, now healed over. As my fingers touched this lump, it yielded slightly. Even though I could feel this anomaly, my eyes could detect no difference between it and the rest of the bark, no matter how minutely I examined it. Then suddenly the lump fell off; when I stooped to examine it, the lump, too, had vanished. Search though I might, there was nothing on the ground but dead leaves and sticks. Just as the thought was occurring to me that my eyes, or indeed my mind itself, was at fault, one of the sticks moved.

If I had not seen the stick move, I would have never noticed it. In colour, form and texture, it was just another broken and slightly rotten stick, about four inches long and half an inch in diameter, looking like any of the hundred other sticks that I could see within reach of my hand. Yet as I picked it up, it felt slightly pliable to my touch, and soft-skinned; in short, it felt like an animal. But still I could see neither arms nor legs, nor eyes nor mouth. It was like no animal that I had ever seen. I turned it over in my hand, and was in the act of bringing it close up to my eye when I received one of the greatest shocks of my life. As I lifted the stick towards my face, I felt a slight wriggle and the stick disappeared. In its place, my hand now sprouted a sixth finger. Between my thumb and index finger, though striking out at a very unusual angle, was another digit, nail, knuckles and all, and of identical colouration to my own. The surprise produced by this was so great that it was all I could do to refrain from crying out, but I managed to control myself for long enough to quickly stuff my hand into one of the small cloth bags I usually carried with me, and was relieved to feel the creature release its grip and fall off. I quickly tied the neck of the bag. I had discovered the greatest master of disguise that nature has yet devised.

By the time I returned to my house with my trophy, I could feel within the bag that the creature had once again changed its form. It was no longer stick-shaped, but had become thin and leaf-like. On carefully opening the bag, I was at first in some doubt whether the creature had not escaped, but I found that it had attached itself to the inner surface of the bag, and now took on both the colour and texture of the coarse cambric of which the bag was composed. When I reached inside to remove it, I was once again startled to see that I had instantly grown a sixth finger. This time my curiosity quickly got the better of my surprise, and I was able to calmly examine this strange creature.

Its resemblance to my index finger was remarkable. There was the nail, there the corrugated skin of my knuckles. Though the finer detail of skin texture was missing, the colour was identical, even to being slightly darker above than below. My false finger was attached almost seamlessly to my hand, though I could in fact feel that I was being gripped with small claws, which, on gently raising the edge of the 'finger' with a small steel probe, I could see beneath. The presence of claws suggested either a member of the Articulata or Vertebrata, but having seen no features which would help me to decide, I could not identify the creature further. The grip of the claws was by no means strong, and there seemed no reason not to pull the creature from my hand, but how was I to prevent it immediately taking on the disguise of whatever next object it chose? The solution that came to me was to fill a large specimen jar half-full of water, into which I plunged my hand. At first, nothing happened. I still appeared to have a sixth finger, albeit that small bubbles were escaping from where it joined my hand. Then, gradually, the finger began to change colour. It grew darker and darker, then suddenly released itself from my hand and rose to the surface.

At last, the creature was revealing its natural shape. Swimming around on the surface of the water was a small brown lizard.

Among the order Reptilia on my island, I have discovered no varanids (which is somewhat to my surprise, as these lizards are common both to the south and the north, and are well known for their ability to swim), neither are there any tortoises (which has also surprised me, knowing how widespread these animals are, being commonly found even on the remotest islands). Apart from the sea serpents which abound in the lagoon, there is but one snake, of the boa tribe, which, though large, appears to feed solely on fruit. I have also discovered several species of small skinks, at least one of them legless, and six species of agamid. This lizard was, I supposed, a type of camelion.

Such a remarkable animal was well worth further study, and I determined to keep it for that purpose. Reasoning that, despite the little lizard's remarkable powers of disguise, it could not make itself transparent, I used a pair of forceps to quickly transfer it from the jar of water to an empty jar; it reacted to its new home by once more assuming the shape and colour of my finger, a bizarre effect to witness. If I were to test its powers of mimicry further, I needed to devise a way of allowing it to change its disguise, yet remain visible. The method I devised was to make a loop from a piece of the red yarn which I use to mend my socks; when the animal was again put into the water and forced to resume its natural shape, I managed to slip this over its head and tighten it around its neck. Now when I took the camelion from the water with my bare hand, I found that my sixth finger was adorned with a ring of red wool, tied just below the fingernail.

Being now sure that I could see through any disguise which the little animal chose to adopt, I experimented by placing it against a variety of backgrounds. Its ability was remarkable. When on sand, it became sand; when on a pile of pebbles, it became a pebble; when on the bark of a tree, it became the bark; when on a leafy branch, it became a leaf. Although the camelion's ability to match the colour of its surroundings was unparalleled by any animal of my experience, its ability to change its size and shape was even more remarkable. It could flatten its body to almost the thickness of paper, or blow itself up to the size of an organdy plum; stretch out to eight or nine inches in length, or contract to just under two. It could assume the smooth outlines of a new leaf or the ragged outlines of a dead one, the jagged shape of a piece of coral rock or the regular curves of a bleached bone. The camelion also had the facility to mimic other animals; I have seen it as a butterfly, a mouse, a spider and, most remarkably, as a snake's head (all the more remarkable because of the rarity of snakes on the island). Many of the disguises are facilitated by the animal's ability to withdraw its limbs into its body, and without the red wool to indicate the position of its head, I often found it impossible to tell which part of the animal was which.

I soon found that, like most lizards, my little camelion was an insectivore, snapping up with its long tongue any fly or beetle which I introduced into the jar, with a speed which defied the eye (no doubt this explained the original disappearance of my orchid beetle). Though I kept a watch-glass of water in its jar, I never saw it drink. I became so fascinated by this little beast that I spent many hours in observing it, and it eventually became quite tame. On being taken from its jar, rather than assuming the disguise of my finger or some other nearby object, it would remain in its natural form, walking around on my desk in the most confident and friendly manner. I grew fond of my little pet, and was alarmed one day when, on looking to return it to its jar, I was unable to find it. I had learned by experience that it was useless to look for the animal itself, but if I scanned the desk for something small and red I would be sure to spot its woollen collar. After much searching, I found the collar caught on a sharp piece of wood projecting from the edge of my desk, but to my dismay I found that the wool had become detached from the neck of its owner. Though I continued searching high and low in the hope that I would be able to find my little friend, I eventually had to admit that the only way I would see him again was if he chose to reveal himself.

When many days went by, with so sign of the camelion, I assumed him to be gone for good. Then one evening, as I was frying up a mess of minnows which I had netted in the lake, I was surprised to see one leap from the pan and on to the ground. Before my astonished eyes the little fish metamorphosed into my lost pet. I had found my little camelion but, alas, he was not long for this world. Though he had escaped the frying pan, his injuries were such that he soon died, and I have to confess I shed tears over his sad demise.

The untimely death of my pet gave me the opportunity to try to unveil the secrets of such a master of disguise, and the next day I pinned out the little body on my table and began my dissection. I discovered that the camelion's ability to change its shape rests largely with the peculiar structure of its skeleton, the bones of which are extremely reduced. The joints, moreover, are not tightly articulated, as is usual among the Vertebrata, but surrounded by extremely elastic ligaments, giving the animal the ability to dislocate its bones at will. Just as a snake can unhinge its jawbone and expand its mouth to swallow prey bigger than its head, the camelion can unhinge almost every joint in its body, including even its vertebrae. Though you may marvel at human contortionists at the fair, their talent is nothing compared with the little camelion. I have named the species *Chamaelio abditissimus*. How common these wonderful reptiles are on my island, I know not. I have not since found another, yet I may be constantly surrounded by them.

Chapter 28

OUR ORIGINAL PLAN HAD been to first explore the shore and the low country, then undertake a thorough investigation of the mountain. Charley had already climbed to its peak; on our second day on the island he had scrambled to the very top, hoping to see a ship, or perhaps distant land. He saw only the sail of the prau slipping northwards over the horizon, but had become fascinated with the fumaroles ('smoke holes' he called them) that he had seen around the peak. Most were small, he said, no more than cracks in the rock, from which issued jets of hissing steam, but there was one big one, a round black hole some three yards across. If you stood close enough to the edge, he told me, you got soaked through from the white clouds of vapour swirling round its mouth, and you could feel on your face the heat of the molten rock within. The hole was, he assured me, quite large enough for a man to fall into. I was eager to see these features for myself, but such a climb was for me a major expedition. My age, and my years as a recluse, had enfeebled my limbs, and I found the ascent of even a moderate slope a difficult and tedious affair. Nevertheless, early one morning about two weeks after Charley's return, I agreed to his suggestion that it was time to explore the mountain more thoroughly. After filling our pockets with ship-biscuits and a flask of water, he and I set off together up the mountain.

Charley was soon lost from sight. He had little patience with my infirmities and strode on ahead at his own pace. It took me over an hour of breathless scrambling until I eventually reached the lower limits of the dildoe trees, and saw Charley resting in the shade of one. As I came closer, I could see that he had fallen asleep. In repose, was he once again the boy who had first caught my eye, then my heart, those many years ago in Macassar; or was it another boy I saw, the boy who entered my heart one summer's day in an English garden, and had never left it? The thought returned to me that I remembered from my first days at Shrewsbury school; rich or poor, virtuous or wicked, happy or sad, all are one in sleep. But awake, which was Charley? I knew from the first that he had always been careless of others' lives, whether men or beasts. I had at first explained this as the result of untutored ignorance; now I was beginning to see it as a presence rather than an absence, as deliberate cruelty rather than simple lack of compassion. How else could I explain his attempt to abandon me on the island?

Charley opened an eye.

'Ah, you've come at last. Got tired waitin', I did.'

I sat down beside him.

'You must forgive me,' I said. 'The effects of disuse, though they may not be hereditable, can be none the less strongly felt during our own lifetimes.'

Charley gave a small laugh. 'You and your damned Theory. There are more important things than theories. What did your precious Theory ever bring you, old man?'

Very little, I had to admit, and had it not lost me the friendship I most valued? I had not yet told Charley about how Bobby had been forced by Wallace to publish the Theory against his will, and about the letter he had sent me, but now I proceeded to do so. He listened in unaccustomed silence.

'How the inspiration came to Wallace, though, I will never understand,' I said. 'I swear he never showed the slightest interest in the whole thing.'

'Oh, he was interested enough when I told him,' said Charley.

'You told him? When?'

'Let me see now,' said Charley, 'When was it, around '57?'

I asked him to explain further.

'I was still havin' a fine old time with Jim Brookes,' he said, 'when who should front up in Kuching but our old friend, still looking for his birds and butterflies. It would have been about a year since I'd left you both in Macassar, and mighty surprised he was to see me. And mighty cheesed off he was too. With you I mean,' he added, poking a finger at me. 'You should have heard the names he called you.'

'Why with me?'

'He was still thinking it was you that stole me away from him, wasn't he?' said Charley with a laugh. 'But he was interested in the Theory, all right, even though I don't reckon he even understood half of it.'

Now it was clear to me. Though Wallace's intellect could not grasp the meaning of the Theory, his memory retained it; like a trained parrot, he could memorise words without understanding their content. When the time came round, he was able to repeat what he had heard from Charley, what Charley had heard from me, almost word for word.

Charley raised himself to his feet and, still chuckling at the memory of Wallace's anger, set off towards the top of the mountain.

Since Charley died I have been forced to shift for myself, and have gradually found that my strength of limb has returned, and my stamina also. As part of my investigation of the land cucumber, I have spent much time cutting down and dissecting a number of dildoe trees. It was while I was engaged on one such lengthy task, not far from the very spot where Charley met his unfortunate end, that, neglecting to take stock of the passing of the hours, I discovered that by the time I had completed my investigations, the sun was only a couple of hand's-widths from the horizon. I had less than an hour to descend the mountain before nightfall, an event which occurs with great rapidity at these latitudes. I set off immediately, and made the lower slopes by dusk. Taking my bearings by the large fumarole on the mountain behind me and the evening star to the west, I was confident of reaching home without difficulty. As I picked my way carefully among the rocks and bushes (gadzocks seldom climb to this height, and there were none of their well-marked paths to follow), I became aware of an unpleasant smell. I had previously noticed that several of the smaller fumaroles on the far side of the mountain gave out a sulphurous smell, but this was not sulphur, it was ammonia. As I rounded a large bush, I was suddenly startled by what I took to be a small bird flying up from behind a rock just before me, straight towards my face. I ducked my head and it missed me, but it was immediately followed by another bird, and another. Within moments a whole stream of the things was flying over my head into the darkening sky, and I realised, when I looked more closely at their fluttering flight, that they were not birds, but bats. The creatures were emerging from a wide crack beneath the rock, which was also the source of the, by now, almost overpowering smell. The crack was clearly the entrance to a cave. More bats continued to stream out for at least half an hour; by my reckoning, there must have been tens of thousands of them. By now the night was almost pitch-dark. Tying my handkerchief to a bush, I once more took careful bearings, resolving to investigate the matter at length the following day.

The crack in the side of the mountain proved to be about two feet high by six wide, wide enough for a man to crawl down. It was not vertical, but angled inwards at about twenty degrees. Due to its narrowness I could not see far down it, but a long branch thrust into the hole met no resistance. This time I had come equipped with bullseye lantern and some rope; I would soon find out where the bats were coming from.

I had no need of the rope. The crack soon widened, the slope remained gentle, and after first crawling, then walking and scrambling about a hundred yards down a narrow tunnel, I found myself in a cavern. How large it was I knew not. My lantern, fuelled at that time with the somewhat smoky oil from cocoa-nuts, was not bright enough to penetrate more than five yards into the darkness. Though I could see well enough that I had emerged from the tunnel into a cave, of this cave I could see neither roof nor farther wall. My eyes were watering so freely from the ammoniated fumes, it was only by constant blinking that I was able to see at all. But 'filling the air with barbarous dissonance', I could see the bats. Hundreds were constantly swooping in and out of my lamplight, clicking and squeaking and flapping, while hundreds more clung to the near wall like tiles on a roof.

As a child in England I had been familiar with the flitter-mouse, and knew of its habit of catching moths and other nocturnal insects. In Australia I had met others of its tribe, and also gigantic bats known as 'flying foxes', which roost in the bush in vast, stinking camps. In the East Indies I had come across similar bats, and even eaten of their flesh (which varies much, from loathsome to delicious). The bats in the cave were mid-way in size between the two. They were stout animals, their bodies about the size of a large rat, though their wings seemed disproportionately long, and their fur most lustrous, being somewhat the colour of polished mahogany. They had the face and dentition of a flying fox, being long in the muzzle and with sharp, even teeth, yet their large eyes had a mild-mannered look which belied their apparent ferocity. I had no difficulty in examining the animals, as they, like most of the island's inhabitants, were exceedingly tame, and had no objection to being plucked from the walls of the cave where they were hanging.

Just as the walls and ceiling of the cave were covered with bats, its floor was equally well-covered in bat dung. The cave was their primary latrine, and an unbroken carpet of guano stretched away into the invisible distance. The guano was the source of the smell I had first detected, and which, since I first entered the cave, had caused my eyes to water freely. As I peered into the darkness, it appeared to shine with a thousand sparkling jewels. Imagining this to be an effect of my tears, and perhaps the flickering effect produced by the wings of the bats, I blinked hard. I blinked again. Though my vision had cleared, the jewels were still there, shining like golden beads on the floor of the cave. Bending down to one of them, my lantern close to my face, I blinked again. It was not a jewel at all. It was a beetle.

I had at last discovered the home of the golden scarab. Almost overwhelmed as I was at my discovery, the cave was no place for a man to stay long. I needed light, and I needed fresh air. Scooping a dozen beetles into my pocket, I scrambled back through the tunnel. Outside, the morning light was already bright and flat. I carefully extracted one of the scarabs from my pocket, holding it by its carapace between my finger and thumb, its stout legs waving slowly in the air. There was no doubt that this was the insect which Charley had first shown me so many years ago. It seemed to be formed of purest gold. It was about the size of an English dor beetle, though somewhat more rounded in shape and smoother, without any of the corrugations found on the wing-cases of dor beetles and other chafers. The specimen Charley had showed me, and the one we had bought from the one-eyed sailor, had been dried and set; I had not been able to look beneath their wing cases, nor inspect the dorsal surface of their abdomens. But when I took out my knife and tried to prise apart the wing cases of my living specimen, I discovered that they could not be opened. The two wing cases were completely fused together, nor could they be lifted away as one from the abdomen. If there were wings beneath the wing cases, they were useless. Here was one surprise; all previous dung-beetles I had seen were strong fliers, yet these beetles had completely lost the ability to fly. In my subsequent investigation of their habits, several more surprises awaited me.

*　　*　　*

All the scarabs that I have ever seen (including our *Copris lunaris*, dear Bobby) make balls of dung and bury them as food for their larvae. I soon discovered that in the cave there was none of that activity; indeed, what could a beetle there bury a ball of dung in, but more dung? Instead, the beetles laid their eggs directly on to the cave floor. Though twenty minutes was the longest I could endure in the cave at any one time, I made several return visits, and was able to watch a beetle engaged at this task. I could detect neither pattern nor plan. The beetle simply scattered her eggs willy-nilly, clearly trusting that wherever a grub might hatch there would be food aplenty. And so it was; while the surface of the guano was scattered with adult beetles, below it seethed with grubs of all sizes. I took up a handful of them. They were typical scarab larvae, with fat white bodies curled into the shape of a C, small brown legs and brown head, showing no sign of the magnificent rayment they would adopt as adults. The dung also contained numbers of large round cocoons, which I found, on breaking them open, to each contain a single scarab pupa, of a pale brown colour.

Though the golden scarabs exist in countless thousands inside the bat cave, I never found one, either larva or adult, outside the cave. The beetles appear to spend their entire lives in the total darkness of the cave, the larvae feeding on the constant supplies of fresh ordure brought in by the bats, the adults creating more larvae. The beetle larvae undoubtedly provide the bats a useful service, cleaning up the excrement which might otherwise rise so high as to completely fill the cave, but the larvae are by no means totally beneficent. Woe betide any bat which falls to the floor, a fate which is not unusual, especially among the young of the species. They are immediately set upon by a swarm of larvae. The animals have no chance of escape, but are quickly pulled beneath the surface of the dung, where they are eaten alive by hundreds of tiny jaws. During even my short visits to the cave, the leather of my boots was clearly abraded by the small but numberless bites of the beetle larvae.

But if the bats pay a high price for a fall, the beetles pay a high price for their board and lodging. They, in turn, are eaten by the bats. The floor of the cave is constantly astir with beetles freshly emerged from their cocoons (there is no night and day in the cave), yet almost as fast as they emerge, they are gobbled up by the bats, thousands of which are constantly flying round in the cave and swooping down on the beetles. That some beetles escape to continue the race is certain, though I would wager little on the chances of any individual surviving. Here was a nice thing, that the bats should consume, through the intervention of the beetles, their own excrement; but I later discovered yet another twist to the bats' unusual economy.

A microscopic examination of fresh bats' faeces from the cave revealed, to my surprise, not a trace of the chitinous skeletons of beetles, though there were small seeds of several kinds. This puzzled me. The bats I had previously been familiar with were either of the small insectivorous type or of the large fruit-eating type. Here was clear evidence that these bats ate both, but it appeared that the faeces from the bats' entomological repast were being excreted somewhere outside the cave. Of the fruit trees on the island, there are three *Ficus*, another with leaves resembling a fig but fruit more like a rumbullion, being sour-skinned and filled with sweet, seedy pulp. These trees grow together, not in a forest, but in a number of small scattered groves on the north-eastern end of the island. Though I had often sought the shade of one of these groves by day, I had never visited one at night.

On the day of the next full moon, I gathered together some things and set off for the middle of the island, intending to spend the night beneath one of the groves of fruit trees, and hoping that I would find the place where the dungbats, as I had now named them, came to feed. Arriving an hour or so before sunset, I spread out my small tarpaulin beneath the trees. The ground was comfortably carpeted with fallen leaves, and I had brought with me for my supper some fish and cold potatoes,[48] after which I ate some fruit, of which large quantities had fallen to the ground beneath the trees. That many of these fruit appeared to be partly eaten gave me hope that I was at the right place.

As the sun set, the full moon rose. Crickets began to chirrup. From far over to the west, I could hear the sharp croaks of the frogs in the lake. When the moon had risen less than a hand's-breath into 'the starry cope of heaven', the dungbats arrived. There was no missing them. Though silent in flight, as soon as they landed on a tree they immediately began to chatter and talk and squabble and scream as loud as a troop of monkeys. Just as I had watched the dungbats streaming from their cave for a full half-hour when I first discovered them, they continued arriving at the grove over a similar period. Each bat, on landing at a tree, but before commencing to feed, carefully pulled itself into an upright position, and defecated. Small dark pellets came rattling down through the leaves on to the ground beneath. Each patch of moonlight sparkled with glistening grains of gold.

This was where the beetles from the cave ended up. The glittering specks in the soil where the trees grew, which I had previously dismissed as pyrites derived from the weathering of the native rock, were formed of the chewed-up remains of golden scarabs. As well as eating the fruit of the trees, the bats fertilise the trees on which they feed. The trees feed the bats which feed the beetles which feed the bats which feed the trees which feed the bats. A nice relationship, would you not say, Bobby? I think it might even beat your cats and clover.[49]

---

[48] There is no other reference to growing this vegetable on his island; the 'potatoes' may well have been wild yams.

[49] An example used in *The Origin of Species* to illustrate the interconnection between different and disparate species. The more cats there are, the fewer voles, the fewer voles, the fewer holes for bumblebees to nest in, the fewer bumblebees, the less clover will be pollinated; thus the more cats, the less clover.

On my several visits to the dungbats' cave inside the mountain I gathered quantities of golden scarabs, both in adult and pupal stages. Hoping that they would metamorphose and emerge, I kept the pupal cells in a tray of sand in my house. I had noticed among the adults in the cave that there appeared to be no differentiation between the sexes. When, some three weeks later, the first adult beetles began to emerge from the sand tray, they were all identical, and all of them, as soon as they emerged, began to lay eggs. They laid their eggs without mating, scattering them haphazardly over the sand in the tray just like the one I had observed in the cave. That the eggs were fertile I had no doubt, for within a few hours each egg had hatched into a tiny grub which immediately started to burrow into the sand. It thus appeared that all the scarabs were both female and self-fertile.

Evolution is a response to change, natural selection assuming the role of gardener, constantly weeding out the less-fit individuals and allowing those better adapted to survive and reproduce. But what if there is no change? What if a species' environment remains constant, day after day, year after year, millennium after millennium? The cave which the golden scarabs inhabit is surely such a place. It is of constant temperature and humidity, there is a constant supply of food, there is a constant pressure of predation from the bats. The species has reached a perfect equilibrium with its environment. Just as the beetles have no need for wings, they have no need for variation. They have evolved beyond sex. One might justifiably say that the golden scarabs have evolved beyond evolution.

That sexual reproduction is not universal is a subject which you and I discussed at some length in Australia, Bobby. Many lower animals reproduce by simple fusion, and many insects are wholly or partly parthenogenetic; within the plant kingdom, reproduction by non-sexual means is even more common. What, then, is the advantage of sexual reproduction? It is surely that sex, by combining in the offspring different combinations of the characteristics of each parent, leads to variation, the main engine of evolution. But if it is sex which gives a species enough flexibility to cope with changes in its situation, to evolve, does this mean that without sex, there can be no evolution? I think that this may well be so.

But if the beetles cannot evolve, how can they have 'lost' attributes which must surely have been possessed by their ancestors, namely the powers of sight and flight? I have already spoken of my discovery that the elytra of the golden scarabs are fused, and I soon found from my dissections that the wings beneath the elytra were, as I suspected, reduced to no more than fleshy buds. The deficiency of eyes was also common to all members of the species. While it is undoubtedly the case that beetles living in total darkness, and in an enclosed space, are in no way disadvantaged by these losses, I cannot but ask myself how this state might have come about, and my answer is at distinct variance to your own, my dear Bobby. Although some variation, and hence selection, might occur in parthenogenetic populations, it will necessarily be less than in one which reproduces sexually, in which the offspring inherit a mixture of traits from each parent. It is therefore clear that the loss of both wings and eyes in the scarabs must have preceded the loss of sexual reproduction. The answer that you have given to how such losses occur, Bobby, is that they can be best explained by the effects of disuse. Here I find myself in emphatic disagreement. You have said in your book that a functioning eye would not be injurious to animals living in the darkness, and suggest that its disappearance cannot be due to selection, but is probably due to disuse. In making this suggestion, I fear that you have betrayed your own faith. A little further thought would reveal that any organ which is of no advantage to its possessor, is *necessarily* of disadvantage. Were my golden scarabs to possess eyes or wings, which are of no use to them, they would be employing in their development resources which might otherwise be put to more profitable use, in the development of, say, a better digestive system, or a larger reproductive system. Furthermore, in accounting for the loss of an organ or faculty as the effect of disuse, you are going directly contrary to the empirical principles on which the Theory is based. As you have yourself said, there is no evidence that disuse, or indeed use, has any *hereditable* effect. To suggest that it does so is to sacrifice observation for speculation, and return to the theories of Lamarck. I would like to discuss this with you further, dear Bobby. I would like to have discussed it with Charley. It is a shame that Charley could not live long enough to see the golden scarabs.

We have not much time now, the mountain and I. From the void we are born and to the void we return, and what comes between is of little importance. Yet nothing to me is more important than that my story be told. To keep my manuscript safe from the things that are to come, I have been experimenting. I am now decided upon the matter. My manuscript will be placed within a glass jar, its stopper sealed with sticky propolis stolen from the nests of my carpenter bees. It will be bound around with a layer of soft bark from the *Pisonia* tree to keep it safe from hard blows, and tied with the tendrils of the floating water-lily. It will then be put into a section of bamboo, plugged with a stopper I have carved from the wood of a dildoe tree and sealed with wax and oilskin. Soon, when I have finished my story, I shall wade out to the edge of the reef and cast my words into the currents. And so that its finder will know that my story is not a fraud, nor the ramblings of some clever lunatic, before I seal the jar I will place within it a specimen of the golden scarab. I have named the species *Copris darwinii*.

Chapter 29

BY THE TIME CHARLEY and I reached the upper slopes of the mountain, I was exhausted.

'Come on, old man,' laughed Charley. 'You're huffin' and puffin' almost as much as these smoke holes.'

We had already reached the part of the mountain where the fumaroles began. The scalding steam that issued from small holes in the rocks condensed into plumes of white vapour, some giving forth a sighing or whistling sound. Our path so far had taken us across the grassy plain at the foot of the mountain and well up into the zone of afforestation that extends right to the top. Few trees grew close to the fumaroles themselves, but around each were a variety of smaller bushes and creepers, their foliage kept constantly wet from the continuous condensation of steam. Most noticeable among these plants was a bindweed or convolvulus. Its enormous, trumpet-shaped flowers seemed out of all proportion to the rest of the plant, hanging like so many white bells from the slender stems of the plant.

'Did you ever do this?' said Charley. He plucked one of the flowers from its plant, bit off the base and sucked.

As a boy in England I would suck the sweet nectar from the flowers of the common woodbine. I reached out to pick a flower, not noticing the small fumarole it grew beside. As I felt the steam scald my hand I gave a loud yell.

'What a noisy old chap you are today,' said Charley, his grin suggesting some amusement at my discomfort. He plucked another flower and sucked out its nectar.

277

'Come along,' he said. 'There are plenty more of these near the big one.'

I pulled myself to my feet and followed him up the mountain.

Charley's big one was indeed an impressive sight. It lay on a flattish part of the mountain, though one side was slightly higher than the other, giving the impression of a cave. It was about four yards across. The steam that billowed from its invisible depths formed ragged curtains as it emerged into the light. Festooned around this giant fumarole were dozens of the giant convolvulus flowers.

'Help yourself, old man,' said Charley, and he reached out towards one of the flowers.

Why did I push Charley into the scalding, scorching hole? What were my thoughts, and what were his? (Why is the old man so close behind me?) Did I push him because it was he who had caused us to be marooned on this deserted island? (What is that look on the old man's face?) Was it because he had tried to abandon me, so far from men, and from where I might never return? (Why has he raised his hand?) Did I want to kill him because I was angry, because he was so short with me, because he laughed at me and scorned me, I, who had been so good to him, who had looked after him and taught him so much? (This is not a good joke, old man.) Was it because Charley robbed me of that first golden scarab, which he had promised would be mine, and made me waste sixteen years of my life? (Get your hand off my chest, old man. Don't push me.) Was it because of the gadzocks? Charley would surely have killed every one of them on the island, every one of them in the world, if I had not done what I did. (My feet are slipping. The earth itself is slipping away.) It was all of these reasons, but none of them. (Oh my God, I'm falling.) There was but one thought in my head as I saw Charley standing there at the edge of the fumarole, as I took that single step towards him. (The steam, it's hot, I can't see anything.) There was but one thought as I saw the surprise

278

on Charley's face as he felt the pressure of my hand on his chest.
(I must save myself. Surely I can save myself.) One thought, as I
saw surprise turn to horror as Charley lost his balance, grappled
thin air, and began to fall. (Yes! There's a rock, a handhold. I
can grab it.) One thought, as I saw him topple and twist, saw
him grasping at the rocks. (Ah miracle, I've grabbed the rock.
But the pain.) My thought was of you, Bobby. (A wave of
purest pain is sweeping through my hands, surging down my
arms, crashing into my brain.) This was for you, Bobby. (The
rock is scalding, as hot as the steam.) This was our revenge,
Bobby. (My fingers are burning, my very lungs are being seared
within. I must hang on.) This was our revenge on Charley for
having stolen my gift to you. (Don't let go, you will fall into the
hole.) If Charley had not told Wallace about the Theory, as they
lay together in Kuching, 'Imparadis'd in one another's arms'.
(Don't let go, you will die.) If Charley had not lied to Wallace,
telling him in that note that it was I who had stolen him away.
(I don't want to die, I don't want to die.) If Charley had not sent
him that note, Wallace would not have been jealous, would not
have wanted to get even with me. (I'll let go with one hand,
but the pain redoubles in the other.) Charley must have told
Wallace about my affection for you, Bobby. (The pain is too
much, I have to let go, I have to let myself fall.) Wallace had no
interest or understanding of evolution, but he had stored within
his memory Charley's words. (Please stop the pain. Someone
stop the pain.) He wanted to get even with me for stealing
Charley from him, and he decided to use those words against
me. (Death will stop the pain. How strange to think that Death
could be a friend.) The one way he knew he could hurt me was
to try to hurt you. (I see my hand above me release its grip. The
pain has stopped). Did you not think it odd that Wallace should
use the very phrases we had ourselves used in our discussion?
(Death takes my hand.) Did you not think it odd that he should
send his version of the Theory to you, Bobby? (Death's touch
is cool.) You were my friend, and by causing you pain, Wallace

knew he was hurting me. (Into Death's arms I fall. Into the black depths I fall. Into Death.) You see, Bobby, it was really all Charley's fault.

The mountain sees, and the mountain knows. Only death will wash the blood of Charley from my hands. Each night I awake to the sound of Charley's single scream echoing in my head, the sight of his face looking up at me, his hands grasping in vain at the scalding rock as he vanished into those 'rifted rocks whose entrance leads to Hell'. But things are as they are. For stealing the Theory, Charley had to die, and my own end is coming soon, the mountain tells me so. The mountain gives, and the mountain takes away. Poor Charley, I had no choice. It may have been Wallace who made you reject me, Bobby, but it was Charley who gave him the power to do so. The mountain gave me the golden scarabs, and it took Charley. Soon it will take me too. Each day it speaks to me a little more, each day a little louder. Will you one day thank me, Bobby, for planting within you the seed of the Theory, your mighty oak from my small acorn? It brought you fame such as few men know, fame that will surely live beyond your death, and mine. Or were my words like the seed of the strangler fig of tropical climes, which, sprouting on the branch of some mighty forest giant, grows stealthily to entwine its trunk and overshadow its crown, and, over slow decades, take the life from it? Did I take away your quiet life, Bobby, or worse, did I take the life of your God? Was it a gift, or was it a curse?

It long puzzled me how the flower of the giant convolvulus is pollinated. I presumed that, like most flowers, the nectar that is produced at the base of the flower proves an attractant to some insect or a bird which, in taking the nectar, transfers pollen from one flower to another. The pollen is contained, as is usual among this family, on stamens near the opening of the flower, but the tube is too long and narrow to admit anything but the slenderest bill or proboscis. I am aware that, in South America, the pollination of many flowers is undertaken by large moths, similar to hawkmoths, whose tongues can uncurl to prodigious lengths, and it seemed not unreasonable to assume that similar insects might occur on my island. I have recently discovered that this is not the case; the truth is even stranger.